MR IN

Neil Cross was born in Bristol in 1969. He now lives and works in London.

MRS. ·BETWEEN

Neil Cross

MR IN-BETWEEN

V

VINTAGE

Published by Vintage 1999

2 4 6 8 10 9 7 5 3 1

Copyright © Neil Cross 1998

The right of Neil Cross to be identified as the author of
this work has been asserted by him in accordance
with the Copyright, Designs and Patents Act, 1988

First published in Great Britain by
Jonathan Cape in 1998

Vintage
Random House, 20 Vauxhall Bridge Road,
London SW1V 2SA

Random House Australia (Pty) Limited
20 Alfred Street, Milsons Point, Sydney
New South Wales 2061, Australia

Random House New Zealand Limited
18 Poland Road, Glenfield,
Auckland 10, New Zealand

Random House South Africa (Pty) Limited
Endulini, 5A Jubilee Road, Parktown 2193, South Africa

Random House UK Limited Reg. No. 954009

A CIP catalogue record for this book
is available from the British Library

ISBN 0 09 977871 8

Papers used by Random House UK Ltd are natural,
recyclable products made from wood grown in sustain-
able forests. The manufacturing processes conform to the
environmental regulations of the country of origin

Printed and bound in Great Britain by
Cox & Wyman, Reading, Berkshire

One *Adrenochrome*

When the man was dead, Jon was compelled to tidy up the mess he'd made in the process of killing him. Because the man had put up something of a struggle there was a fair amount of furniture to be straightened, photographs uprighted and pillows to be fluffed, which he went about with efficient detachment born of a sense of contractual and personal obligation. He knew that little touches, insignificant in themselves, could be surprisingly effective in context of the whole. It was a question of presentation.

When the flat was tidy, he took the corpse beneath the armpits and hauled it with some difficulty into an armchair. Then he set about doing to it exactly what the Tattooed Man had asked. It took a long time and considerable skill. When it was done he stood, wiping the blade of the scalpel on the arm of a chair, walked to the kitchen on stiff legs and washed his hands in cold water, soaping them with washing-up liquid. On the squeezy plastic bottle there adhered a yellow price sticker, its legend blurred beyond legibility, corners curled to reveal its white underbelly. Returning to the living room he stuffed his things into a small army-surplus rucksack. He picked up the tape recorder which sat on the coffee table, rewound the cassette then replaced it. He took care to balance on top of the cassette player the printed card that read 'Play Me' in such a way that it would not be toppled by a draught.

He took a moment to scrutinise the result. The Tattooed Man had asked for something besides a compensatory death. He wanted to open perceptual doors for those in whose honour it had been conceived. He wanted them to sleep with the lights on for the rest of their lives.

Jon pulled on his overcoat, slung the bag over his shoulder and left the flat. He walked down three flights of steps and out on to the street. He paused to nod hello to a smartly dressed old woman who passed him on the threshold, her face smooth and fragrant with powder that had made a small stain on her Burberry scarf. He lit a cigarette and began to make his way home.

By the time he had settled on the train the amphetamines he had injected that morning were beginning to wear off: his upper arms began to twitch and his spit felt thick and sticky. He removed a pewter hip flask from an inside pocket, took a swig, winced, replaced it, then awkwardly opened a newspaper across his knees. Smoking and drinking and reading about murder and corruption and celebrity, sex and money and fame, he whiled away the journey. By the time the train pulled into the station, he was beginning to feel better.

Although the station was three miles or more from where he lived he decided to walk, putting off the amphetamine comedown and its paradoxically restless ennui. The city centre was bathed in a dirty sodium halo. He walked past taxi ranks and multi-storey car parks that gradually gave way to the area he called home. Decaying Victorian tenements circled in a slow vortex towards a brutal, atavistic henge of tower blocks. This was where the classes merged. Pubs and wine-bars stood at different faces of the same corner. The stench of kebabs drifted in malodorous eddies past Italian restaurants. Puke stains on grey doorsteps.

He knew that his house would have been a disappointment to anybody who suspected the nature of his profession. The professional killer of the popular imagination lived in splendour just the wrong side of vulgarity: luxurious white fur and black leather, high windows, chrome accessories thrown in for the express purpose of reflecting cruel, passionless features.

Mirror-lensed sunglasses and elegant cheekbones. Distantly, he found this amusing.

He lived in a converted three-bedroomed terraced house whose scrupulous order, sharp lines and hygienic soullessness invited notions of a meticulous and ordered mind. It existed in a continuum of timeless stasis, of preservation. It was free of dust because it was devoid of life. There was a monolithic television, a stereo almost ostentatious in its minimalism. There was an armchair and a sofa. There were neat bookshelves, each book with an unbent spine. Perfect and unread.

It was showroom neat but had none of the essence of the new, of the carefully chosen statement of status. It was odourless and the light it contained was ancient, the quiet light of a deserted attic, where there are no eyes to employ it.

He let himself in, took off his overcoat, hung it in the hallway, walked into the living room and sat in a black leather armchair which, like many of his possessions, had been a gift from the Tattooed Man, who genuinely seemed concerned at his lack of interest in the *little luxuries*. From his pocket he took a short, silver tube with a spherical end the circumference of a pencil and laid it on the coffee table parallel to a mirror with an ironically elaborate frame, another obscure whim of the Tattooed Man. From the same pocket he removed a self-sealing plastic bag and tapped on to the mirror a small pile of amphetamine sulphate, which he arranged into two lines with a razor blade. He snorted the powder through the tube and sat back, wincing and sniffing. In time the speed entered his bloodstream and charged his viscera with palpitating energy. He picked up the mirror, stared at the reflection of his eyes and said his name. The personality that the name belonged to stared silently from deep within the blackness at the back of his eyes, which were the wrong eyes. They had the unspecific mildness of a kitsch Christ rendered in Catholic tat. While his face was sombre and inanimate, these eyes reflected back at him the tentative self he adopted whenever he stepped outside this lifeless mausoleum. He was neither particularly suited to the social milieu he chose to haunt, nor particularly unsuited. He was seldom first to get in a round, never the last, neither irritatingly witty nor lumpenly dull. He affected vague support for a football team. He never told jokes, but laughed or groaned or grimaced as necessary at the jokes of others. Even mean drunks did not become jealous if he engaged their wives in conversation, and women did not fantasise about him, even when fantasy cast-lists were stretched to desperate limits. The memory of him seemed to slip from the consciousness as if he had never fully occupied it. He registered on the cornea but slid from the cortex.

Only once had somebody enquired what he did for a living. It was during the blue last-orders haze of a Friday evening, before the Chinese take-away and a sweating, football-song stagger to some house to view a forgettable, pornographic horror movie.

Fat Dave, fresh from a diatribe about Pakis (he wasn't a racist mind you, there were some smashing Pakis about), drew on the soggy stub of a cigarette, leaned his elbow in a pool of warm lager and said, 'What about you, then, Jonny? What is it you do, again?'

Jon took the cigarette from Dave's hand, drew on it, handed it back and said, 'I'm an assassin, Dave.'

Gordon the Gofer spat lager in a wide, briefly iridescent fan, wiped his lips and said, 'Oh yeah? Pays well does it?'

Jon nodded seriously and said, 'I do all right.'

'Tax free as well, I expect,' suggested Jagger, luxuriating in his wit.

Jon nodded. 'Unless MI5 ever ask me to do a job.'

'Oh yeah? They do that, do they?'

'Not as yet. But you never know.'

The bell rang last orders and, pausing on his way to get a final round, Jagger said, 'How do you do it, then – offer to buy them a drink and wait for them to die of boredom?'

'Or surprise,' added Fat Dave.

'I've got a couple of targets for you,' suggested Nelson gamely. He had recently suffered the ignominy of his wife running off with an older, fatter and poorer man, resulting in the widespread and oft-voiced conclusion that said man was hung like a carthorse and went at it like a pneumatic drill.

'I expect he gives a discount for mates,' said Dave.

'Only for bulk orders,' said Jon.

'Hurry,' said Nelson morosely. 'This offer must end soon.'

The conversation steered inevitably to a discussion of public figures deemed worthy of murder. It was generally agreed that there were not a few, although Fat Dave's quite disproportionate loathing of and apparent wish to systematically mutilate John Noakes was the cause of some concern. By the time the subject of discussion had moved off at a tangent, the question of Jon's employment had been forgotten, and aside from a short-lived fashion for referring to him, obscurely, as the Avon Lady, was not mentioned again.

Eighteen months after the conversation had taken place, the cuckolded Nelson murdered his runaway wife and her sexually precocious lover. He was picked up by the police the following morning, still drunk, waiting alone outside the George and Dragon for it to open. There was a bloodstained hammer on the back seat of his Ford Orion and a small triangle of scalp in his pocket.

Murder was easy. As Nelson demonstrated, it tended to be a depressingly vulgar crime. Usually the murderer was known to the victim, often intimately. Frequently the parties involved were drunk. More frequently the murderer was a lamentably stupid creature: the crime, though endlessly fantasised about and mulled over, was committed in haste and fury and drunkenness. Although a modicum of planning (even as rudimentary a detail as disposing of the body) greatly increased one's chances of avoiding detection – even investigation –

murderers tended to be squeamish cowards horrified by the results of their own orgasmic release of rage and most murderers, simply, got caught.

Even the vocational killers, the serial- and mass murderers and assorted oddities, were brought down less by the cunning of the Constabulary with its DNA fingerprinting, psychological profiling and dogged persistence, than their own largely unconscious drive to get caught, get punished and get famous. Hence the tell-tale reek of rotting flesh from an anonymous house, the letter to the *Mail*.

However, for *professional* killers, the clear-up rate was improperly modest, even though in most instances 'professional' was something of a misnomer, usually little more than a euphemism for 'paid'. If a job was carried out properly and efficiently, only liaison with clients carried any real risk. On top of this the police were somewhat less interested in gangland murder – criminals despatching other criminals – than in domestic killings, and not only because the latter were, on the whole, easier to clean up, in both senses of the word. They looked on gangland murder as an ongoing process of social Darwinism. Indeed, retired inspectors would talk openly and fondly of the days of the Krays and their ilk, gangs who monopolised crime and thus made life easier for all concerned, at least in so far as there were rules which everyone obeyed and no shortage of professional gentlemen more than willing to punish those who didn't. Modern gangland – being modern – had less of this spurious romance, and there was little unofficial fondness for urban scum, but a certain amount of self-regulation was allowed. Young thugs with a sawn-off and a motorcycle (young men 'known to the police') could kill other young thugs with relative equanimity, so long as they didn't allow their egos to become too large and their bragging too public, so long as the reputation which preceded them didn't do so to the extent that it became an embarrassment to the police, and so long as the people they killed weren't going to be missed by anyone sensible. The police preferred to concentrate on catching only the idiotic and brutal, while blaming declining moral standards and, like every other sector of society, the government.

Amphetamines hammering in his veins, Jon walked upstairs. He paused outside the Oblivion Suite with a junkie's craving for the infinite space that lay within. Briefly he rested his forehead against the door, then went on to the bathroom and showered and shaved and changed. Naked, he was incongruously slight. He wore the finger-traces of scar tissue across his chest and ribs and back, testament to knives and teeth and glass.

He craved the Oblivion Suite, but the Tattooed Man wanted to see him later that night. Since he didn't care to wait, he went to the pub. Stepping from the crisp night air into its smoky cacophony was a blunt, physical blow. For a second he couldn't draw the miasmic atmosphere into his lungs. He shouldered past shouting strangers and stood at the bar, lighting a cigarette to help counteract the speed-fuelled shaking. A pint and a double to chase. He sat next to the pinball machine. Two young men, porcine faces made hideous by some fundamental internal ugliness, snorted and cursed as they took it in turns to hump the table with enthusiastic abandon. The machine replied with delighted bell ringing and flashing lights. When one of them asked if he could set his drink on Jon's table, Jon remembered to call him 'mate' when answering. Not to include this pacifying rune counted as heresy in the unwritten cabala of such places.

Somebody put money in the jukebox. Over the blare of cheap music Jon could hear two sour, overweight men, one balding with Victorian sideburns, the other with flesh the texture of supermarket cheese and a long comb of nicotine-yellow hair scraped and greased across his bald pate. They were exchanging manifestly psychotic fantasies of revenge against women who had done them little harm, dressed as sexual boasts, dressed up as *stories*. Jon listened and knew that they were impotent, that they spent endless flaccid hours on the bog with increasingly violent pornography, that at heart they were rapists, that they would never be anything but rapists even if the act of hatred was never carried out.

Later, Fat Dave spotted him across the bar and beckoned for him to come and sit among his menagerie of corpulent gargoyles in football shirts. Jon made a space on the table by piling some empty glasses into one another and squeezed into the corner. Everyone said, 'All right, Jon?' in turn, and he smiled tightly and offered round his pack of cigarettes. Fat Dave got in a round and Jon monitored the conversation, which was about marriage, a favourite subject.

'It's fucking kids, innit,' said Jagger, scowling into his beer.

'That's what does it,' agreed Nigel, sagely.

'I'll never have fucking kids. Never,' added Jimmy the Scot, who was Welsh.

'You fucking couldn't if you *tried*,' said Jagger, and the table erupted into laughter, in the light of which he unashamedly basked.

'No, I mean it, like,' said Jimmy the Scot.

Fat Dave set a pint before Jon. 'Keith's missis just had a nipper,' he explained. Keith had been a Mate. If there was one thing a Mate could do that was worse than Getting Married, worse than Taking the Piss, worse even than Going Queer (which had actually happened in the case of a former Mate, Gordon, henceforth Gay Gordon, whose name was only mentioned in hushed, embarrassed whispers), it was Having a Kid. Having a Kid was the ultimate betrayal.

Keith had proposed to his wife live on breakfast television, while a cherub-faced presenter jammed a fat microphone beneath his piggy nose (which, at twenty-eight, was relief-mapped in vivid purple). Even that had been OK. Proposing on the telly was quite a classy and romantic thing to do. Keith had blown away wassname who'd since become his missis, and you had to hand it to anyone who had the bottle to blow away a bird in front of the whole fucking *country*. Before she stammered her answer, Keith's beloved's eyes had flitted nervously towards the camera, and thus into the homes of the nation. She had struggled to fight back tears. If you were honest about it (you'd probably had one too many, like, but be *honest*), it was moving. Many of Keith's Mates had bought boxes of Milk Tray decorated by a functionless purple ribbon that day. Even more had intended to, and had spent the remainder of the day vaguely troubled that they had forgotten something. For a while all this actually elevated Keith's standing in the community; having a Mate who had appeared on telly was something special, it tinged him with greatness, with glamour. Now he'd gone and Had a Kid. It was unforgivable.

Besides, only last month Jagger had appeared on a TV quiz show based on luck (computerised dice) and judgement (If I was to give you a piccolo what would you do with it? Would you a) wear it, b) play it, or c) take it for a walk?), demonstrating considerable composure even in the presence of a woman with thighs like concrete coated in peach skin and teeth as lustrous as a hospital sink. Jagger's glamour was therefore of awesome power. He shone. That bird, you know, the one on the programme, she'd given him the fucking come-on, a bird like *that*, in front of everybody, in front of the nation. Naturally, in the face of this, poor Keith's slide from Matehood to Wankership was swift and assured. He would carry this stigma with him for the rest of his life.

Untouched, Jon's glass gently turned on its axis, like a planchette on a Ouija board.

'I see,' he said. He had a sudden, graphic flash of where he had been and what he had done that afternoon. He took a long, gulping draught of beer.

'Seen the last of him, like,' elaborated Jimmy. 'He might as well be dead.'

At twenty past eleven, Jon and his companions left the pub. The others staggered in the direction of the chip shop while, all but unnoticed, Jon hailed a passing taxi. A police car screamed past, followed by an ambulance. Jon gave the driver the Tattooed Man's address and sat back in a seat that smelled faintly of vinyl, ash and vomit. He gazed sombrely ahead as the taxi's path was crossed again and again by cheap cars driven by men too witless to care they were drunk.

The Tattooed Man lived in a Victorian mansion house set in a large garden which was demarked from the pavement by a crumbling wall. The street on which it sat was lined by similar buildings, most of which had been converted into flats, evidenced by gaggles of dustbins that huddled in the corners of concreted drives. The road was lined by gnarled and twisted trees which lifted kerbstones with their roots. The Tattooed Man's house had a history in which, despite ironic intimations of things best left unsaid, Jon could summon little interest, partly because he could sense its questionable history in the oblique quality of the shadows it cast across the clipped lawn and gravel drive, lined by beds of flowers withdrawn as autistic children, and in the way its moist limestone blocks crumbled to the touch. On the front lawn stood a ragged topiary cockerel, an obscurely salacious presence.

An insipid light glimmered through a chink in the downstairs curtains, then the Tattooed Man came to the door, bathed in the sudden radiance of a security light. His grin was triumphant and affectionate. When he smiled his eyes crinkled pleasantly, the furrows running deep in leathery flesh. He might have been sixty, with cropped grey hair thinning at the temples. For all his urbanity he had about him something of the thug, an imposing physical presence. The bridge of his nose was fleshy and much broken and his hands were gnarled and callused. His teeth were almost childishly small, chipped and stained like little ivory pegs. His voice was deep, with an aftertaste of irony and accent. Sometimes when he smiled and flashed those childish teeth he resembled a Victorian street urchin, some malevolent imp grown subtle and deathlessly old.

He took Jon's hands in his and shook his head from side to side in silent admiration. Jon smiled in return and followed the Tattooed Man into the house. He led him through to the kitchen, at the outside door of which whined an Alsatian, half-rampant, ears pressed flat to its head.

The Tattooed Man walked to the door and, nudging the dog gently to one side with his knee, turned the key in the lock and yanked it. The dog poured through the gap like sinuous liquid and, nose to grass, followed a meandering path to the pool of deep shadow beneath the apple tree where, haunches trembling, it defecated. Through the window, Jon could see light reflecting from the back of the animal's eyes, giving them an unearthly radiance.

'Look at him,' said the Tattooed Man from the door. 'He's embarrassed. Silly sod.'

Jon opened the fridge, pushed aside a large jar of mayonnaise and removed a cold beer. The dog, as if to suggest that its interest in the garden had been instigated by any number of factors besides the need for defecation, was sauntering about in casual circles, ears half-cocked.

'Come in then,' the Tattooed Man called to the dog. 'Come in, boy.'

The hound looked coquettishly over its shoulder before padding off to the far end of the garden, where it sat with an air of petulant challenge, a military tilt to its jaw.

'Look at him,' said the Tattooed Man. 'Look at the bastard.'

'I'll get him,' Jon volunteered. The Tattooed Man shook his head and said, 'Sod him. Let him freeze,' and closed the door.

Jon followed him to the front of the house, where one of his drivers was lounging in front of the television. As they entered, he grabbed the remote control and hit the mute button. He acknowledged Jon with a small nod before facing the Tattooed Man.

'Do me a favour, Phil,' said the Tattooed Man. 'The bloody dog's playing up again. Give him ten minutes and let him in, will you?'

Phil nodded. 'Will do.'

'Thanks.' He turned as if to leave. 'What are your hours tonight?'

'I'm on till eight,' said Phil.

'Right you are,' said the Tattooed Man.

'Cheers,' said Phil, and turned the television up. The sounds of televised boxing faded behind them as Jon followed the Tattooed Man through to the silent heart of the house, a library of rich, dark mahogany. Leather-bound books stretched to the high ceiling. The spines of some, high in the shadows, had grown white with mould which partially obscured Latin titles stamped in tarnished gold leaf.

Jon pulled a high-backed chair to the enormous reading table as the Tattooed Man produced a decanter and two tumblers. He poured whisky that had the colour of honey and the consistency of mercury. He pushed a glass across the table and sat back, massaging his lower lip between thumb and forefinger. 'How did it go?'

Jon sipped whisky. It cut through his drunkenness like a burst of intense light. He told the Tattooed Man all about it.

Sweating and trying to scream and mesmerised by his eyes. The impressive gush of black, rich with corruption and thick with the secretions of his earthy life; soiling himself as his hands clawed and crabbed and twitched. And the final burst of intense purity that passed into Jon like a rush of heroin, like wings bursting from his back.

When he had done, the alarm on his watch sounded, like impish giggling.

The Tattooed Man pulled open a drawer and withdrew the parcel of velvet and leather which contained his works. Neither man spoke again until the Tattooed Man, veins livid on a wiry arm, released the tourniquet with his teeth and let loose an orgasmic grunt, ejaculating blood into the syringe in a single smooth effluvient.

Some time passed. Jon smoked a cigarette. The Tattooed Man gazed at the ceiling and through it. He offered the syringe, his blood congealed like rust along the length of its needle. Jon took it, laid it on the table and reached for the rest of the works, the spoon, the cotton gauze and the lighter. With a flick of the wrist the Tattooed Man pushed across a foil envelope. It nearly overshot the table, saved only by a clumsy lunge and a lucky shift of weight. Jon wiped a fleck of spit from the corner of his mouth and wordlessly began to prepare the injection. The Tattooed Man watched silently until, as blood oozed forth to fill the vacuum, he said, 'Bad blood,' and smiled, paternal and bestial.

After some time, Jon reached for his drink, succeeding only in knocking and nearly toppling it. His hand was the colour of pork fat. A lazy, amber droplet ran down the side of the tumbler, negotiating the gradations and contours of its relief, settling in a bead on the dark wood of the table.

He wiped viscous, white saliva from his mouth. He reached into his pocket and withdrew a small bundle of kitchen paper secured with black insulation tape. It was stained by a dark circle that lightened towards the edges, fading eventually to cheap, dirty pink.

The Tattooed Man rubbed sweat from the tips of his fingers with his thumb, took the parcel and tugged at the tape which bound it. He gazed at the contents and exhaled a luxurious, appreciative breath. Then he looked at Jon and said, 'Me and my mementos.'

Jon wiped his palms on his shirt and did not answer, except to mutter, 'Bad voodoo.'

The Tattooed Man placed his trophy in the drawer and pushed it closed.

Jon did not know how long he and the Tattooed Man spent

together that night. Time took on a peculiar quality, and he could not judge the passage of what seemed unmoving, to have happened not as a sequence of events but as a dawning revelation that he felt he had always known, could not imagine not knowing. At some point the Tattooed Man said, 'I'll have you driven home,' and was at his shoulder, helping him to his feet, supporting his weight.

He led Jon to the hallway, where Phil was still sitting smoking his way through a pack of Benson & Hedges, reading a pornographic Japanese comic, which he stuffed into his pocket as he stood. Phil had a lean face in which were etched all the worry lines of an industrial ancestry, but his hair was an incongruously cherubic tangle and his eyes were the colour of bleached denim.

The Tattooed Man patted the back of Jon's neck and opened the door for him. 'Here you are,' he said. 'Here you go. Get yourself to bed.'

Jon could barely feel his lips. His eyes were smoky and dry. The light in the hallway was too bright. His feet were a long way away.

Phil jingled his keys.

The Tattooed Man touched Jon's shoulder. 'Sleep with the light on,' he said, then led him by the elbow over the threshold. It was the darkest and most silent part of the night. As Phil passed him, the Tattooed Man grabbed his sleeve and quietly said, 'Look after him, Phil,' before closing the door.

Phil made no attempt at conversation. Jon sat beside him, his eyes glazed and his jaw slack like a caricature of an idiot. His head bobbed loosely when the car hit a pothole. Phil helped him to his door, and taking Jon's weight on his shoulder, fished around for the keys in Jon's coat pocket. The Jaguar sat predatory and sleek, purring in the darkness of the empty road behind them.

'Thanks, Phil,' murmured Jon.

'You're welcome,' hissed Phil in a late-night whisper, fiddling with the lock.

'Do you know who I am?' slurred Jon, as Phil slipped out from under his arm.

'You're Jon,' said Phil.

'No, who *I* really *am*,' said Jon.

Phil opened the door and helped Jon inside. 'All right, Jon,' he said. 'Shush now. Quiet, now. Let's get you in and to bed.'

Jon stumbled over the threshold.

'Do you need any more help?' said Phil.

Jon shook his head, leaning against the wall.

'Are you sure?' said Phil. He made a comical face as Jon closed the door on him. Then, jingling his keys, he walked to the car.

Jon fell against the wall. He stumbled to the kitchen and threw up in the shining sink, running the tap to wash away the thin bile. Then, beneath the frigid glare of the strip light, he stripped naked, and, shuddering in flurries that made his teeth click, walked through the lifeless front room, up the stairs, and into the Oblivion Suite.

Two For Ever and a Day

It was in the bleak midsummer that the timeless threads of his life began to tie together, to make something strange and half-familiar. It was a small coincidence, but it was a small coincidence in which he perceived the machinations of something impersonal and terrible.

On a Saturday afternoon, on his way to Fat Dave's, Jon's passage was blocked by a small crowd that had coagulated about an old man who lay half-spilled into the road. His legs were awkwardly folded beneath him and one trouser leg was hiked up his shin, revealing a brown, ribbed poly-cotton sock gathered in a pool about his hairless, very white ankle. It was clear that he was dead, despatched perhaps by a heart attack merciful in its instantaneous savagery. Nobody in the crowd, which gazed at the corpse with bovine vacancy, had either attempted first aid or called an ambulance. Instead they scabbed around him like paid mourners or village idiots. Jon tried to squeeze through them, causing a domino-spread of awkwardly corrected balances, and was struck in the cheek by an elbow, for which he received the mantric apology, 'Oh shit. Sorry mate,' to which there was but one possible reply, 'Don't worry about it,' as he shouldered on. Something within him recognised the voice even before the man reached out and touched his shoulder. Its tone touched a dizzying string of recognition and connotation and in the passage of half a second, as he turned to face the man, he was bombarded by the memory of smells and sounds that belonged to another life.

'Jesus Christ,' Andy's voice broke to a fragile falsetto on the final syllable. 'Jon?'

Jon looked into familiar eyes, the eyes of a boy set in a man's flesh, eyes that had crossed time. He smiled without knowing if the smile was genuine or merely a Pavlovian reaction, a deep association of this face with the act of smiling. 'Hello, Andy,' he said. 'How are you?'

They pushed from the crowd and faced each other.

'Jesus Christ,' said Andy in the same strangled falsetto. 'Look at you. You grew up.'

For the first time in many years, Jon thought he might cry for what he had become. Instead, he shrugged, the smile stiff on his lips. 'Not so you'd notice,' he lied.

There was too much to be said, things to be explained, excuses to be made. There was nowhere to begin. There was not enough time, or too much. Unspoken memories: youthful dreams of escape.

'Listen,' said Jon, and a cloud passed over the insipid summer sun. Distantly, the sound of an approaching ambulance. 'Do you fancy a pint? If you're not too busy.'

Andy's hesitation was slight, but it cut through Jon like cheesewire. 'Of course I'm not too busy.'

They walked in uncomfortable silence the few hundred metres to the pub, masking their awkwardness with cigarettes. Once, Jon caught their reflection in a shop window, and was sad.

The pub was an old man's place; dark and quiet, pools coupons, dogs curled at Hush-Puppied feet. They walked to the bar.

'What are you having, then?'

'Put your money away,' said Andy. 'The first one's on me, mate.'

He tried not to notice that Andy paid with a pile of loose change, counting out the coppers and silver after excavating three tarnished pound coins. They sat in a quiet corner and silently supped the heads from their drinks.

'The first pint I ever drank in a pub was with you,' said Jon eventually. 'Remember? It was in the Crown and I was sick.'

'Of course I remember. Two pints of cider and "whuff".' He made a vomiting sound then blushed and sipped gently, and looked up from the glass. He wore a moustache of froth. 'Hang on,' he said. 'That was your first time in a pub? You used to tell me that you drank in pubs *all the time*.'

'I was lying. You were always in pubs and I felt stupid.'

'No, I wasn't. I'd had a couple of halves with my old man before Sunday lunch, that was all.'

Jon bristled. 'You used to tell me that you and your dad used to drink in there every Wednesday night. You were on the darts team or something.'

'I was trying to be grown up.'

Jon produced his cigarettes, offered them. Andy accepted with a self-reflective smile. 'And if you wouldn't have started me on *these*,' he said, 'I might have been able to give them up by now.'

Jon made a face of exaggerated incredulity. 'You used to smoke like a chimney.'

'Only because I thought I looked cool when I was lighting up. I used to give myself a terrible headache.'

'And you could always tell when you'd nicked your mum's', said Jon, 'because she smoked menthol and you'd put them in a Benson & Hedges packet, and when people asked you why the filter was white you said they were duty-free.'

Andy groaned, his hand across his mouth.

'How is your mum?' said Jon.

'Oh, she's fine. Still the same. Does the bingo.'

'And your old man?'

Andy drew hard on the cigarette. 'Just the fucking same.'

'You don't see them much, then?'

'I take the kid round to mum's on a Saturday afternoon when the old man's out on the piss.'

Jon let this sink in.

'The kid?'

Andy shook his head and beamed in pride, more, Jon thought, for the power of revelation than the satisfactions of fatherhood. 'A girl. Kirsty. She's nearly three.'

'Kids. Jesus. You're married then?'

'Seven years. Remember Cathy Reynolds? In the year below us?'

'Cathy *Reynolds*? After that night with the phone you used to deny you even fancied her!'

'Well I did fancy her. Bumped into her a couple of years after I last saw you and one thing led to another, y'know. Bob's your uncle. Married with a kid. Before I knew it.'

After I last saw you. As if the parting had been a watershed: the passage from one world to another.

'What about George and Mildred?' This had been Andy's name for Jon's foster parents, and they had loved him for his innocent cockiness in using it, for the fondness it implied. The unique power of names. When Andy was around they had referred to one another thus, 'George, it's Andy for our Jon.' 'I'll put the kettle on for him, Mildred.' 'Sit yourself down, Andy. George'll make you a cup of tea.'

'They're dead,' said Jon.

Jon found the loss in Andy's face hard to bear. He was uncomfortably certain that Andy had for a moment entertained the notion of turning up on their doorstep, a pushchair in one hand and the toddler in the other, greeting them with a smile and 'Hello George, hello Mildred,' achieving a kind of continuity, a sense of himself as the boy of whom they had been so fond, grown older but unchanged in essence, still eminently recognisable.

'Oh, Christ, Jon. I'm sorry, mate. When?'

Jon shrugged and smiled bloodlessly. 'It must be ten years.'

'Ten *years*?'

'Time flies.' He said this in a half stoop, standing and draining his pint. 'Same again?'

When he returned, Andy had his head in his hands. He looked up and rubbed his eyes. 'Ten years.' He took the pint. 'How long has it been since I saw you?'

'I don't know. A long time. Years.'

'Eleven?'

'Twelve.'

'No, it must be eleven,' Andy said. 'You were there on my twentieth. Remember? Lee Clarke took a beating on the way to the pub.'

'That was your *nineteenth*.'

'It could have been. I don't suppose a year either way makes much difference.'

They knew this was not true.

Silence.

'So what have you been doing for eleven or twelve years?'

'Oh, you know. Getting married. Having a kid. What about you?'

'You don't want to know.'

'The last I heard you were going to university.'

'That wasn't to be.'

'What stopped you? You were always the brainy one. We all thought you'd end up being a doctor or something.'

Old dreams. 'You know how it is. Things happen.'

Andy let it pass. 'So what do you do, since you didn't grow up to be a doctor?'

Jon shifted in his seat. In the far corner an old man sent up a cry of delight as the fruit machine hacked up a small handful of coins. He began to pump them straight back in. 'Nothing much. I make a few quid here and a few quid there.'

'I know you,' said Andy. 'I bet you're making a killing on the quiet.'

The second pint disappeared quickly. Jon said, 'Same again?'

'No. it's my shout.'

That meagre pile of coins. Andy's incipient embarrassment. 'Come off it. You've got a wife and kid to support.'

Andy looked briefly irritated. 'I can afford a couple of pints.'

'Don't be stupid. I'm flush. I had a bit of a win last night.' It was not quite a lie: he would have won had he played Fat Dave and his friends that afternoon. 'What's it to be? Same again or what?'

Andy sighed. 'Go on then. Cheers.'

'Anyway,' said Jon upon his return, setting the glasses on the table, 'I never paid back that twenty quid you lent me to impress Michelle Thompson.'

Andy laughed. 'That was twenty quid well spent, wasn't it?' he said with gregarious sarcasm. 'If I remember right, she ended up going off with some bloke from Exeter and you ended up getting sick all over the shirt I loaned you.'

'Oh shit,' said Jon. 'I forgot about the shirt.'

'Rum and black,' said Andy. 'My mum went mad.'

In this manner they passed the afternoon. Regret for the things they had not done was reserved for the unspecific haze of inebriation; an empty carton of cigarettes, a fresh pack open on the table. Andy leaning on his palm, his elbow wet with spilled lager. A sigh, the death rattle of nostalgia. 'It's good to see you again,' he said. 'No, I mean it,' he insisted. 'It's really good to see you again. It really is. I didn't know how much I'd forgotten. What a laugh we had, like.'

'It wasn't all a laugh,' Jon reminded him. 'Most of it was fucking diabolical. I wouldn't be seventeen again for anything.'

'No, it was,' Andy agreed. 'I mean, it was fucking diabolical and all that, but we made it a laugh. You can make things a laugh when you're a kid.'

'Come off it, Andy. What have you got to be maudlin about? You're married. You've got Cathy wassname from the year below.'

'Reynolds. No, don't get me wrong.' He waved his cigarette a little too expansively and frowned. 'Don't get me wrong, like, she's smashing. I love her to pieces. She's my best friend. And Kirsty. It's smart being a dad. Fucking smart having this tiny little thing that you've made. I'd do anything for her. I made her *alive*, like. Me and Cath made her *alive*. That's a smart feeling. S'amazing if you think about it. But it's not having a proper *mate*, is it? It's not like having a mate.'

'I don't know,' Jon said.

'You will,' said Andy with assurance. If he could have known how much, in that second, in that tone of voice, in that expression, he resembled his father, he would have been filled with something like hatred. Then he laughed out loud and said, 'There must be *somebody* who'd have you.'

'I don't know about that.'

'Don't be daft. Of course there is. There's someone for everyone somewhere. Having someone,' he regarded the smoked-out stub of his cigarette with disdain, and lit another, 'who knows everything about you. That's smart.'

Jon thought of the Tattooed Man. 'I suppose it must be.'

'Someone you can really *talk* to, like. I'm not just talking about someone you can fart in bed next to. Someone you can talk to.'

'You're a lucky man.' Once it was said, it sounded absurdly adult and paternal. Andy didn't seem to notice.

'Am I fuck,' he said, with resignation. 'I'm skint. I've got a kid being brought up on the social and a car that packs up every fucking fortnight. I'm losing my fucking hair and I'm getting fat.'

'You've got Cathy Reynolds from the year below.'

Andy pressed his lips together and hung his head. 'How long for, though? That's the question, innit? How can you keep it going when you're in each other's way twenty-four hours a day and you haven't even got the cash to nip out for a pint? Cath gets all her clothes handed down from her sister. I'd kill for a few quid in the bank. Kirsty need new clothes every other day. How can I keep it going when it's like that?'

Jon knew nothing of such things. The people with whom

he fraternised spoke of their wives seldom and, if at all, disparagingly.

Suddenly he was possessed by a memory so powerful and immediate as to verge on the tactile. A school corridor, a pulsating crowd pressing claustrophobically close as he curled on the floor around the savage boot of Christopher Aitken. The crowd parting. Andy, broad-shouldered and tall, the fashionable shoes he was so proud of, the skinny tie, the blue blazer with the unravelling school badge. He looked first at Jon, grazed and dishevelled on the floor, then at Christopher Aitken. Christopher Aitken, two years their senior, never knew what hit him. This vivid image of his friend began gradually to fade until once more Jon saw him as he had become. His blond hair was cut short, and was thinning at the temples. At the crown, the pink skin of his scalp was visible. Once effortlessly athletic, he was now heavy-set with pasty skin and the beginnings of a gut hanging in small rolls over the edge of his jeans.

Jon had loved this person, or the person this man had been, more than he had ever loved another human being.

'I'm sorry,' he said.

'Fuck it,' said Andy. 'I think I must be a bit pissed. I shouldn't go on like that.' He looked at his watch. 'Christ. Look at the time. She'll be thinking I've run off with a stripper.' He stood and picked up his jacket.

'Well, it was good to see you,' Jon said, for lack of anything better. 'Take care, mate. Look after yourself.'

With the jacket half on his shoulders, Andy paused. 'Look,' he said, 'I'll give you my address. Why don't you come round for tea tomorrow?'

Jon shifted in his seat. This is what people did. What mates who had grown up together did. He doubted his capacity to function in such a context. The world in which he moved had become so familiar he had almost forgotten that it was not his, that he despised Fat Dave and Jagger and Jimmy the Scot. 'Tea?'

Andy leaned on the table. 'Yeah, you know. Meet Cathy and Kirsty and that.'

Weren't children supposed to have a sense of things that bordered on the psychic? Would the child be *scared* of him? He determined to decline, to bite down on his embarrassment until Andy had walked through the pub door and back into that other world. He even opened his mouth to answer, then again he remembered those eyes enraged by his pain and humiliation. 'Of course,' he said.

'Nice one.' Andy stooped and ripped open the empty cigarette packet. He patted his pockets, made a face and wove to the bar, returning with a red Biro. He scribbled for a second, then handed the dissected fag packet to Jon and said, 'Give me a call tomorrow.'

'About lunchtime,' said Jon.

Andy paused at the door, fumbling with the buttons of his denim jacket. 'Nice one,' he said again, and stepped outside.

Jon drank alone until ten thirty, then walked into the damp but tepid summer evening, drawing his jacket about him and huddling within as if for protection. He walked to Fat Dave's flat. The door was answered by Jagger, who had his hand on his zip.

'All right, Jon?' he said. 'You've just caught me on the way to the bog, mate. Go through and they'll deal you in.'

Dave's flat was ripe with the grey odours of unwashed humanity and malnourished dogs. A desiccated turd lay in the hallway against the skirting board, from which peeled wallpaper that had once been garish but was now a step away from dust. In the front room, Fat Dave and friends were huddled about a table with affected looks of intense concentration. Dave glanced up and offered a can of Special Brew. 'What happened to you this afternoon?'

Jon shrugged. 'You know.'

Much nudging and winking.

He sat at the table, sipping thick, catarrhal beer, and picked up the cards Dave dealt him. They were unpleasant to the touch. They began to play, and steadily he began to lose a great deal of money.

He was full of unspecific and inappropriate shame as he stepped from the taxi the following afternoon. Andy's house was an identikit council property surrounded shabby clones which lined a shabby street in the middle of a shabby estate. It was definitively the kind of place where one might *end up*. It was not a place of transition. It was a place where one made the most of things. It was the kind of place where neighbours burgled neighbours, or accused neighbours of burgling neighbours, where a car was, at best, a temporary purchase, where playgrounds were littered with the detritus of hopelessness, used condoms like eviscerated slugs, the odd glue bag fluttering in the breeze as if at the racial memory of flight, where children with Victorian faces smoked stolen cigarettes while ogling stolen pornography.

He walked up the garden path and rapped on the door. He was excruciatingly aware of something in the house going tense. Andy answered the door. They smiled at one another.

'Come in. Take off your coat.'

The living room was small, almost filled by a brown corduroy three-piece suite and a television. There were pictures on the wall that Jon knew, with an ache in his testicles, had been hung there to *brighten up the place*.

'Sit down.'

'Cheers.'

While he was half-way to sitting, Cathy walked into the room. Her hair was washed and pulled into a ponytail and she was wearing a sweater and jeans. She smiled and said 'Hello' and Jon said 'Hello' back and she said, 'Make yourself at home,' and he sat. Then she bent, heel to haunch, and poked her face around the corner of the door, into the hallway. 'Are you going to come in, now?' she asked. Then she turned to Jon and said, 'She's ever so shy.'

A small child toddled into the room, on the edge of balance, stubby arms stretched horizontally, massive head lolling, her sticky face radiant with the joy of her achievement. In one fist she clasped a lollipop, which had smeared sugar around her mouth. There were even sticky bits of it in her hair. Jon was discomfited by the confidence with which Cathy scooped her up and into her arms. 'Say "hello".'

The child gurgled. 'Lo,' she said, and buried her face in her mother's breast.

Absurdly Jon found himself wanting the child to like him. He wished he knew how to make it happen. He imagined some simple conjuring trick might be appropriate, such as producing a fifty-pence piece from behind her ear. Instead he smiled a rictal smile and gave a single, staccato wave. 'Hello,' he said.

'Lo,' said the child.

'Hello,' repeated Jon. He felt frozen in a moment he could not escape. He sensed that something was required. 'She's lovely,' he said. He could scarcely believe that he had voiced the word 'lovely' without caustic intent. His voice sounded comical and clumsy, as if the words were the wrong shape for his lips.

Cathy laughed. 'She's a little terror.' She nuzzled her daughter's face. 'Aren't you? Aren't you a little bloody terror?' She set the child on the floor and Kirsty staggered precariously behind her father's legs. Andy made a neat manoeuvre and scooted behind her, took her beneath her chubby arms and swung her in an arc above his head. Jon caught Cathy's eye as the child yelled her delight: the danger of falling, the safety of her father's arms. The exquisite uncertainties of childhood.

'I know,' Cathy said. 'He's an idiot.'

The child showed Jon her dolls, all of which were unclothed, and only some of which had heads. Andy sat across from him and they talked. Cathy produced a pot of tea on a tray and sat, largely in silence until Andy related the circumstances of their meeting, when she contradicted him and once slapped him on the arm in mock outrage.

'He thinks I fancied him when we were at school,' she told Jon, 'but I thought he was a poser and a big-head.'

Jon confirmed that Andy had been just that.

'He used to have these shoes,' she said. 'These *blue* shoes with buckles on them.'

'They were good shoes,' protested Andy.

'They were bloody *horrible*,' Cathy corrected him. 'They were like something out of *Star Wars*.'

'Hang on a minute,' Andy answered. 'If you didn't fancy me, how did you come to notice my shoes, for God's sake? Do you always pay such attention to people's footwear?' He looked at Jon for confirmation of this minor victory.

'I wasn't *looking*, especially,' Cathy pointed out. 'You just couldn't miss them. They were that horrible. People laughed at you on the street.'

Jon agreed that this was not an unreasonable point.

Andy protested with further circumstantial evidence: 'She wrote my name on her biology book,' he told Jon.

'I did *not*.' This was when she slapped his arm.

'He probably hasn't told you this,' Jon told her, 'but one night I spent a whole evening watching him get drunk so he could find the courage to phone you. In the end he passed out.'

She seemed unsurprised, indeed vaguely affronted. 'He used to follow me around school as well,' she shuddered. 'It was a bit creepy.'

'Christ,' said Andy. 'Who's full of herself tonight?' He looked very pleased.

Presently she left to bathe the child, and put her to bed

before preparing the dinner. She declined Jon's offer of some help, which he had assumed would be expected and welcome. She was, according to Andy, 'funny about the kitchen'.

They drank Jon's wine with the traditional Sunday meal. When Jon expressed his appreciation there was a slight awkwardness and he regretted opening his mouth. He couldn't seem to find the right thing to say. He felt himself to be an accessory to their conversation rather than a part of it, someone whose function was to listen to the jokes and appreciate occult references to years past without ever actually being central to the discussion.

Cathy wouldn't let him wash up. She brought them a beer and a glass each, and disappeared into the mysterious kitchen, about which she was funny, but in which way she gave no clue.

They lapsed into silence. Andy's joblessness fell heavily between them, like an unspoken bereavement. Eventually Jon spoke. 'Listen,' he said. 'I've got a few friends here and there. I might be able to sort you something out. It won't be much.'

Andy set his beer on the floor. 'What sort of stuff?'

'I don't know, this and that.' He seemed to think. 'You're good with cars, aren't you?'

'Well, I don't know about *good*. . .'

'You can make cars that don't go, go, can't you?'

'Well, yeah. I suppose so. Yeah, I can. I'm all right at that. If it can be done, like.'

'I'll see what I can do. I'll have a word with somebody. It might just be a bit of temporary cash-in-hand. Off the books, you know.'

'That's fine,' he said. 'Anything.'

'It could lead on, though,' said Jon. 'Depending on how things work out.'

'Course,' said Andy. 'Course.'

He looked at Jon with embarrassingly naked gratitude and something like wonder before calling for his wife. She walked into the room drying her hands on a dishcloth. Andy explained to her almost word for word what Jon had told him.

She looked at Jon with newly serious appraisal, an indication that she was aware that relationships had changed, that he was moving from Andy's past into their present. He sensed for one illogical second that she had some intimation of the future this would involve, and that it frightened her.

Later that week he sat at the Tattooed Man's kitchen table, a mug of coffee in one hand, a newspaper spread open before him, upon which the Tattooed Man dropped an A4 jiffy bag. Jon removed the documents it contained, examined them. Names, addresses, photographs.

The Tattooed Man waited for him to digest the contents, then said, 'I went out of my way to promote good will with these wankers. They're part of a *Welsh separatist* movement, would you believe.' Jon nearly choked on his coffee, spat some across the paper. The Tattooed Man indicated with a wave of his hand that he thought he had seen everything. He tapped the side of his aquiline, much-broken nose and smiled with singular malevolence. 'I don't think any particular subtlety is called for in this instance,' he said. 'I think it would be best all round if you just kicked the living shit out of them. You might as well leave them alive to tell the tale. But not necessarily psychologically intact.'

Two days later in a tower block in Cardiff Jon spent fifteen tiring minutes beating three men senseless with a series of blunt objects. First there was a baseball bat, with which he struck at knees and ribs and necks, then, when this was finally torn from his grip, a short rubber cosh kept in his back pocket. Finally there was a sock filled with snooker balls, which he was forced to intercept and wrest from the hand of one of the men, shattering bones in the process. The man lost his balance, fell into the sofa. Jon swung the makeshift cosh in a wide arc that terminated in the side of the man's head. The man collapsed with astonishing certitude, like a cow stunned in a slaughter house. The dreadful, dull concussion brought a momentary stillness to the room. Jon was out of breath and in a degree of pain. He took a moment to regain his breath, half-crouched in the mess of upturned and broken furniture, between the remaining two men and the door. Each of them was exhausted and clearly terrified. There were flecks of blood on the walls.

When Jon had done, he taped the oldest of them, half-conscious and dishevelled, to a kitchen chair, then sat and smoked a cigarette. The first man was still and silent. It was possible that Jon had swung the snooker-ball cosh with too much prejudice. The other man lay quietly on his back gazing blankly at the ceiling, one arm crossed loosely on his chest. He would require a short convalescence, and perhaps counselling. He had begged for his life and Jon had let him. He had shit his trousers and Jon had laughed.

When the cigarette was smoked, Jon kneeled before the man taped to the chair and said, 'This was a goodwill gesture. If I have to come back I'll cut out your tongue so you won't be able to scream, and so I'm able to really take my time and enjoy myself. Do you understand?' He took a knife from his back pocket and unfolded it before the man's eyes, so close they crossed trying to focus on it. The man whimpered and struggled. He was trying to say 'please'. Very quietly, Jon said, 'I'll cut your fucking face off. Do you understand?'

The man was unable to nod. He lacked the strength. His head lolled on his chest and he shuddered and wept for his humiliation. Jon lifted his face and spat in it.

As Phil chauffeured him home he became aware of a pain deep in the muscles in his back, as if something had ripped there. It was an unfamiliar pain and a nagging one, present even in his dreams that night, absurdly and comically symbolised by a pair of lurid blue shoes with buckles on the side.

Three   The Good Thing

Grey rain lashed the bay window. The topiary cockerel in the garden had its spindly bones whipped this way and that. A pleasant whistling emanated from the chimney, like that made by a child blowing across the rim of a bottle.

Phil the driver placed a tray on the coffee table and poured the Tattooed Man and Jon a cup of tea. The Tattooed Man, legs crossed, a *Daily Telegraph* folded on his lap, thanked him. Phil replied with a tight acknowledging smile and closed the door behind him.

'Put a record on,' said the Tattooed Man, reaching out for a cup and saucer, on the edge of which balanced two chocolate Hobnobs.

Jon walked to the wall and ran his finger along ranked compact discs. 'What do you want?'

'I don't know. Something a bit cheery.'

'Show tunes?'

The Tattooed Man placed the saucer on the floor and joined him. They stood side to side, in each other's force field, and gazed blankly at the numberless thin spines.

'I'm up to here with show tunes. And this sounds like cocaine psychosis. The trouble is', he said, 'that I'm bored with all of it.' Finally, with an index finger he levered a CD from the shelf and handed it to Jon. 'I haven't heard this for a while.'

It was *Hunky Dory* by David Bowie. The Tattooed Man not only had David Bowie's autograph but a photograph of David Bowie signing it. Bowie's haircut and impossible degree of emaciated ethereality dated it sometime in the early 1970s. Jon was not sure if this was some kind of long-running, arcane private joke.

'Right, then,' said the Tattooed Man, and took a satisfying half-moon crunch from the biscuit, catching the crumbs in an open palm. 'This friend of yours. Do I know him?'

'No.'

'Why not? Have you been keeping secrets?'

'Of course not. I just haven't seen him for years. We were at school together.'

The Tattooed Man drained what must have been scalding hot tea then leaned to pour another. 'A good friend, was he?'

'He looked after me.'

'That's one of the things I like most about you,' said the Tattooed Man. 'Your sense of obligation.'

Jon protested weakly. 'It's hardly obligation.'

'Loyalty, then. If you prefer.'

Jon shrugged. 'I don't know. I just know him.'

The Tattooed Man smiled. 'Good enough. I'll see what I can do.'

Jon scratched his cheek. 'I don't think he's up to anything too strenuous. Morally.'

'I don't have any vacancies for moral philosophers.'

'You know what I mean.'

'Of course. I always know what you mean.'

'He's got a kid.'

'Phil's got kids. Hundreds of them, if I remember correctly.'

'He's not like Phil.'

'Nobody's like Phil,' said the Tattooed Man. They laughed.

'Andy's not weak,' said Jon. 'It's just . . . his kid. I know his wife.' He shifted in his chair. He became aware that he was sweating and that his cheeks were hot. He hoped the Tattooed Man hadn't noticed and knew that he had.

Again, the Tattooed Man laughed, then wiped the corners of his eyes and said, 'I'm sorry. I shouldn't. It's just nice to see you getting out and making friends of your own. It'll do you good. It does me good to see it.'

Jon was unsure whether he was being ridiculed. He didn't altogether understand the Tattooed Man's sense of humour. Sometimes he doubted whether it actually constituted a sense of humour at all in anything but the most cosmetic sense. When the Tattooed Man laughed, which was often, it was seldom a laugh that seemed to stem from immediate stimuli: he laughed at a notion, a connotation that reflected at a cracked tangent from the words he used to articulate it. Sometimes Jon looked at the Tattooed Man's teeth and gums as the lips pulled back and was fascinated by the feral savagery and joy he saw there. He was reminded of the fairground automata that had terrified him as a child: laughing crones and clowns that had come, to him, to encapsulate the very essence of intelligent malevolence.

'Don't take the piss,' he said.

The Tattooed Man knuckled his eyes again. 'I'm not,' he said. 'Well, not in a nasty way. You've got to admit it's odd. Mr Zen gets sentiment.'

'I haven't changed.'

'I'm not saying that you *have*. You should be happy that you still have it in you to surprise me after all these years.'

Jon chose his words carefully. 'I couldn't think of anything that would surprise you,' he said. 'I wouldn't want to try.'

'Everything surprises me,' said the Tattooed Man, 'if I look for surprise. Sometimes I'm surprised to find out how old I am.'

'How old are you?'

'Ancient.'

'Too old for David Bowie.'

Dark shadows in the fleshy folds at the bridge of his broken nose, the furrowed brow of a retired pugilist rolling a cigarette with thick fingers. 'Never too old to rock and roll,' he said.

Jon laughed and shook his head. 'I never know', he said, 'if you're trying to be eccentric.'

The Tattooed Man brushed crumbs from his lapel. 'That would be pretentious of me, and I've no need to pretend to you that I'm something that I'm not. You know everything that I am.'

'I don't know if I do,' said Jon. 'I don't know if I see things the way you do.'

The Tattooed Man produced a pack of cigarettes, unwrapping the Cellophane seal with a spatulate, yellowed nail horny enough to blunt scissors. 'Which I still don't understand,' he said. 'Did you read none of the books I gave you?'

'Of course. I read all of them.'

'And you found none of them illuminating?'

'I thought they were all very good.'

'However?'

Jon took a cigarette from the proffered packet, tapped its filter on the coffee table to settle the tobacco. 'I don't know,' he said. 'None of it seemed relevant to me. I don't identify with universal concerns.'

'None of it moved you at *all*?'

Jon shook his head. 'I might be articulate,' he said, 'but I'm a vulgarian and a thug at heart.'

'You try to be,' conceded the Tattooed Man, 'keeping company with scum and wankers.' He said this with a twist of disgust. 'I wish you wouldn't. I really do. They give me a pain on your behalf.'

Jon lit, inhaled, exhaled. Paused. Inhaled. Exhaled. 'They keep things real,' he said, and knew that the flush had drained from his face. He could feel his bloodlessness.

'Scatology is no escape from metaphysics,' said the Tattooed Man darkly, in the portentous manner he adopted when he was least self-conscious, when what Jon suspected was his fundamental, contemptuous self flickered in his scowl. 'That's intellectual and existential cowardice at its very worst.

Immersing yourself in vomit and shit is a cowardly tactic to avoid confrontation with what's truly important.'

'Like what?'

Darkness seemed to pool at the Tattooed Man's feet and he swelled with it, drawing substance and nourishment. 'God,' he said. 'Death. Love. The Devil.'

'Those things don't mean anything to me.'

The Tattooed Man shrank into his anger like water folding about itself before coming to the boil. 'Those things mean something to everyone, whether they know it or not. Only an idiot thinks otherwise.'

Jon feared to answer. The Tattooed Man closed his fists on his fury. Jon's heart beat heavy beneath his ribs. 'They don't mean anything to me,' he repeated.

The Tattooed Man stood and bellowed the agony of release. One of his knees upended the coffee table and in the perceptual slow motion clarity of shock, Jon watched the teapot spin as it fell, a corona of golden liquid arcing behind then briefly encircling it in a spiral before it hit the carpet and gushed forth its contents.

Head lowered bullishly, the Tattooed Man advanced upon him, meaty hands drawn into scarred fists. 'What do you mean,' he whispered, fury laced with almost petulant sarcasm, '"*they don't mean anything to me*"?'

Jon's testicles shrivelled into his body and he felt tiny and fragile. The Tattooed Man towered above him. 'Don't you know what you are?'

Jon forced himself to meet his gaze. He knotted his fingers and spoke quietly. 'I know what I am,' he said.

Something flickered in the eyes of the monster the Tattooed Man seemed to have become. Jon thought that perhaps it was pity. Whatever it had been, the Tattooed Man was already drawing the anger back into himself, shrinking and folding within it as Phil the driver kicked open the door. He carried a handgun that had an absurd, spindly proboscis of a silencer which, legs spread, he levelled at Jon.

Jon looked into his face. Phil's eyes were as lifelessly alert as lollipops. Phil was not visible in them.

'It's all right, Phil,' said the Tattooed Man with an oddly dissipated wave.

Phil glanced uncertainly at the Tattooed Man, then back at Jon.

'I got carried away,' said the Tattooed Man, addressing Phil in the contrived colloquialism he used in the presence of those whom he deemed otherwise incapable of comprehending him. He privately addressed Jon and a cabal of others in a way that was formal in presentation but intimate by implication. There were still others, of whom Jon had only peripheral knowledge, before whom the Tattooed Man pretended nothing. Jon understood that not all of them were friends or allies.

The Tattooed Man had adopted the uneasy, nervously over-casual tone of a teenage babysitter disturbed *in flagrante*. 'It's my fault,' he said. 'You know how frustrated I get with Jon sometimes. It's not his fault. It's mine. I shouldn't interfere. I'm a nosy old woman.'

Phil's hand began to tremble and he lowered the pistol. 'Oh, fuck,' he said, with something like shame, as he replaced the gun in the holster he wore beneath his arm. 'Oh, fuck. I'm sorry, Jon.'

Jon waved away the apology with a cold hand. 'No problem,' he said.

The Tattooed Man put his arm paternally about Phil's shoulders. 'Jon understands,' he said softly. 'You did well. That was quick off the mark.'

Phil wiped his mouth with the back of a hand. 'I spilled my tea,' he said.

The Tattooed Man chortled. 'Never mind. So did I. I'll mop it up later.'

'That's all right,' said Phil. 'I'll do it.'

'Rubbish. Go and put your feet up.'

'Right you are,' said Phil. He looked sheepishly at Jon. 'I'm really sorry, Jon,' he repeated.

'There's nothing to be sorry for,' said Jon.

'No hard feelings, then.'

'Don't be stupid. It's forgotten already.'

'Right you are. Cheers.' He closed the door respectfully and silently, like someone leaving a confessional or entering a public lavatory. Once more, like a cloud of ancient dust whipped into a loose vortex by a breeze, the peculiar intimacy settled about their shoulders and altered the quality of the light.

'I'm sorry,' said the Tattooed Man, head hung low.

Jon looked at his hands. They were trembling. 'You scared the shit out of me,' he said.

The Tattooed Man looked about him as if surprised that he still stood, then sat and for a moment was silent. 'I only get angry because I want the best for you. I don't like you hating yourself. It hurts me.'

'I don't hate myself,' said Jon.

'It's not enough to know yourself,' insisted the Tattooed Man. 'You have to *revel* in what you are. I hate to see you associating with scum because you're scared to admit what you know. They don't keep you real, they keep you in the mire. It's I who keep you real.'

Jon did not intend, and had not expected, such a level of audacity and bitterness in his reply. 'I'm not like you,' he said. 'There's something inside you. You're driven by will. But I don't have anything inside me. I don't make choices like you do. I'm incapable. So what would you have me do? Attend the ballet with hit men and Shakespeare with assassins? It doesn't make any difference. All places are as one. I only pretend in order not to disappear entirely.'

The Tattooed Man listened, chin resting on fist, staring at the wall. Finally, he answered, 'You're just not admitting to yourself what you are.'

Exasperated Jon said, 'Then what am I?'

The Tattooed Man knotted his fists in his lap. 'An uncommonly loyal friend. A man with sufficient will and love to do things he considers questionable because the consequent self-hatred is secondary to his love and sense of duty.'

Jon laughed, then, absurdly, tears welled in his eyes and he blinked several times in rapid succession. He felt the Tattooed Man's walnut-knuckled hand spread across his back. 'Come on, Jon,' he said. 'Come on. You know all this. It's not as if you haven't heard it before.'

Jon sniffed, wiped his nose. 'I'm sorry,' he said. 'I don't know what's wrong with me.'

The Tattooed Man became both more casual and distant, closing the perceptual door upon his self. 'There's nothing wrong with you. Why you of all people are hung up on all that macho shit is beyond me. There's nothing wrong with crying. It's about time I saw you have a good sniffle. It'll do you good. You can't keep everything bottled up all the time. It'll kill you.' He stroked Jon's hair, forehead to nape, in long, gentle waves, Jon wanted to nuzzle into the palm of his hand like a cat. 'I know there's a lot you haven't told me. I wish you'd talk to me.'

'It was seeing Andy,' confessed Jon, simultaneously demon-strating trust and servitude by offering his weakness. 'I remembered what I was like as a kid.'

Jon's memory of early childhood had always been the colour of weak tea gone cold. When he considered the institutional-ised child he was assured he had been, he might have been remembering a lost brother. He sometimes thought he vaguely remembered meeting his foster parents for the first time, although this half-memory too was without colour and even sentiment, for he could not have known then who they were to become. His first true memory of himself was also a memory of Andy. Twelve years old and in school uniform, one of them far bigger than the other, both with bad haircuts and scuffed shoes, schoolbags slung over shoulders, *faux*-nonchalantly sharing a cigarette as they sauntered home. The image had the ghostly colour of a Polaroid left too long on a window sill and was accompanied only by the muted sounds of traffic. Jon could not remember what he had sounded like, what the pitch of his voice had been. What he had talked about.

'Come on,' soothed the Tattooed Man. 'You've got to know everyone you were in order to love who you are. Sunday supplement psychobabble, but applicable none the less.'

'There's nothing in me to love,' said Jon.

'If you are capable of loving, then you are capable of being loved,' said the Tattooed Man, deliberately, Jon realised, avoiding the deepest intended meaning of his statement. 'Do you love me?'

'You know I do.'

'I know I know. And do I love you?'

Jon nodded.

'Your problem,' said the Tattooed Man, 'is that you insist on associating love with weakness. But so long as your love is a product of *will* it becomes a thing of power. Don't you think Lucifer loved the angels cast out with him? Weakness is a product of sentimentality: Phil loves you, you've done no end of things for him, but he wouldn't have hesitated to kill you just now. He wouldn't have stopped loving you, either, or for that matter started hating himself. That's strength. That's love.' He sat, lit another cigarette, then, with a passing look of ironic exasperation, picked up the ashtray from the carpet. A small mound of ash had settled into the deep pile. 'And that's why I'll look after your friend,' he continued. 'Because you're loyal to me for no other reason than you love me. If you did what I asked only because you were scared of me, I'd despise you.'

Jon smiled. His lips were stiff. 'Thanks,' he said. 'It means a lot to me.'

'That's why I'm doing it.' He took a long draw on the cigarette, tipped a small tube of ash into the ashtray. 'There is one thing, though,' he said.

'Anything,' said Jon.

Carnivorously the Tattooed Man gazed from beneath his brow. 'If I asked you to kill him, would you do it?'

Jon did not pause. 'In a second.'

The Tattooed Man nodded, and slapped Jon's back. 'I know,' he said, and went to change the record. The shadows cast by the cockerel played across his back and the expanse of wall, like the flickerings of blank celluloid, ancient and scratched and projected on a screen. A map of nerves.

The following Monday Andy started work in a garage owned by the Tattooed Man. Jon turned up at lunchtime. Andy's legs were visible, clad in already filthy overalls and steel-capped workboots, protruding from beneath the bonnet of a battered Volvo estate. Jon ignored him for the moment and motioned silently for the other two employees, Gibbon and Rickets, to join him in the 'office', a tiny room strewn with papers and half-empty mugs of tea. They did as they were told, after exchanging an eloquent glance. Gibbon, a graceless ginger monster, put the kettle on to boil after wiping his hands on a filthy rag, then sat in the greasy revolving chair while Rickets perched on the end of the table, pushing aside a tottering, dog-eared sheaf of loose papers.

'What can we do you for?' said Rickets, scratching an armpit, his casualness a transparent over-compensation. The only thing beautiful about him was his extraordinarily lustrous skin, black beyond black, within which Jon could see swirls of colour, like light refracting from a puddle of oil. His teeth were yellow and cracked like antique ivory.

'I've come to have a word.'

'About what?' said Rickets. Rickets was a bad man. He was the worst kind of man. He was a man who had voided himself

40

of conscience, leaving only a sense of warped humour unburdened by anything but the most cursory irony. He had done bad things and dreamed of doing worse. He would erupt into petulant temper and injure another human being, any human being regardless of sex, age or race, for no reason other than proximity, than sheer joyless malice. He was scared of Jon. He did not properly know how to be scared.

'I take it that you're aware that Andy's a friend of mine?'

Gibbon paused in the act of pouring boiling water into a cracked mug. He and Rickets exchanged a momentary glance. Something passed between them.

'No,' said Rickets. 'I didn't know that.'

'I thought you might like to.'

'Yeah. Right. Thanks.'

'Then I can assume that it goes without saying that he'll be treated with a great deal of respect.' He glanced out of the office window, which was so grimed with exhaust-fume grit it framed the garage in haze like a Victorian photograph.

Gibbon spread his hands. 'Of course. No need to ask.'

Jon nodded, looked at Rickets, who scratched his woolly head then nodded in return.

'Nice one,' said Jon. He left the office struggling with a small smile.

Through the grimy window, Rickets watched his retreating back. 'Wanker,' he said, raising a rigid middle finger at waist height.

Jon squatted and tapped Andy's shin. 'Hello, tosser,' he said. 'Fancy a pint?'

Andy wriggled from beneath the car. He sat up, wiping his hands on a greasy rag. 'Is it lunch already?'

Through the window Andy caught Gibbon's eye and performed a short mime that somehow communicated exactly this: 'I know I'm not finished yet but would it be OK if I went for lunch?'

Gibbon raised an affirmative thumb and smiled before half-turning and exchanging rapid words with Rickets. Andy returned the gesture, which Gibbon acknowledged with exaggerated *bonhomie* before turning once more.

He and Rickets continued to converse quickly and quietly. They did not look at Jon.

The pub was busy with lunchtime custom. Jon perched on a stool with a worn velveteen cover, elbows resting on the dark varnish of the round table while without comment Andy bought them drinks and a sandwich each.

Andy chinked his glass against Jon's. 'Cheers,' he said. 'I can't tell you how much I appreciate you sorting me out like this.'

'As long as you're sorted.'

'Well, put it this way: I'm more sorted than I was.' He tore a chunk from the sandwich. A tiny sliver of ham rode on his chomping lips like a cowboy in some hellish rodeo. 'At least there's light at the end of the tunnel.'

Jon bit from his own sandwich and tried to chew without expressing the dry disgust he felt. 'Do you owe money?'

Andy shifted. 'A bit here and there. You know.'

'How much is a bit here and a bit there when it's at home?'

Andy told him.

'I didn't know it was that bad,' said Jon. He took a sip of tepid bitter, then reached into his jacket pocket.

Andy raised his hands before him. 'Hang on,' he said. 'No way. I can't accept anything else from you.'

'Don't be a moron,' said Jon. 'I've got more money than I know what to do with. Let me help.'

Andy averted his eyes and ground his teeth. 'I couldn't,' he said. 'I couldn't just take your money. It's a lot of money, for fuck's sake. It's a lot of money. I couldn't.'

Jon sighed. He was unaccountably irritated. 'Look,' he said, 'once you've got yourself together you can start to pay me back. If you want I'll take *interest*, for Christ's sake. The money might as well be doing something useful in the meantime. I'm never going to spend it.'

He watched as Andy silently debated with himself. The agonies of pride that cannot be afforded. The relief of being shown a way out, of surrendering a responsibility that cannot be met.

There was something foreign inside Jon. It was not pity because there was within it a complex thread of pleasure, a satisfaction to which he did not want to admit because he feared to understand it. He did not know how best to compose his face. In a moment it had passed. He had no wish for it ever to return.

Andy met his eyes. Tentatively: 'Are you sure?'

'I wouldn't say it if I wasn't.'

'I'd pay you back.'

'If you like.'

'It would make a difference.' Andy conceded quietly. 'It would make all the difference.'

Jon opened the chequebook, scribbled in it with a black Biro. 'Buy Cathy something,' he said. 'Some clothes or something. I don't know. A dishwasher or something.'

Andy took the cheque, smudged its edges with oil. 'I don't know what to say,' he said. Jon reached across the table, placed a hand on his shoulder and said nothing. Somebody walked into the pub and for a second they were frozen in this meagre intimacy.

Later, Phil was noticeably nervous as he and Jon dressed head to toe in black bikers' leathers. Before he squeezed his head into the helmet, he said, 'What's he up to with this one? It doesn't make any sense.'

Jon pulled on a gauntlet. 'I don't know,' he admitted, checking that the glove was snug. He squeaked when he moved, a bathetic note of low comedy to offset his sinister appearance. 'He's beginning to move in mysterious ways.'

Phil concurred with a muffled grunt. 'Fucking right he is. This is just beyond me. Way above my head.'

Jon pulled on his own helmet. 'Let's get it over with.'

They walked from the derelict house, pushing aside the creaking iron gate. Phil mounted a black Suzuki motorcycle, kicked it into life, and Jon settled behind him. They leaned into the curve as the bike turned right, then straightened and weaved like an irritable meat-fly through the congested traffic of a main arterial road. Half a mile further, they pulled up across the road from a high-street building society.

'They're late,' said Phil with a note of panic.

Jon clapped his shoulder reassuringly. 'It'll be OK.'

'We're a bit obvious here, aren't we?'

'One minute,' said Jon. 'We'll give them one minute, then we'll leave.'

Phil gunned the engine. Jon was uncomfortably aware that its roar had attracted the attention of several of the bored customers who formed the building society queue, and perceived the minute flickers of trepidation which passed among them. One or two of the staff, alerted by the slight shift in the hormonal balance of the air, glanced up with more recognisable anxiety. Jon dismounted and, kneeling, made a mime of fiddling with the bike's exposed chromium engine. Phil was tapping his feet.

A red Ford Escort pulled up outside the building society. Jon tapped Phil's leg. From the car spilled four men in ski masks, hurried and spiky with adrenaline. Carrying sawn-off shotguns, they bustled clumsily through the smoked-glass doors of the office. From the street the pandemonium inside was pantomimic and surreal: pensioners freezing, hands on heads, women scooping children from the floor, young men emasculated and terrified, muzzles waved and brandished and gloved fingers pointing this way and that.

Jon took a moment to get his breath, then stood, opened the bike's saddle-bag and withdrew a conscientiously oiled semiautomatic pistol. He tucked it under one armpit as he dodged traffic, then held it aloft as he walked through the smoked-glass doors. For an extended fragment of time, all activity froze. He held the pistol high and steady and let it bark twice. The first of the ski-masked men folded violently at the waist as the impact drove him into the wall. A fine spray of blood rained slowly upon the customers who by now were stretched across the floor. Hands over heads, arms folded protectively about children too scared to sob. The second burst of fire, as decisive an exclamation as the first, sent the second man spinning on his axis like a spastic ballerina, sawn-off spinning gracefully from his hand. The third was in the process of turning, raising his gun, when a third burst, more accurate, shattered much of his head. The fourth had been given perhaps two seconds in which to react: he spun on his heel, gun in one outstretched hand, and discharged both barrels. Although the shots hit the wall behind him, something hot and sharp, like a tiny meteor shower, rained on Jon's back, pittering and pattering against the motorcycle helmet. He drew an unhurried aim on the fourth man, who was running for the door. Glass shattered in his wake like crashing surf and cascaded in jewelled shards about his head as the jumping muzzle pursued him. When the line of fire crossed his shoulders, he was rammed head-first through plate-glass and on to the pavement, coming to a twitching halt across the bonnet of the red Escort. The horrified, pasty-faced young man at the wheel, who only that morning had woken thrilled with his new role as Driver, reversed with a smoking banshee wail into the traffic, letting the corpse slide from the bonnet into the gutter.

It had taken considerably less than ten seconds. Jon turned and sprinted on to the street, the beginnings of a crowd scattering like water the moment he did so. He clambered on to the back of the revving motorcycle, and Phil accelerated away. At the appointed place they dumped the bike, clambered over a fence and into a trading estate where a van was waiting. The back doors opened as they approached, and closed behind them as they threw themselves in, to the smell of white spirit and stripped pine and the hammering of exhilarated hearts.

'I couldn't believe it,' said Phil. 'There were four of them. I admit that I was ready to call it a day there and then, I mean there were four of them and we were only expecting two, but Jon here walks in, cool as a bloody cucumber, and takes them all out before you can say Jack Robinson. It was the most beautiful thing I've ever seen. It was beautiful. It was like a film.'

The Tattooed Man grinned wolfishly, and poured Phil a whisky. Jon had spent much of the afternoon having shrapnel removed from the back of his arm. He was wearing a white T-shirt and jeans, both of which had been taken from the Tattooed Man's wardrobe. Jon's own clothes had blood on them and had since been incinerated in the basement.

'You played your part, too, Phil,' said the Tattooed Man. 'That was a beautifully arranged get-away. Pretty impressive all round.'

'Cheers,' said Phil. He was still shaking.

Jon sipped whisky.

'You shouldn't be drinking,' said the Tattooed Man. 'Not on top of all that medication.'

'Come off it,' protested Jon. 'I'm toasting myself.'

'And so you should,' said the Tattooed Man. He stood, glass in hand. 'To Jon,' he proposed.

'To Jon,' agreed Phil.

Jon wiggled his glass beside his ear. 'To me.'

'You did a good thing today,' said the Tattooed Man.

'I know,' admitted Jon. 'And after that I killed some people.'

The Tattooed Man frowned. 'Enough booze, I think.'

Jon waved him off. 'I'm sorry,' he said. 'I shouldn't try to joke. I'm not very good at it.' He raised his glass. 'To the good thing.'

'To the good thing,' echoed the Tattooed Man and Phil.

The next day, the newspaper headlines were exactly as the Tattooed Man had predicted, indeed seemed to want. Perhaps even require. They were variations on a theme of 'Bizarre Gangland Murder Puzzles Police', sub-headed 'Lone Gunman Kills Three, Injures One', jazzed and teased into varying degrees of vulgarity dependent upon the price and size of the paper in question. He was third headline on the television news, at least until the afternoon when a corrupt government arms deal and the death of a minor television personality shifted him in the running order. In the *Sun* the last paragraph of the leading article was devoted to unashamed celebration of the previous day's deed. The next day speculation had spread to the broadsheets. Eye-witnesses were interviewed by television journalists and asked the inevitable question: 'How did you feel?' More than one, interviewed in the safety of their warm house and with more than a day's hindsight, spoke of feeling oddly *safe* the moment Jon burst in and started firing. By the following week, the subject of vigilantism was the talking point of a daytime television discussion programme. The gang-war speculation quietly ended. The popular mind wanted something else and relentlessly pursued its desire until it took on tangible form. It was revealed by an eager media that the three dead men had boasted two sentences for rape and one for murder between them, not to mention a string of convictions for robbery with violence.

At short notice and with little preparation, he was asked to complete two broadly similar jobs. It was as if they represented a last-minute idea of the Tattooed Man's: as they were about to board a ferry to Zeebrugge Jon put to sleep a Dutch child pornographer and two of his entourage. Phil did well to get him away. Two days later he dumped on the steps of Bristol Crown Court the shattered corpse of a hit-and-run driver who, after drunkenly ploughing through and killing two of a queue of children at a bus stop, had been released from custody to national disgust after serving six months in an open prison. By the end of the third week, a figure clad in leathers and brandishing an Uzi stood behind a cowering, indecisive Prime Minister in a *Times* cartoon, the word 'justice?' in gothic script scrawled across a war-torn banner which fluttered behind them.

Jon was mystified, but not unamused. He kept the *Times* cartoon. He had no idea why the Tattooed Man had wanted such a thing done, since it served no purpose nor furnished any advantage of which he was aware. He half-suspected the whole project to be an exercise in whimsy. Perhaps the Tattooed Man, for his own reasons, perhaps with no motivation other than the amusement afforded by secret, skilful manipulation of others, was playing a game with British public opinion. Perhaps he was doing it merely because it had occurred to him that he could. Jon found the idea intriguing and oddly disturbing. He thought of the Tattooed Man's smile, of that mixture of atavistic savagery and intellectualised ironic distance. And then he thought of him saying, 'You've got to *revel* in what you are.'

At this, the strange joy left him, replaced by a fragile, distracting unease, so that, during the self-imposed quarantine he undertook to allow his recuperation, he would often find himself in the bedroom or the kitchen or the hallway, wondering why he was there, and what was the nature of the thing he had come here to do, but had forgotten.

Finally, as he stood, confused, in the hallway, the telephone rang. Passively, he stared at it. The receiver seemed to shiver with its impatience to be held. With its craving to discharge the voice of the Tattooed Man into the hollows of his cranium.

He took half a step towards it. He knew that the Tattooed Man was at the other end of the line. Jon could picture exactly his stance, the way he clasped the receiver loosely at his ear in an almost effeminate posture. After five or six rings, the brow knitting darkly with frustration. After ten or eleven the redundant consultation of a wristwatch. Dumping the receiver heavily back into its cradle and stalking moodily into the kitchen to brew a cup of tea.

He knew that he should answer. His stomach knitted in fondness and fear and he wished that he might merely reach out and lift the receiver, but he could not, although he could not be sure why. After a while the ringing stopped. Jon remained unmoving, a helix of remorse twisting through his intestines. He knew that the Tattooed Man would not enquire after his whereabouts. The Tattooed Man understood the necessity of retreat, but he understood the subtleties of betrayal also, the minutiae of contempt.

Something began to gather at the base of Jon's skull, in the darkness at the back of his mind. It was pre-orgasmic and dizzying, like the precursor to a madness which might build in his head before exploding with the furious beauty of napalm.

There was within him a kaleidoscopic multiplicity of things he did not understand. He did not feel able to contain it. He did not feel able to bear it, that he was capable of even such tiny betrayal.

He removed his clothing and walked upstairs and into the Oblivion Suite. It was like dying.

Four The Oblivion Suite

The Oblivion Suite was a place of indeterminate dimension. Every surface was mirrored. Dim, concealed lighting allowed unbroken reflection. Some of the mirrors were flat and flawlessly reflective. Others were warped, producing distorted monster images. Still others were cracked and crazed, creating tiny homunculi, perfect in every detail, the sparse hair on Jon's chest, the many scars that marred his skin, the dark thatch of pubic hair, so that it was impossible to judge which image was tiny and close and which was large and distant. Naked, the frigid glass numbed his flesh as he lay flat and spread his arms in a gesture of welcome or surrender. His image spiralled infinitely about him, like the heavenly host in some lunatic's rendition of heaven. As the chill numbed his bones he began to lose sense of a physical self. He became nothing but eyes regarding an endless parade of selves that would never be, or which had been and had passed away. They regarded him with the passionless pity of a Renaissance Christ.

For a period without thought and thus without time he levitated, a single fixed point about which the cascading, vertiginously regressing images revolved. He underwent movements of epiphanic intensity. He and the multitudes of himself wept as he surrendered his hold on the guilt that had begun to fruit in his stomach like a tumour. Hallucination followed epiphany, and he was visited by armies of demons and legions of angels, each of which burned his corneas with their majesty and unbearable beauty, and each of which wore a parody of his features. These twisted *doppelgängers* burned with an unbearable mercy or were tortured and twisted by hatred but each, in its way, mocked and taunted him with what he was and what he was not, with what he had been denied the freedom to be. He underwent the stigmata, bled from hand and foot and side. He displayed the crown of thorns in negative, a succulent perspiration of berries oozing forth across his brow, ripe juice spilling in thin rivulets the length of his nose, the curvature of his lips, into his hair, the line of his jaw. He underwent the torments of hell, and wept and tore at his flesh because he knew he endured it in the name of others, who he did not and could never know. He burned for the sins of those he had killed and for the evils of those he loved. His flesh blistered and split and his throat parched and he brought time to that timeless place with a cry, by imploring the mercy of a God who could not have been more distant.

At some point time returned, leaking into the Oblivion Suite like odourless gas. He came back to himself. He became aware of the stiffness of his limbs against the mirrored floor, which had again become substance beneath him. He felt, for a second, that he had recreated the world. He crawled like a babe to the door, which was like a portal into corporeality, opening on to a dawn-lit, deep-carpeted hallway which seemed absurd and half real. Standing and taking tiny, painful steps, his muscles knotted with cramp, he walked to the bathroom and turned on the light, revealing a room lightly sugared with a trace of dust, his own ancient skin cells fallen still as if *in memoriam*. In the mirror he saw that he had grown a short, scruffy beard, and that his hair was tangled and knotted with sweat and blood. He was desiccated to a kind of newsreel emaciation, as if his living skin had mummified on his bones, dried to leather. His cheeks were hollow and shadowed. Eyes that had become accustomed to gazing into a space that was not truly there testified to a mixture of listlessness and vague reproof, as if the things they had gazed upon rendered all else pitiable. He moved as if possessed by the malevolent spirit of an old man.

He was cold, and hugging himself produced no warmth. He ran the tap and poured a tooth-mug full of stale water, painstakingly rinsing his mouth although his etiolated frame begged to bend to the lightly musical flow, to let the water pass uninterrupted into his cramped gut, to let the urgency of osmosis spread in a visible bloom of colour from his guts to the soles of his feet and the curve of his skull, to inflate the withered lobes of his ears and mother-of-pearl nails. Obscurely, he longed for the taste of vinegar. For a delirious moment, in which he had to extend a hand to the cistern to steady himself, he was visited by two images, sufficiently intense as to be hallucinatory. They were simultaneous, like one piece of scratched film played over another. He heard the parched, crucified Christ beg for water, for release from his torment, only to be mocked by a sponge soaked in bitter vinegar. He saw the American soldiers who, upon arrival in Dachau, numbed by the horror that had transpired there, brought with them a talismanic offering, a fragment of the reality in which they had believed and which this terrible place had proved a lie. Young men who had travelled across the sea to witness history spasm and twist in ways no God could have allowed, offered to colourless, hairless skeletons in striped rags and wooden clogs the gay talisman of American candy bars. Half-human, wretched things, whose presence in such a place made them appear in newsreel as ghostly, saintly creatures with eyes that testified not to the fact but the meaning of what had happened there, were offered chocolate bars. There was no JHVH to avenge them nor Christ to caress their shaved and fleshless heads with hands wounded in the name of all who had died here and all who had killed. Instead there was American candy. Out of the mighty came forth sweetness. The sweetness of freedom, the primary coloured gospel of abundance, of a mythical place where goodness was enough and innocence sacred. Although starved for so long, although deprived of sweetness of any kind, the survivors had no need of American candy. Instead they asked for vinegar because they craved the familiar bitterness of that which was used to mock Christ in his death agonies.

Jon had an image of a young soldier, so intense the rips and stains and repairs in the boy's uniform could be discerned, the scuffs in the leather of his boots, not yet old enough to shave, yet who had encountered carnage on a scale hitherto undreamed, gazing at the unwanted candy bar in his hand. He saw there the true nature of the horror which would never leave his dreams. He had never seen this image, either in newsreel or newspaper, but knew none the less that it was true. For a moment he felt the whisper of the soldier's ghost pass through him like a breeze, raising a thrill of goose bumps the length of his spine. He knew that it was the weight of such memories, of things that should never have been which happened on a scale that should not have been possible, which had somehow formed the creature that he was. He thought for the remains of that giddy moment that he might be an angel, an agent of vengeance against those who had used up all the love there was and rotted in a miasmic superfluity of hatred and wilful idiocy. He thought of the Tattooed Man and longed to curl himself beneath that fierce and paternal arm and find solace there. The hallucination faded.

He ran his head beneath the tap, cursing and spluttering, then allowed himself to swallow a mouthful of water.

He showered, washing the dried faecal matter from his inner thighs and buttocks and the blood from his forehead, hands and feet. Clear-headed beneath the massaging flow, he supposed that in the passion of hallucination, he had clawed the marks of Christ into his own flesh and was glad that the thing which felt such things had left him.

As the daylight gathered strength, it became clear that the damp summer had slipped into another winter that was little more than an administrative convenience, the bureaucratic memory of seasonal shift. The evenings would be darker and the meagre drizzle would become not so much colder as marginally more irritating. The planet, meanwhile, continued to wobble unsteadily about its fat axis like an alcoholic bag woman. He saw through the window that most of the leaves had fallen from the tree in his neighbour's garden, and those few that remained were gold and russet and as good as dead. The world was the washed-out grey of a bad water-colour.

After showering and towelling dry he took a set of electric hair-clippers and shaved his head to an eighth of an inch of stubble. Then he lathered and shaved his new beard. The reflected face he saw displayed nothing but the most academic interest in itself. Shaved and drained of personality, it might have belonged to a demonic statue churned up by a spade or a boot in the deserts of the Middle East.

It was some time before he was fit enough to leave the house, which he would not do until the full sense of solidity in the world had returned to him. For days he continued to slip into mildly hallucinatory states, which were marked by an uncharacteristic willingness to make metaphysical suppositions. He heard voices in the corners and saw movement in the periphery of his vision. He imposed on himself a regime of bastardised yoga. The muscle fibre beneath his skin had the consistency of wire rope coiled about itself, like a nest of cybernetic snakes. The small puckered wounds that dotted his shoulder and upper arm had begun the slow fade from rude purple to the lividity of white scar tissue. He felt like he had sucked time into himself, solidified it by exercise of an ego-less will.

When he was ready, he dressed and jingled his keys in his pocket as he stepped outside. Cars drove past and did not register that he existed. Strangers passed him on the street, and did not guess that he had for a time stepped out of the world. A mongrel pissed against the stem of a lamp-post and did not whimper and scuttle from him. He had to sidestep to avoid curled turds and deep roadside puddles that a bus might run through, soaking him. He carried a handwritten list in his pocket that read 'batteries, shaving-foam, new razors', because for some reason these were things he often forgot to buy. He waited at the corner while the traffic passed, then, when the red man was replaced by his green counterpart, he crossed amidst a small crowd of others. In the shop he thought he had the right change but didn't, and after painstakingly counting out coppers, found himself eight pence short. He checked all his pockets in turn before producing a twenty-pound note and some clucks of impatience from the queue behind him. Walking back into the world was like walking into a sandstorm. There was no way to protect yourself from it. A composite of sheer, abundant power and insidious intrusiveness, it found every crack and crevice. By the time he lit his first cigarette, what he had undergone began to seem distant. He wondered at the fact that the wounds of Christ had reduced him to tears, although he knew that Christ had been nothing more than another revolutionary megalomaniac who died mocked and deserted, unable to make sense even of his own suffering. Whatever it was that had been in him, leading him to believe such things, had passed away into the private infinity of the Oblivion Suite.

When he got home, he opened all the windows in the house to let out the dead smell, put the shopping in the cupboards (neat ranks of tins and sauces and bottles, labels forward), then phoned Andy. The phone was answered on the fifth ring. He heard the clearing of a feminine throat, slightly impatient, a half-whispered, 'Hello?'

'Hello Cathy wassname from the year below,' he said. 'It's Jon.'

He heard her smile, found himself picturing her eyes folding into crow's-feet at the corners, her scrubbed skin, her hair pulled into a practical but deliberate and neat ponytail. The faint smell of baby on her clothes. He was a little surprised to find out that he was smiling in response.

'Where have you been?' She spoke in the same cracked whisper, exasperation and perhaps, he thought, surprised pleasure raising its tone half an octave. 'We thought you'd been kidnapped by aliens or something. Andy's been out of his mind with worry.' She stifled a laugh. 'Pacing up and down the room calling you a bastard and wondering where you'd gone.'

He laughed. 'I'm sure it wasn't that bad.'

A muffled snort, like a hand was pressed across her mouth between the receiver and her lips. 'Sorry,' she whispered, 'I've just got the little one to sleep.'

'She's not ill, I hope.'

'No, just a bad-tempered little madam. Where have you been?'

'Not far. I'll explain when I see you both. How are things?'

This time he heard or thought he saw her smile spread right across her face, dimples in her cheeks, and he knew that her eyes twinkled within their nest of crow's-feet. Oddly, he thought of Father Christmas. Although her answer was confined to a single word, 'Yeah,' Jon was almost shocked at the depth of fondness he heard there. He wanted her to say 'Yeah' like that while Andy stood at her side, with his burgeoning beer gut and his thinning hair and his wispy gingery-blonde moustache, and he wanted to be able to smile back and hold them at arm's length, one shoulder each, and look in their eyes and see himself reflected there. He very badly wanted nothing bad ever to happen to either of them. He did not want for them ever to have to say anything but 'yeah' in that precise tone of voice ever again.

'Listen,' she said, 'I don't know if you realised, but it's Andy's birthday a week Tuesday. Next Saturday we're having a bit of a do round our place. Not much: you know, Kirsty at my mum's, a few friends round. Andy would be chuffed to nuts if you were there. He really would.'

His hand was cold round the phone. 'Of course I'll be there,' he said. 'The last time I celebrated one of Andy's birthday's he was about half as old. . .'

'And half as fat,' she finished. He could smell her perfume, a warmth just beneath and behind the lobes of her ears, and Andy's smell, fresh sweat and grease that was ingrained into the whorls of his hands.

'What time?'

'Any time. Seven. Half past.'

After confirming, he ran out of things to say. He had nothing to talk about. He wasn't even sure what day it was. He found himself wondering why he had phoned when Andy would obviously be at the very job Jon himself had acquired for him. There was a curious feeling in his stomach.

With the phone back in its cradle, he perched on the edge of the coffee table watching a triangle of light cast by a window shift slowly across the carpet. He thought about himself. When this was no longer absorbing, he walked to the bookshelf and surveyed the ranked volumes which the Tattooed Man had given him. Some were handsome hardback editions, some of them, he knew, worth some money, while others were cheap paperbacks apparently picked up on a whim. He thought of the Tattooed Man queuing in W.H. Smith's, a paperback in one hand, a packet of mints in the other and a *Daily Telegraph* folded beneath his arm, while those queuing before him and those queuing behind him did not suspect for an instant the nature of the thing in whose shadow they stood. He smiled fondly. The book he chose was one of these paperbacks, one which fell open at a particular page, as if the Tattooed Man had passed on a well-used volume. It was perhaps another of the self-referential in-jokes that brought the Tattooed Man such evident pleasure: Milton's *Paradise Lost*. Jon let the book fall open in his hand. One line was underlined, and in the margin next to it was a meticulously inscribed exclamation mark. 'Which way I fly is hell,' it read; 'Myself am hell.'

This time, Jon thought he might get the joke.

He arrived at Andy's and Cathy's at ten o'clock in the evening because he wished to avoid any possibility of being the first to arrive. The thought of sitting with the two of them, excited and a little apprehensive, anxious that all would go well, making stilted conversation which fell silent every time a car slowed outside, filled him with a dread whose depths knew no bounds. He had actually woken in the middle of the night in a clammy sweat at the thought of it.

He could hear the music from half-way down the street. There were lights flashing in time with the bass drum, intermittently illuminating the living-room window, behind the darkness of which he could discern shifting figures. There was already a smattering of pleasantly strained, atonal singing rising above the music. The song he recognised as a 1970s' disco hit to which, at his first school disco, he had tried to dance. He had been so heroically inept at producing anything even vaguely recognisable as what might, even with charitable intention and in the dark, be called a dance, that – as he devoted the entirety of his concentration to willing his arms, legs and hips not only to do what he wanted them to, but to do it in a co-ordinated fashion and, if possible, in time – his schoolmates, one by one, had stopped dancing and gathered in an awe-struck circle about him. His ineptitude was such that his audience which, after all, was comprised of adolescents whose savage sense of humour knows nothing of the sensibilities of others, were struck dumb for the duration of the song, which perchance, was called 'He's the Greatest Dancer (that I've ever seen)'. As it faded to silence, somebody (he never knew who) said, in a paradigm of perfect comic timing,

'I bet his mum does the laundry by throwing him in the bath with it and turning the radio on.'

He hadn't been the kind of sensitive child driven to solitude and ultimately adult bitterness by such an event. He had forced himself to laugh along because he perceived, accurately as it turned out, that this would be the best way to diffuse the situation, a pre-emptive strike against the prolonged agonies that would follow a public display of humiliation, of being a little boy in front of all those little girls who at the time seemed like impossible, unattainable ideals of Womanhood. Still, he had never danced publicly again. Possibly he was saved from the worst traumas of adolescence by the fact that by the age of thirteen he had spent a good deal of his life in institutional care.

This train of thought, the association of images and smells led from thoughts of events once so important, now sufficiently distant to be gently amusing, invoked other, gentler memories: as an adolescent Andy had danced with an utterly arrhythmic yet blatantly unselfconscious series of pneumatic thrusts and wiggles. Somehow he convinced all who gazed in wonderment upon him that this obscurely pornographic series of jerks and grunts was actually dancing. He carefully calculated his entrance to school discos, which were held in the sports hall. He swaggered in late, brandishing a half-bottle of vodka which he had taken great pains to smuggle in with the express intention of producing it as if it were the most natural thing in the world, and from which he swigged with fire in his throat but impassive stoicism on his face. For a while he wore the worst footballer's perm Jon had ever seen. He had bought the kit from Boots one Saturday, and when it had gone awry had called in maternal aid. He looked, Jon recalled, like an absolute wanker. With his disastrous hair, blue shoes and ecstatic pelvic thrusts, Jon actually used to feel sorry for him on such occasions, until the night when, extraordinarily, Andy lost his virginity. What had really rankled Jon is that they'd taken out a bet on that very occurrence. 'Tonight's the night,' said Andy. 'Now or never, innit?'

'A tenner on it,' said Jon amicably, making no attempt to hide his scepticism. To *plan* the loss of one's virginity was a quixotic crusade indeed. Come midnight he was in debt to Andy to the tune of forty-five pounds. Only six months later (six months representing a considerable passage of time to teenage boys, for whom the transition from climbing trees to obsessive interest in the cut of one's trousers might measure to the outside world the length of perhaps one Easter holiday, while representing to the subject an almost geological time-shift), Andy himself had been horrified at what he called his 'Kevin Keegan stage'. He referred to it, under duress, in an embarrassed mutter, and always qualified it away into nothing-ness with surprisingly creditable sociological contextualisation: 'Everyone dressed like that. It was fashion, innit?', and so on and so forth, until his embarrassment became so palpable the subject was changed. He had the perm cut into what he considered to be a kind of punk look, but not so much as to upset his mum, and which nevertheless resembled, for a period at least, nothing other than a radically trimmed home perm. Once, a group of them, drinks barely touched, was forced to leave a pub because Andy caught sight of the girl to whom he had lost his innocence and by whose favour he so extravagantly won a bet. He didn't want to speak to her. He was embarrassed. He was ashamed. Not by any of the usual catalogue of post-adolescent cringeworthy memories, prema-ture ejaculation, terror-stricken, limp penis, Marks & Spencer's underwear with a Yogi Bear legend revealed to history at the bottom of a school field. He was embarrassed about the clothes he had been wearing. Jon suspected that his disproportionate shame about the Kevin Keegan period actually constituted a genuine trauma in his life. It was one of the key events by which he would always understand and measure himself.

As Jon walked up the short garden path, he remembered

that he had actually owned some photos of Andy wearing that very disreputable bubble-cut. Although, like the Tattooed Man, he had always been compelled to preserve any image of the past, he had ripped them into tiny pieces which he burned in an ashtray until they were nothing but ash. It was a solemn occasion, a proof to Jon of the depth of his friendship. He had forgotten all about it.

It was pissing down. He rang the bell. Andy opened the door. Still chubby, a couple of days' growth of gingerish stubble, his face lit up like a baby shown a shiny rattle. His eyes were crystal blue and beautiful. 'Fuck me,' he exclaimed. 'It's Bod!' He sang the theme tune to this very cartoon, the protagonist of which was a bald-headed boy with a very round head. Andy found this unbearably amusing. He was wearing what was clearly a new shirt, purple cotton with white cotton detail like Roy Rogers, open at the neck to reveal the links of a St Christopher medallion. He had a packet of cigarettes in his top pocket, a half-smoked filtertip in the corner of his mouth and a bottle of Newcastle Brown ale in his fist. He extended his arm, bottle still in hand, and rested it on Jon's shoulder. He leaned forward, put his beer-and-fag-and-aftershave smelling face next to Jon's and said, 'What on earth have you done to your fucking hair?' He fell into Jon with the unbalancing force of his amusement. 'You look like Mr Fucking Potato Head,' he said. 'Like something from One Flew Over the Whatsit Nest. Cuckoo.'

'Are you going to invite me in out of the rain,' said Jon, 'or do you expect me to stand here and get pissed on while you stand there and laugh at my haircut?'

Andy placed his arm fully about Jon's shoulder and Jon allowed himself to be led inside.

There were brightly coloured crêpe-paper streamers hanging from the banisters and balloons parading the hallway and stairs. The front room was almost dark, but he could see that there were perhaps thirty people in there. Some of the furniture had been pushed to the edges of the room, some of it moved upstairs and out of the way. Hired disco lights throbbed red yellow blue red in the corners. In the middle of the floor a woman of perhaps sixty who had clearly already drunk more than was good for her was dancing too close to a youth of possibly seventeen whose face, even in the darkness and intermittent flashes of coloured light, was clearly rigid with terror and embarrassment. Her wide buttocks, in a black dress, shifted sinuously and drunkenly in half-time to the music, attempting to make a smooch of some Hi-Energy confection, while his bony and still childishly narrow arse was set rigid, moving through an arc of about twenty degrees, and that obviously under some protest.

Small groups of people gathered around the stereo, attempting to read cassette boxes as they talked and drank and spoke and occasionally listened to each other. Others sat on the carpet or the three-piece suite, which now lined the walls, or stood in corners. Jon guessed that most were either relatives or neighbours. The party had that particular spread of ages, not to mention a certain degree of salacious cackling, which characterised such a milieu.

A girl whom Jon assumed to be the youngest at the party swept her fringe from her eye and swigged from a bottle of cider, a cigarette held self-consciously in her other hand. She was taking advantage of the opportunity to flirt in absolute safety with one of the younger married men. The man's wife glanced at him. Jon could tell she felt sorry for him as well as irritated. The girl took an almighty puff on the Silk Cut followed by another swig from the bottle. Her parents had allowed her to come, Jon guessed, because they knew that Andy and Cathy would let her enjoy herself without letting her do *anything stupid*. She was going to be so ill tomorrow, it was quite possible that she might have learned her limit, and bear it in mind at future parties where no adults would be present, thereby saving on all the expense and bother of taxi fares and a Boots' home pregnancy-testing kit.

'Wanna drink?' said Andy, slurring a little more with every swig. 'Inna kitchen. Help yourself, mate.' He patted Jon's back between the shoulder blades.

Jon walked through to the kitchen, where Cathy and a small group of friends were sat around the table sharing two-litre bottles of wine. He plonked the carrier bag he was holding on the table. A slightly expectant silence fell among the women. The woman to Cathy's left took a gulp of wine and wiped the back of her hand across her lips. 'This is Jon, is it?' she said in a whisper that was meant to be heard, nudging Cathy with vaudeville exaggeration. 'You're right,' she said. 'He's *lovely*, isn't he?' The women cackled and howled and screamed and slapped the table and spilled wine.

Jon panicked. He fought a momentary urge to run, acknowledged that such a course of action was all but impossible and resigned himself to the novelty of the situation. It was a long time since a woman had claimed to find him attractive. Indeed it was the first time in many years that his presence had been fully registered by those who didn't know him by professional reputation alone. Attempting to be charming was not something he was accustomed to, but he hung his head modestly and said, 'If that's what you think, I'd better have a glass of what you're drinking,' and the table erupted again into laughter. To avoid meeting anyone's eyes, he looked around the kitchen. Everything was new. He glanced at Cathy and her look confirmed what he had perhaps arrogantly assumed. He had paid for this. He had given someone a kitchen. A kitchen. Cooker and freezer and fitted cupboards. A portable television. A microwave oven.

'I'm glad you could come,' said Cathy.

'Wouldn't miss it for the world.'

'Plenty of booze in the fridge,' she said. 'Help yourself.'

'We've all got a head start on you,' said the woman who had

passed comment upon him. 'You'll have to go some to catch us up, love.' Raising of bottles and a spontaneous chorus of approval.

He opened the fridge. It was taller than him by several centimetres, and a good deal wider. It was a peculiar kind of excessively technological white, as if it had been carved from a single gigantic denture. From its cavernous maw he withdrew a can of lager, one of a regiment that stretched in an orderly fashion back to the fridge's far horizons. The doors were filled with wine and spirits, and mixers lay flat across the bottom shelf and in the salad compartment. There was also a carton of Lo-Fat yogurt and a green apple.

Cathy peeked into the bag he'd brought. 'More wine?' she said.

Jon shrugged. The music in the front room silenced for a moment, and there was a brief interlude where all the human social noise could be heard in its comforting familiarity. 'I haven't been to a party like this for a long time,' he said, and cracked the can of lager. He poured half of it down his throat in a sequence of oesophagus-freezing gulps, then burped into the back of his hand.

'Well, take your bloody coat off at least,' said Cathy, looking up from the bag of booze. 'People'll think we're so desperate for friends we're letting in the local dossers.'

He shrugged off his coat, looked for a place to drape it before stuffing it on top of the fridge like hand luggage in an overhead compartment. He had to stand on tiptoe to do it properly. As he did so, punctuated by small groans as he stretched and reached and stuffed the overcoat into the small gap, he said, 'There's a bottle of Johnny Walker in there and I brought some Absolut as well, but I'm afraid I've already started on that. And a bottle of', he was grateful that his back was turned as he worried the overcoat further into the gap than was absolutely necessary, 'Southern Comfort.'

He heard the bag rustle as she removed the liqueur. The

table in unison cooed something approximating 'ooooh, Southern Comfort,' as if it was as rare as bananas in wartime.

'I *love* Southern Comfort,' Cathy said.

He had no choice now but to turn and face the table, so he busied himself first by lighting a cigarette then passing the packet round. When this was done, he said, 'Yeah, I know. It's a present.'

He had not yet properly looked at her. Her hair had been cut into a chin-length bob which he knew was probably practical, but because tonight was a party, it framed her face and gleamed a deep mahogany. She was wearing the type of little black dress and carefully chosen accessories that she read about in *Cosmopolitan*, and which she believed to represent a level of sophistication to which she could aspire but never truly possess. She was wearing make-up that she had painstakingly applied, and had gone out of her way to mask the mole on her right cheek of which he knew she was acutely conscious. 'How did you know I like Southern Comfort?'

'Everyone likes Southern Comfort,' said one of her friends confidently, as if such a statement represented a logical necessity. Jon looked at the speaker, who was looking to the woman at her right. They were sharing a private joke. Southern Comfort apparently had a peculiar significance to them that could never truly be articulated. The full implications of being the solitary man in a room full of slightly drunk heterosexual women, all of whom were friends and neighbours, probably utterly conversant in the minutiae of each other's sex lives or lack thereof, began to dawn on him. He was an object of sexual curiosity. This was an extraordinary situation, not an altogether unpleasant one, but he genuinely wished that they'd tire of it soon, or that someone better-looking or more charismatic might come along and start telling risqué jokes or whatever it was he was expected to do.

'I thought you told me,' said Jon.

'I don't think so.'

'You must have. Or Andy.'

'Either that or you've got a bloody good memory,' she said, and when she smiled he saw that there was a small lipstick stain on her front teeth. It broke his heart.

'That's possible I suppose,' he said, self-consciously raising an eyebrow that was intended to be ironic and enigmatic but felt grotesquely distorted. He reached out and grabbed the vodka by the neck, tucked it under his arm, hand burdened both by the cigarette and the half-finished can of lager. He leaned across the table and with his free arm removed from the bag the third of the four bottles therein. 'I'd best be off to see the birthday boy,' he said. 'Does he still like this stuff?'

She laughed and said; 'He loves it. With a bottle of that in his hand he feels like a teenage punk-rocker on heat . . .'

'My God!' screamed the woman at the far end of the table, 'get a couple of glasses down him quick!' and once again there was much shrieking and table slapping and low-heeled shoes being stamped against the floor.

'Birthdays are a time for fantasies to be fulfilled,' Jon said. He did a little wave and walked from the kitchen. During another break in the music (a diminuendo as some absurd American rock ballad prepared to crank up the bombast to a blood-vessel-threatening level), he heard one of them comment on his passing, 'He's got a lovely little bum, hasn't he?' He wondered if people often passed such comment without his noticing. For a moment, when the music burst into its guitar-and-voice-and-drums-and-a-heart-so-big-the-world-will-end-should-it-be-broken crescendo, carrying him away on an emotional level too basic to be modified by ironic distance, he rather hoped that this was the case. He knew it was not. Being in the presence of Cathy and Andy had solidified him. He knew that even for the women who had striven in such a calculated fashion to find something in him which they found physically attractive (it was, after all, a party), he would never again cross any of their minds unless he was mentioned by Cathy, and even then would not be pictured with any clarity. In this house, within these walls, they had trapped something of his essence like a genie in a bottle.

As he entered the front room, more couples were dancing half-time as the aspirant operatic rock star's voice trembled with grandiose passion. Andy, with three friends, was head-banging. John grabbed him by the back of his cowboy shirt. His face was flushed and beaded with sweat. He looked like an anthropomorphised tomato from some ill-conceived advertise-ment. His hair was in sweaty spikes, and he was breathing in a strained manner that might have been alarming had Jon known a little less about how people breathed before they died. 'You'll give yourself a brain tumour,' he shouted. Then he held out the Jack Daniels and said, 'Many happy returns, you sack of shit.'

Andy looked at the bottle with an almost feral intensity and broke the seal with his teeth. 'I love this stuff,' he yelled, the metal lid still between his teeth. A bead of sweat had gathered like a dewdrop at the end of an eyelash, and the disco lights were reflected there in miniature. He took a swig, then with drunken pride gave an honest and comprehensive introduction of his friend Jon who he'd told everyone about, which was drowned by the music. Most of them got the gist: some nodded their heads and smiled, or raised a glass or can or bottle. The young girl caught his eye, smoothed her skirt with her palms and wriggled deeper into her chair, and attempted to light a cigarette in a flirtatious manner that, in its lack of practice, spilled over into Hollywood melodrama. Andy put his hands on his knees and bent to face her. 'You'll lose your bloody eyebrows if you carry on like that,' he shouted, 'you stupid little mare. Your mum'll have my bloody guts for garters.'

Her brow clouded with a potent, unstable mix of rage and worse, the humiliation of someone whose deepest, dearest, most heartfelt wish is to be considered an adult and whose endlessly rehearsed, endlessly considered, agonisingly gauche pretence has been ridiculed by adult thoughtlessness. She looked venomously at Andy and hissed, 'Grow up, you wanker,' taking a defiant draw on the Silk Cut, expelling smoke through tight lips.

It occurred to Jon that he had more in common with this girl than anyone else present. Each was feeling their way tentatively through a world of which they had little knowledge, to which they feared they could never truly belong. Except, of course, that she would one day grow up and such parties as this would bore her in a way she could never now begin to comprehend, whereas he would always be a spook in the corner whose smile fell from his lips the instant there were no other eyes to see it. He sat next to her. She moved to one side to accommodate him. 'What are you doing hanging around with a bunch of old farts like this?' He nodded at Andy, who sat on the floor in front of them. 'You should be in some flashy night-club or restaurant being wined and dined by some millionaire who lights your Silk Cut with a gold lighter.' Without really intending to, he had said almost exactly the right thing. She perked up visibly. If there was one thing that makes isolation in a social situation bearable, it was to be convinced (by oneself but preferably by another) that the reason you were so out of place was that nobody there had the wit or insight to understand you. When she asked for a sip of his vodka, he could hardly do anything but oblige, but he diplomatically took the bottle from her the moment he observed that her throat had closed, effectively refusing admission to any more alcohol. Andy watched all this with a nodding, village-idiot smile. It was a very old smile, belonging to a young man. Jon upended the bottle down his throat, then reached to swig from the Jack Daniels. He and Andy passed the bottles between them and effectively ignored everyone else, with the exception of the girl, who was attending with the intensity of the very drunk and who, having more cunning than either man had ascribed to her, swigged from a cider bottle she had concealed down the side of the sofa every time she judged herself to be in their blind spot. After a while, Andy was so drunk that he was actually trying to push cigarettes on her. She began to slide into the chair, her eyes rolling in her sockets. She tried to draw on the cigarette and missed, her hand flopping limply over the side of the sofa.

Cathy and her friends descended upon the party proper. Obviously they had merely beaten a tactical withdrawal to the kitchen in order to get some serious drinking out of the way before descending upon the makeshift dance-floor like a murder of crows behind a tractor. There was a brief, brilliantly organised *coup* wherein the stereo was reclaimed from the ruling powers and Thin Lizzy's 'Whiskey in the Jar', a song for which, happily enough, Jon nurtured a groundless but passionate dislike, was stopped mid-chorus. Within another five seconds, Diana Ross was singing 'Where Did Our Love Go', and the women had embarked on what was to prove to be something of a danceathon. Individuals left to pour drinks, run to the toilet, light cigarettes, but the group danced all night. To Jon, the fact that people genuinely seemed to extract pleasure from the act of dancing with friends, not as some atavistic mating ritual (which he understood only a little more), or even as a form of aerobic exercise, but for the sheer joy of clumping together into a loose group whose boundaries might be confined to a dance-floor upon which there was barely room to shuffle, or more diffusely spread across an entire night-club, was absolutely and singularly unaccountable. He associated dancing with one thing: young men ineptly attempting to signal to young women their sexual availability, as if the virtue of a spotty youth out in his best shirt and tanked up on cider had ever actually been in question. That just sort of standing in a loose circle with a couple of friends, shuffling with an occasional twist of the hips when there was a favourite bit, could constitute anything like fun for its own sake distantly troubled him.

He and Andy sat talking over what it soon became clear was Cathy's favourite tape (she appeared to know every word to every verse of every song, and occasionally broke off from an in-dance conversation to dance alone, eyes closed, mouthing the doggerel to herself as if it were scripture). As they became more drunk, Jon found his gaze increasingly drawn over Andy's shoulder, to the group of dancers, whose exuberance and enthusiasm to be together seemed limitless. Their almost uniform choice of *the classic little black dress* added an obscure element of poignancy of which he was aware, but which he did not fully understand. In such a small group, that there was such wide variation of hair and skin colour, of posture, of shape, of size, of sense of rhythm, of elegance and clumsiness, all tied together by a shared dress sense, made something in his stomach ache. All dancing in different ways to the same song. He ran his palm over the stubble on his head.

'Why the skinhead, then?' said Andy.

Jon shrugged, belched the unpleasant taste of neat vodka and stomach acid. He was grinding a cigarette into an overspilling ashtray. 'I don't know,' he said. 'Practical.'

'Bollocks,' said Andy. He pointed a wavering finger like a drunk in a bus station, addressing somebody only he could see. 'I wanna know what you've been up to. Where've you been?'

'Nowhere interesting.'

Andy struggled to open a pack of cigarettes, removed two and placed one butt-first in Jon's mouth. 'Your problem is', he said, and waved the cigarette like a mini baton, the drunk's rhetorical tool, 'is that you haven't told me anything about what you do or what's happened to you in the last few years. I'm your mate, right,' he said, and patted Jon on the shoulder, thereby crushing the as yet still unlit cigarette. 'And I don't give a shit about what you do. I don't care if you're a fucking lollipop man or . . . It's just, you know, you've done so much . . .'

His face brightened. 'Seen the kitchen? That's down to you. Bought the kitchen. Cath couldn't believe it at first, you know, you turn up out of the blue and bingo whatsit, I've got a job . . . We couldn't believe it. Saved us, like. Proper mate. Kind of friend who don't ever let you down. Might take the fucker ten years to pop up like Indiana fucking Jones and save all and sundry, but you can be fucking sure he'll be there. Trust you, like,' he said with surprising vehemence, and emphasised his point, such as it was, by striking the carpet with the flat of his hand. 'I told Cath all about you,' he said, 'only about a month before you turned up. When she found out I met you that afternoon, she was worried you'd be a bad influence.' He lifted the half-empty bottle and tipped it, his ironic laughter causing some to bubble from his throat and down his chin. 'That's a laugh. Bad influence. Bless her.'

'Christ,' said Jon. 'Give you a couple of drinks and off you go. You've got a world full of best mates until you wake up.'

Andy buried his face in his hands. Jon was slightly scared that he was going to start crying in his drunken sentimentality, which was not without historical precedent, but it was a false alarm. Somebody walking back from the toilet nudged Andy forward and he rocked like a weeble. Jon saw that he was stretching the skin around his tired, blood-red eyes with his yellowed fingertips. 'We were worried,' he said, in a very small and very sober voice. 'We didn't know what had happened to you.'

Jon knew that this was something that Andy had to be drunk in order to say, rather than that he was saying it because he was drunk. The distinction, ostensibly subtle, was fundamental, and opened before him a vertiginous abyss, threatened to transport him to an undiscovered country for which there were no maps. 'Come on, mate,' he said. 'Don't be dumb. Stop it now. Shut up.'

Before anything else could be said, a hand closed around Jon's wrist and one of the black-dressed dancers was trying to

71

pull him to his feet, jerking her head in the general direction of the dance-floor. Jon groaned so that, if she was especially sharp sighted, she might have seen a slight flutter of contempt pass across his lips. He looked despairingly at Andy, who winked and mouthed the eternal credo, 'I think you're in there, mate.'

She looked back at her friends and laughed. Dancers paused and gave a round of applause. She had very big, very even teeth and bent forward slightly when laughing, clasping her thighs. She couldn't believe she was doing this, her laugh said, she really couldn't believe that you lot of drunken mares had put her up to this. I'll get you back, the laugh said. The dancers clapped louder. She pulled Jon to a half-crouched position. He had yet to think of something that might enable him to escape the hell that this woman was trying to lead him to. She turned once more to her friends, 'This is like trying to unblock a bloody sink. . .' and back again to Jon. He could see a wickedly confident light in her eye, fuelled both by her own surprise at doing what was clearly for her an unusual thing and the approval of her friends, who continued to look on and clap their encouragement. Jon had no choice but to allow himself to be pulled to his feet. For some reason, he was surprised that she was shorter than him. Looking down, he could see the crown of her head, and felt a stab of ambiguous pity for her that she had made such public efforts to entice to the dance-floor the one man who for all the world could not be made to dance.

She tugged on his hand. 'Come on, love,' she said, 'we don't bite.'

He shuffled from foot to foot. 'I'm not a very good dancer,' he pleaded. He honestly believed, when progress to the dance-floor seemed inevitable, that he had never been so scared in all his life. As soon as he caught Cathy's eye, he knew that she saw some of this, although once again the smile did not alter, nor was there even some more subtle clue, not even the infinitesimal shifting of weight from one foot to another. She took a single step forward and touched her friend's shoulder, nodding at the half-comatose figure of the young girl, whose eyes had rolled to show the whites.

Cathy said, 'I think we'd better get madam some fresh air.' She looked at Jon: 'Jon, could you help her out to the garden and get her a glass of water or something. Be a love.' Jon wanted to fall at her feet and weep with gratitude. Instead, he looked at the other woman with soulful apology. She looked at him like he was mad. She laughed and again glanced back over her shoulder before speaking. 'Bloody hell,' she said, 'cheer up. It's not the end of the world.' Then she took another man's hand, a father or a neighbour or an uncle, and proceeded to lead him to the makeshift dance-floor. Not without effort Jon, Cathy and Andy raised the girl to her feet. One way or another, her arm was slung round Jon's neck and he walked her, half-conscious, in the direction of the garden. He opened the door and watched her sit, shuddering in the first cold blast of fresh early morning air. She hugged her knees to her chest. Jon retrieved his overcoat from above the fridge and wrapped it about her shoulders. She snuggled into it, nuzzling her cheek against its soft weave. She was so drunk that to move her mouth was an effort beyond her capabilities. Jon poured her a glass of water and held it to her lips. She took a tiny sip, swallowed, licked her lips. He tipped her chin with his finger and said, 'Once more, it'll do you good,' and she took a second, obliging sip. He stroked her brow, brushing her sweaty fringe from her face.

'I told you you'd be good with kids,' said Andy, who was standing behind him, a bottle in each fist. 'Nothing to it. You're a natural, look. Proper nurse.' At this point the girl leaned forward and threw up across the threshold. Jon wrapped her in his arms and said, 'Come on, stand up. Let's get you into the garden. You can get it all out of your system in the fresh air. Best place for it.'

He walked her to the bottom of the small garden. She was

bent double as if cramped, and was repeating something softly and rhythmically. He stopped and bent so that his ear was level with her mouth. She was repeating 'It's horrible' over and over again. He couldn't resist a laugh. He even moved to rustle her hair again, but was acutely aware of Andy's eyes upon him as he too stepped into the garden, sucking breath between his teeth and wrapping about his shoulders an old coat retrieved from some kitchen cupboard. Jon sat on the narrow strip of grass just outside the patch of light cast through the kitchen window. Andy plonked himself next to him and groaned, stretched his neck. Jon heard bone click. They allowed the girl to undergo the painful but inevitable rite of passage, the indignity of pacing the damp grass on all fours, pausing only to strain, puking and hacking her guts somewhere behind them. Occasionally, one of them would turn to her to offer a brief word of comfort and encouragement, but the desired effect of this was somewhat undermined by the little snorting laugh they shared between them when they had done so. They passed the Jack Daniels between them, blowing on their numb fingers when they had taken a swig and wincing as they passed it along. After a pleasant interval of this, Jon lay back and looked straight up. It was a relatively clear night, and through the haze of low cloud and electric light pollution, he could see several of the brighter stars. They snuggled into themselves, cupping free hands around cigarettes.

Eventually Andy handed the bottle over and spoke in that particular and uniquely soft tone of voice reserved for drinking alcohol outside, late at night on patches of grass, in the winter. 'The fresh air did me good,' he said, the banality given weight by the special tone in which it was broadcast, which contained a certain indefinable intimacy. The girl retched painfully and noisily. 'That's right,' encouraged Andy, 'bring it all up.' For the twentieth time tonight, they found this hilarious.

At length, the girl crawled over to Andy and put her head in his lap. Before he could speak she had fallen asleep. He raised his eyes to the sky in mock exasperation. The girl snuggled for warmth and he tucked Jon's coat more tightly about her. Jon craned his neck to see, and drew on the cigarette. Its tip glowed bright in the darkness. Jon lay flat once more. He found the bottle with his hand and managed to glug a good mouthful without lifting his head, which he still considered a pretty neat trick if he thought about it.

'Is she a neighbour or what?' whispered Jon, in that same hushed voice.

'Family,' said Andy. 'Cathy's sister's eldest.' He gently stroked her head with one hand, lit another cigarette with the other. 'I'm going to have a hangover and a half tomorrow,' he said, examining the cigarette as if he had not the faintest idea of where it had come from. He scratched his chin. 'Sorry about going on a bit in there,' he said. 'I think I'm pissed.'

'That's all right. There's nothing you said that I'd like to think you didn't mean.'

Andy shifted uncomfortably. 'We just wonder,' he said at length. 'You've done all this for us. Have you really got no one?'

Jon scowled. 'Not so you'd notice, no.'

The pause that followed lasted the length of the cigarette, plus a period which marked the evaluation of how wise it would be to light another one. Andy lit, inhaled. Jon could feel him thinking. Finally he said, 'Are you a poof?'

Jon barked, although he was not amused. 'Does it matter?'

A long pause.

'No.'

'Well, then, why ask?'

'Because you're my mate and I don't know a single fucking thing about you.'

Jon sat up, and saw that Andy was gazing at him with sober intensity. 'What does that mean?'

'You're never on one level,' said Andy. 'You always seem to be thinking about ten different things at once.'

75

'What do you want? Life's complicated. Surprise surprise.'

'It's not that. Look,' he said, 'Rickets, I mean, he's a fair enough bloke but you know he can be a bit of a wanker. Well, he's an arrogant, jumped-up little shit really, isn't he? Except when you're around. He treats you like royalty.'

Jon shrugged. 'It's cold. Let's go inside.'

'Oh, bollocks to that,' said Andy, and ground out the still fresh cigarette in the freezing grass. 'Look, I don't give a toss. I really, honestly, genuinely don't give a toss. I just,' and here he dipped his head, 'look, I love you. You're my friend. You know. Anything could have happened to you. Nobody even knows where you live. You disappear for a couple of months and your name begins to creep into Rickets' conversation in the past tense, you know, and this big fucking grin all over his face. Anything could have happened. We had no way of knowing. We were worried.'

Jon took a protracted swig from the bottle. He didn't want to be clear-headed. He wanted to be drunk. He wanted to be dizzy and he wanted to see double. He wanted to pass out and he wanted Cathy to come out and sit out here with them on the grass and say 'yeah' the way she'd said it a week or two before. He wanted to get up and walk through the house and through the front door and into a taxi and never see Andy or Cathy or the kitchen he'd bought them ever again.

He massaged his neck. 'Look,' he said, 'point one, for what it matters, I'm not gay. But if being straight means sleeping with women, I'm not that either. It's sort of complicated. All the rest is details. My address is no big secret. You and Cathy can bring Kirsty round for tea if you like. Stay the night. The big secret is that I'm a sort of overpaid personal assistant for a pretty big businessman, which is why Rickets is scared of me. I represent the boss. All right?' He stood, and brushed moisture and grass stains from his arse. 'Let's get your niece inside.'

Andy lifted the comatose girl and carried her back into the house, upstairs and into Kirsty's room, removing her shoes, tucking her up tightly in a clean duvet and leaving a jug of water, a glass and a packet of Anadin Extra on the floor next to her.

As he was about this, Jon remained in the kitchen. He retrieved another beer from the fridge. Cathy walked in. He looked at the floor. She was flushed with alcohol and exercise, and her previously immaculate hair was ratty and wet. He could smell the fresh sweat beneath her perfume. He knew that she could tell he wanted to look at her, or that he was reluctant to do so, which amounted to the same thing. He wished that this shared knowledge was the intimate thing it might have been. He wished he could tell her that, more than anything else, he wanted to rest his head against the warmth of her naked belly and allow himself the dreadful intimacy of touching and fixing in his memory every inch of her skin. He wished that this yearning could be simple, that it could be something as human and as everyday and as monstrous as lust, which drove friends to terrible betrayals. He wished he could explain to her.

She waited until he raised his eyes from the floor and looked at her. 'Has Andy talked to you yet?' she said, and sipped from a tumbler of Southern Comfort and lemonade which she held against her breasts. The ice cubes tinkled.

Jon sat at the table and buried his head in his hands. Anything to avoid looking at her. 'Yeah,' he said, tilting his head just enough to take a sip from the top of the beer. 'Everything's sorted.'

'He loves you,' she said.

He pressed his eyes with his thumbs and bit the tip of his tongue. 'I love him too.'

'That's not the point,' she said. 'He knows that. I know that. Everybody knows that.' She pulled up one of the chairs that Jon had bought her. It screeched across the floor. 'You've got no idea what a bloody mess everything was before you showed up,' she said. 'It got so I couldn't stand the fucking sight of him.'

At this Jon looked up, and saw that her face did not match the ferocity of her words. Instead there was a kind of gentle surprise, as if she'd given voice to something she'd never quite acknowledged. 'He hadn't touched me for months, but that got to be a blessing. I caught him crying', she said, 'on the bog. Trousers round his ankles and head in his hands.' She drained the glass, ice and all. 'I would've left him at the first opportunity.'

Jon was nodding. He wished he was deaf. 'He loves you,' he said, quietly. He was ashamed.

She reached out and took the beer from his hand. Either her finger brushed his or the minute static charge of her dress raised the hair on his knuckles. She sipped. 'That's the point,' she said. 'That's what made it all so fucking unbearable. All he wanted was to make me happy, but he associates love with *doing* something, with actually going out and physically doing something to show it. He thinks he's thick and that anything which comes out of his mouth is going to make him look like an idiot. About a month before he met you again he started talking about you when he was drunk. All those things you did to look after each other as kids. I know it was kids' stuff, but it means a lot to him. He knew he was making me hate him, and didn't know how to stop. So he started thinking about you, about simpler times. About the mate who was always there to save him and who he was always there to save in return.' She returned the tin. 'And you bloody did. You saved him. Now he wants to help you. He wants to do something for you.'

'He asked if I was gay,' said Jon.

'I think he was praying for you to be gay,' she said.

Jon laughed, incredulous. Massaged his brow.

She insisted that this was true. She was smiling a gentle smile now. Almost nostalgic. 'I think he wanted you to be gay just so that he could tell you that it didn't matter and that he was still your friend no matter what. Do you see what I mean?'

Somebody staggered from the front room and up the stairs and even over the music he could hear them curse as they tripped.

'Let him do something for you,' she said. 'Just something little.'

He wanted to say something witty, non-committal. He wanted what he said to sound offhand and casual, possibly even a little conceited. He either wanted to impress her or to sound like he wanted to. But when he said, 'I don't need anything,' it sounded like the loneliest and most desolate thing he'd ever heard. He finished the beer.

Andy and one of the guests swaggered, arms linked, into the kitchen, wincing in the glare. 'What are you two up to?' said Andy, reaching into the fridge, withdrawing a beer for himself and his companion, who, accepting it, released himself from Andy's grip and swayed on the spot with a look of simian confusion.

'Trying to convince your wife of my heterosexuality,' said Jon.

'Fair enough,' said Andy, and swigged. After a mouthful of lager, he added, 'But don't try too fucking hard, will you?' Andy and friend sat with them. The friend maintained his silence. Every time he took a swig he held the can close to his eye as if looking through a keyhole, as if every time he sipped the beer was a different flavour. The crown of his hair was sticking up and his shirt had come untucked. Andy said, 'Liz is on the prowl for you tonight,' and winked lewdly. 'I'd watch myself if I was you, mate.'

Jon went cold. 'Hasn't she got a husband or something?'

Cathy slapped his arm, laughing and making wide eyes. 'Don't be such a bastard,' she said. 'What's wrong with her? She's lovely.'

'I know,' agreed Jon. 'I know. She is. No, really. She really is. Lovely. It's just that I'm not so good a dancer.'

Andy had informed his wife of Jon's lack of ability to dance in any recognised fashion. She put her hand to her mouth and giggled and then belched. 'You need to let your bloody hair down a bit more,' she suggested and Andy laid his arm across her shoulders and agreed. 'That's what I've been bloody telling him,' he said. 'He can't let it down so he cuts it off.'

'Have a dance with her,' said Cathy. 'Go on. She likes you.'

Jon spread his arms in a silent plea. 'Jesus,' he said. 'I can't dance. He just told you that.'

'You're like an old man,' said Cathy. 'It's a party!'

He scratched his head. 'Can we just forget the whole subject and get back to the party?'

They assented, leaving the silent guest newly comatose, his cheek pressed against the table and a pool of spit gathering at the corner of his lips.

A few guests had begun to drift home. The little gaggle of dancers occasionally whooped and threw their arms in the air, and every now and then it was possible to see a glimpse of whatever man had been sufficiently courageous to surrender himself to them: a flash of elbow, a trainer, a shoe. Cathy and Andy kissed briefly, with evident drunken carnality, before she turned away, not to dance but to refresh her tumbler of Southern Comfort and join a mixed group in conversation in the corner. She sat on a chair and crossed her legs and pushed her sleeve up to her elbow. When she took a sip from her glass, the loose bangles she wore clattered down her arm, and clattered back when she was done. Andy and Jon watched her for a while, as they stood in the middle of the room. Andy had his arm round Jon's shoulder. 'Am I the luckiest fucker in the world or what?'

Jon agreed that he was. They sat on the carpet. Andy scratched deep in the canal of his ear. 'Do you know what your trouble is?' he pronounced after a meditative pause. Jon didn't. 'Your trouble is that you're so fucking self-absorbed you think that everyone's idea of what you are depends on what you do. Everyone knows that what you do isn't what you are.'

These words, these familiar words, shook Jon so that he dropped his can and, as he hastily righted it and rubbed spilled lager into the pile, shivers passed down his arms. He urgently needed to defecate. His mouth was dry.

'Growing up', said Andy, 'is all about learning to know what you are.'

Jon couldn't help it. It was a question he was compelled to ask. 'What do you think I am?' he asked.

Andy spread his arms. 'The most loyal fucking friend a bloke could ask for,' he said, with booming theatricality. Then, more quietly, 'Amongst other things.'

Jon leaped to his feet and walked quickly and stiffly from the room, up the stairs and into the bathroom. He bolted the door and sat on the toilet with his head in his hands, one knee against the wall, the other against the edge of the bath. In his drunkenness, the memory of the Tattooed Man voicing those words, or words so very similar, seemed pre-emptively to be mocking his friend. His two worlds, two lives that should not be true of the same man, seemed to be converging. He thought of the moon moving slowly across the sun, bringing a temporary night, and sometimes blindness to those foolish enough to raise their eyes. He knew that it was his fault. It seemed to him then, in that bathroom with a small basket of dried, odourless pot-pourri atop the cistern, that he had done a terrible thing, perhaps the most terrible thing he had ever done. He could feel the music downstairs through the soles of his boots. Somebody banged hard on the door. He stood and pulled the flush, leaving the bathroom to somebody whose need of it was unquestionably more appropriate, and walked downstairs into the flashing darkness, the smell of cigarettes and alcohol and all those people gathered in the shadows and flashing lights.

He sat on the floor beside Andy, who tapped his knee. 'Taken short were we?' he cackled.

Jon said, 'Can I ask you something?'

Andy nodded heavily. ''Course, mate,' he said. ''Course.'

'And it goes no further?'

'Goes without saying.'

'It might sound a bit weird.'

Andy shrugged. 'Whatever. Go on.'

'Listen,' said Jon, and exhaled. 'I want you to do me a favour.'

'What sort of favour?'

'A weird favour.'

Andy was silent.

'It's like this,' said Jon. Head to foot, he was cold. 'My life isn't what I wanted it to be. Sometimes I forget how weird it's become. Things seem normal that should never seem normal, and have for so long that I forget that things were ever any different. You've reminded me what things can be like. What I want you to do,' he said, and swallowed, 'is promise not to change. Don't let anything about you change, and tell me that whenever I want to I can come round here and sit on the sofa and watch TV or something, even if you haven't seen me for weeks. Take the piss out of me and remind me of all the stupid things I did and all the times I thought I was being clever and you told me that I was being a wanker. Make me feel stupid and embarrassed.'

'Of course I'll do that,' Andy said. Something in his voice suggested that, although he had only a vague understanding of the nature of the pact he had entered into, he was proud and scared.

'Right,' said Jon. 'Change of subject.'

Much later, somebody put 'Staying Alive' on the stereo. Everyone whooped and laughed and even those who knew they couldn't dance did so, distanced from their embarrassment by the irony of their intent. Everyone stood and gyrated extravagantly and began to clap and stamp their feet and chant Andy's name. This was obviously a long-running joke. Photographs had circulated, tales had been exchanged and exaggerated. Andy's every embarrassment was public property. After meeting Jon's eyes, he climbed stiffly to his feet, apparently begrudgingly but evidently fighting a smile. As everyone began to form a circle about him, Jon was forced to stand and crane his neck. Andy stood motionless, arms crossed, legs spread, as if dancing was the last thing he intended to do. Then, as the song reached its first chorus, he suddenly struck an exaggerated Travolta pose, one finger pointing at the ceiling, the other at the floor, and proceeded, move for move, to reproduce exactly the strutting, hip-thrusting stomp of yore, down to the expression of intense concentration. When the song had finished, Cathy joined him, and, red-faced and sweating, he embarrassed and pleased her by strutting around her like an arrogant, libidinous cockerel, at one point even flapping imaginary wings.

Liz's hand closed about Jon's wrist: he looked into her eyes, glinting, mischievously insistent, then back to Andy, who was stomping on the spot and miming an invitation for Jon to join him. He looked again at Liz, and mouthed the words, 'You're going to regret this,' before allowing her to lead him on to the floor. He was given a round of applause. He faced her and she straightened his shirt collar and giggled and he said, 'I hope you're ready.'

His dancing had not improved. People laughed, moved out of his path, patted his back, clapped this particularly poorly judged hip-swivel or that particularly extraordinary elbow movement. People were laughing at him. He looked an idiot. When he had finished, the applause was tumultuous. Liz kissed him on the cheek. He had never been so happy.

Five   Mr Michaelmas

Behind the wheel of the bottle-green Aston Martin, Phil wore a sombre suit, leather driving gloves and no expression. He took the car smoothly over country roads, chasing the beam of headlights into darkness. Beside him sat Jon, similarly clad, similarly expressionless, hands crossed in his lap. Occasionally he sniffed, dislodging tiny lumps of cocaine from his oesophagus.

Behind them the Tattooed Man sat in a silence upon which neither cared to intrude. There was a sense of purpose in the car, an air of expectancy.

The engine purred softly. They passed no other vehicle, saw no signs of life, with the exception of a fox smeared across the asphalt. Its needle teeth were bared in rigor mortis and two paws clawed rigid at the air.

Phil turned the car on to an unmarked track, past an old five-barred gate which hung like a fractured limb. The car bumped over potholes and other irregularities before turning finally on to a gravel drive upon which two other cars – a black Range Rover and a Bentley – were parked at casual angles outside a whitewashed cottage. Leafless ivy climbed its whitewashed stone walls like a network of dried veins.

Phil opened the rear door of the Aston. The Tattooed Man unfolded from inside like something primordial emerging from a pupa. One on either side, feet crunching in the gravel, Jon and Phil accompanied him first to the threshold, then, after a small pause, through the door into the cottage's musty warmth.

Inside it was homely and rural. Horse brasses and dried

flowers and floral prints. They walked through to the front room, in which waited three men. The first sat in an over-stuffed armchair, a tumbler of whisky in his sallow fist. He had the air of one who had slept in his clothes, was jaundiced and pinched at the temples. His hair, thinning to a peak, was combed back, black with oil. As they entered he placed the glass next to an over-stuffed ashtray and stood. He wiped his hands on his trousers, offered one to the Tattooed Man, who took and shook it wordlessly. The man turned and poured the Tattooed Man a drink. Only when the Tattooed Man had accepted it and sat did the man acknowledge Jon and Phil. He spoke with a Yorkshire accent, insinuating as well as dour. He acknowledged them thus: 'Lads.'

Jon and Phil nodded. He turned his back on them and sat.

The second man stood and greeted the Tattooed Man with a vigorous handshake and a beautiful, craggy smile. Between fifty and sixty, he dressed like forty: cuffs just so. Windsor knot. Hair a touch too long and luxuriant. Perhaps a wig. He clasped a firm hand on the Tattooed Man's shoulder. The Tattooed Man, uniquely in Jon's experience, reciprocated. They grinned at one another. The Tattooed Man took a step back. 'You old bastard,' he said, surveying the handsome man's suit. 'You might at least have made an *effort.*'

The man brushed non-existent dust from his lapel and straightened the knot of his tie. 'You know how it is,' he replied, 'the first thing that comes out of the wardrobe.' He laughed and again clapped the Tattooed Man's shoulder.

Jon's sense of decorum was offended. He experienced a twinge of resentment.

The handsome man disengaged from the Tattooed Man and took a step to Jon and Phil. In turn, he shook their hands, meeting their eyes with a twinkle of pleasure in his own. 'It's a pleasure to meet you both at last,' he said, with too much warmth. He inclined his head in the direction of the Tattooed

Man. 'He's got nothing but good things to say about you, you know.'

Before either could reply, he withdrew from them and stood in the glow of the standard lamp. The Yorkshireman stirred whisky with an index finger, which he sucked clean, concave cheeks and thin, bitter lips.

The third man stepped forward from the corner. The sight of him was enough to force Jon to suppress a tiny gasp. His bulk was such that he seemed to fill the room, shoulders stretching wall to wall, head slightly stooped beneath the low ceiling, yet he moved with an elegance too profound to be anything but intrinsic. But it was not this that captivated Jon and held his fascinated gaze. The man was an albino, his skin so smooth and white and flawless it seemed to glow faintly, such that he seemed almost spotlit, highlighted like the central figure in a Renaissance canvas. His face was wolfish, his hair a luxuriant, colourless mane that swept from his temples and fell between the blades of his shoulders. Thin, bloodless lips connoted a permanent, fabulously dangerous irony. His eyes were the lifeless red of wax strawberries. He wore a sporty, navy-blue blazer, from which protruded bone-white wrists and huge, bloodless hands which ended in exquisitely manicured talons. Jon had never encountered such a flawless merge of primal ferocity and intellect.

The albino and the Tattooed Man greeted each other warmly, clasping hands and grinning fiercely like old friends. He stood at the Tattooed Man's side, dwarfing even his physical presence. 'So these are the boys?' His voice was baritone, almost archetypally English: resonant with self-referential irony even when he was not the apparent object of discussion. It was an acknowledgement that his presence was such that he was an unavoidable subtext.

'These are the boys,' confirmed the Tattooed Man.

The albino approached them. The dim light bulb flickered. 'You must be Phil.'

Phil took an unconscious step back, then took the proffered hand, which swallowed his own like a child's. The albino stooped to address him. 'You'll go far, Phil,' he said, 'if only half the things he's said about you are true.'

The Tattooed Man laughed. The albino grinned. Visible goose bumps erupted on Phil's neck.

'Really,' the albino said. 'You have no idea how far you'll go.'

Phil swallowed and thanked him. The albino moved on to Jon. He took but did not shake Jon's hand. He held it between both of his own, and stared at Jon with something like genuine pleasure. 'And what can we say about Jon?' He turned again to Phil, still clasping Jon's hands between his own. 'What is there to say about Jon, eh Phil?' He took Jon's shoulders. Jon had never felt so small or so weak. He felt that the albino could rip him in two like a paper man. 'What is there to say about a man who surpasses all superlatives? If there were more like you, all our lives would be considerably easier.' He stepped back, and his face split into a lupine grin. 'I'm very pleased to meet you, Jon. You can call me Mr Michaelmas.'

'It's a pleasure,' said Jon.

The four men – the Tattooed Man, Mr Michaelmas, the Yorkshireman and the handsome man – exploded into laughter, like adults amused by a child's unconscious irony. Jon and Phil exchanged a sidelong glance, then Jon and the Tattooed Man caught each other's eye for a moment. Although each face remained set and impassive, something twinkled in the Tattooed Man's eye, like a glint of sunlight on the oiled barrel of an assassin's weapon. Then the four men pulled their chairs closer, excluding Phil and Jon. They huddled and talked quietly and seriously. Jon and Phil, for any number of reasons, several of which neither would choose to discuss, contrived to hear nothing but a constant, wordless hum. They stood at either side of the door like night-club security, hands clasped before their genitals, staring silently into space.

Presently, with a hiss of gravel, a car drew up outside. The conversation came to an immediate halt. The four men looked up and towards the window. The Tattooed Man stood and opened the floral curtains a notch with his forefinger. He gazed out, sipping whisky. They heard the night-time sound of a car door slamming, twice in succession, then two pairs of feet, resolutely crunching gravel. A silence fell, which Jon read as the newcomers pausing at the threshold, composing themselves. He imagined how he would feel were he the reason for a gathering such as this, how his heart would be lurching arrythmically as his hand reached forward to take the handle of the door, how his legs would tremble as he took a step over the threshold. He heard the creak of the oak door opening slowly and fatalistically. Another pause. Lips being wiped. The handle of the living-room door turned. Jon and Phil stepped aside to admit two men. The first was a solid, fat man in a navy-blue suit and open-neck shirt. He wore a thick, wiry goatee and rimless spectacles behind which his eyes were quiet and calm, like a player of cards. His head sat massive upon hairy rolls of neck which spilled over his collar. He was balding, greying, cropped to stubble. Chunky gold watch and assorted jewellery, the back of his hands and fingers as hirsute as his chest. He breathed as if something had broken in the gristle of his throat. He paused in the doorway. His eyes settled for a moment on Jon.

None of the gathered men stood. The albino chose not to twist in his seat, but presented the fat man with the vast prairie of his back, the snow-capped peak of his skull.

With one rigid finger, the Tattooed Man pointed beyond him, to the semi-darkness of the hallway, then turned his hand palm upwards and crooked his finger. 'Come in, son,' he said.

A lean, Nordically blond man dressed in jeans and leather jacket entered the room. Eyelashes transparent as fishing line, eyes watery pale behind rimless spectacles. The Tattooed Man smiled at him, eyes crinkling at the corners, then turned his attention back to the fat man, who avoided his gaze by reaching into an inside pocket for a pack of cigarettes as he explained, 'I didn't think you'd mind,' in broad cockney.

The Yorkshireman and the dandy turned the intensity of their gaze upon the fat man. He seemed rooted to the spot by the weight of the astonishing malevolence he saw there. He shifted his bulk from foot to foot. 'If I were in your position,' said the Tattooed Man, standing, 'the last thing I'd want to do is try my patience any further.' He regarded the young Nordic man, who gazed stoically and neutrally ahead, not quite meeting his eyes. 'What's your name, son?'

'Martin.'

'Right, Martin,' said the Tattooed Man, 'I'm going to ask you to quietly leave the room. Do you think you can do that for me?'

Martin opened his mouth to answer, was cut short by the Tattooed Man, who immediately motioned at Phil, a lazy flick of the wrist. 'Don't say you weren't asked, Martin,' he said.

Phil grabbed Martin by the hair, twisting it in his fist and tugging it hard so that Martin was bent double at the waist, hands locked about Phil's wrist. With his free hand, Phil cuffed Martin about the ears, then threw him into the wall. Briskly, Phil patted him down, taking a pistol from him before taking him by the collar and dragging him from the room.

In the hallway, when the door was closed, he whispered, 'Nothing personal, mate.'

'Fuck off,' said Martin. He was flushed and dishevelled.

'Fair enough,' said Phil, and threw him through the front door. Martin half-ran a few steps, waving his arms to catch his balance. 'Go and sit in the car,' said Phil, 'you miserable fucker.' He watched as Martin did as ordered. The car was an old Jaguar. Phil had a fondness for old cars. When Jon had enquired as to the nature of this fascination, Phil had been able

89

to articulate it only by suggesting that it had something to do with steering wheels and the solid way the doors closed.

Inside the cottage, the fat man sat perched on the edge of the sofa, hands clasped in his lap. He was the focal point of a heavy silence. He looked to floor, to ceiling. Into his glass. At the glowing end of a cigarette.

'All right, Jon,' said the Tattooed Man.

Jon followed Phil outside, closing the door of the cottage softly behind him. They stood in the meagre patch of yellow thrown across the gravel by the weak light which escaped the house.

Phil lightly took Jon's shoulder and led him, hushing him silent, away from the house, past the oddly parked cars, to the darkness cast by an enormous, twisted old oak tree. He offered Jon a cigarette. 'What did you think of that albino?' he asked in a whisper so cautiously quiet he had to lean into Jon's ear to be heard.

Jon shrugged.

'Come *on*,' hissed Phil.

'I don't know,' admitted Jon in an equally ragged whisper. He had the odd feeling that the albino was standing at his shoulder, grinning.

Phil lit another cigarette from the stub of the first. 'He put the fucking wind up me, I know that,' he said. 'He gave me the right fucking creeps.'

They looked to the cottage. A shadow passed across the window.

'Come on,' said Jon, and led Phil back to the Aston. They leaned against it, smoking, occasionally glancing at Martin, who sat perfectly still and stiff behind the wheel of a Jaguar, and glancing now and again at the cottage. Once or twice they heard distant, soft laughter.

'I wonder who walked,' said Phil.

'What?'

'One of them must have walked here. One of them must

have. Not enough cars.' He glanced over his shoulder, distantly troubled.

'Perhaps one of them', whispered Jon, 'accepted a lift. Perhaps one of them *lives* here. I don't know.'

Phil looked at him and shook his head eloquently once. 'Oh, fuck this,' he concluded. 'Do you fancy a game of cards?'

Phil strode to the Jaguar, hands in pockets, and kneeling at the driver's side window rapped on it with a knuckle. Although the window slid smoothly down, Martin gazed steadfastly ahead. Only an involuntary tic in his cheek betrayed an awareness of Phil's presence.

'Fancy a game of cards?' Phil asked.

Martin slid his eyes sideways. 'Fuck *off*,' he repeated through tight lips. The window slid silently closed.

Phil stood from the crouch and laughed. He spread his hands. 'Did you hear that?' he asked.

Jon nodded that he had.

'He'll get nowhere with that attitude,' said Phil. He rapped on the window and said, 'Did you hear that? You'll get nowhere with that attitude.' Martin contrived to ignore him still. Phil seemed to find this hilarious.

He and Jon sat in the back of the Aston, spreading the cards between them. With the joker Jon arranged a generous line of cocaine. Shadows moved back and forth across the cottage window, backlit and projected in silhouette across the curtains. Once they heard a raised voice, though what was said neither could discern. The tone of the voice was ambiguous. Neither Phil nor Jon mentioned it. Another time a voice that clearly belonged to the Tattooed Man barked in what sounded like a foreign language, guttural and full of glottal stops. Perhaps it was a joke, because the albino's voice responded with a laugh. Then silence fell again.

After some time, the cottage door opened. The albino stepped outside, pausing as if to take a deep lungful of fresh air.

He walked to the Aston, from which Jon obligingly stepped. 'You might as well stay where you are, Phil,' the albino said.

'Righty-ho,' said Phil.

'While you're here, Phil,' said the albino, 'keep an eye on the Aryan gentleman over there, would you?'

'Of course.'

'He's a laugh a minute, our Martin, isn't he?'

Phil answered with a laugh that was a touch too enthusiastic.

The albino adjusted his blazer and motioned with his head for Jon to follow. As Jon pushed the door of the cottage closed behind him, he had to fight an urge to yank it open again and run blindly into the night.

'We'd like a word,' said the albino.

'Is there a problem?' Jon said.

The albino ruffled Jon's hair like a schoolboy. 'Far from it,' he announced. 'Nothing of the sort. Don't let the thought enter your mind.'

The albino stooped a little further, hung over Jon's shoulder like the big bad wolf. Jon could sense the smile widening. Eyes the intense but passionless red of moulded plastic. An exhalation of hot breath, the albino standing to his full height, laughing. 'He said you were an honest man, Jon,' he confided. 'He said you were the most dedicated he'd ever had. I can see why he loves you.' His teeth were too long. The inside of his mouth and his rolling tongue were rich and moist against the colourless purity of his skin. His broad forehead knitted. 'You're everything I've heard you were.'

Mr Michaelmas took the handle of the door to the front room in his massive hand, and pulled it open. Darkness spilled from the room and wrapped itself around him before rolling languidly along the hallway. Its passage made weak the electric glow of the lampshades. There was a displacement of air, as if something had rushed from the room to cower behind him. The Tattooed Man stepped from the room and softly closed the door behind him.

Oddly, the first thing that Jon noticed was that in his hand he held a syringe. Oddly, because the Tattooed Man was naked. His penis, distended but not fully erect, hung arrogantly across his scrotum. A thick blue vein ran to his glans, upon which a golden stud twinkled in the half-light. He was utterly hairless. His skin shrink-wrapped sinew and hard, shifting muscle.

Jon took a step back and regarded him in silent consternation. The Tattooed Man allowed himself to be gazed upon, smiling indulgently. The albino restricted his attention to scrutinising Jon's reaction. Jon felt giddy: the Tattooed Man, naked and ironically unashamed, his feet sunk in the soft pile of the corridor of a country cottage, floral wallpaper behind him, his earring glinting with the horse brasses. Jon could not look away.

Toe to wrist, wrist to neck, the Tattooed Man's skin was decorated by indelibly etched faces, to which the ripple of muscle lent the illusion of animation. He was tattooed with hundreds of faces, each of them rendered with uncommon skill. Row upon row of faces, a seamless chain mail of portraits. Adult and child, male and female. Among them were dozens of recognisable renditions of his own features, now as a child, now as a young man. Many of the others wore the expression of corpses photographed in a shadowless mortuary. Still others were more sensitive, even sentimental, with the melancholy gaze of faded Victorian sepia. There was no dermis left. He had run out of skin before he had run out of time. Only his wrists, hands and head above the neckline were untattooed. He showed Jon the syringe. 'Succinylcholine,' he said. 'Ten milligrammes for each fifty pounds of body weight produces instant paralysis. For about ten minutes, before the victim's respiratory system gives out, he can experience every second of what's done to him. With the added bonus of complete immobility.'

The albino laughed. His grip grew firm on Jon's shoulders

and all expression fell from his face. 'There are places which one should enter only of one's free will,' he said. He pointed at the door. 'In there. Do you understand the nature of freedom, Jon?'

He awaited a response, which was not forthcoming.

'There is a single choice which determines the course of your life entire,' the albino told him. 'You elect to jump or allow yourself to be pushed. Those who elect to jump are of course free to choose in which direction.'

The Tattooed Man smiled at Jon. It seemed incongruously natural. Relax, the smile said. It's all right.

'Do you understand what freedom is?' petitioned the albino. 'Do you know what a terrible and precious thing it is?'

Jon nodded that he did.

The albino stepped to one side and made an expansive gesture of welcome, opening the door and ushering Jon inside. There was the smell of burning fat.

He was aware of the Tattooed Man's hand resting gently and reassuringly on his shoulder.

Phil watched the darkened windows of the cottage until curiosity became frustration, then eventually an ambiguous mix of concern and a sense of exclusion. He flicked endless cigarette butts absently on to the gravel. He was intermittently aware of the blond man in the Jaguar watching him in the rear-view mirror.

After the passage of some hours, Jon appeared in the doorway and walked to the Aston. He carried a spade in his hand.

'Where the fuck have you been all night?' said Phil.

'In there,' said Jon with an unfamiliar grin.

'Fair enough,' Phil sulked. He rolled his eyes. 'Be like that.' He nodded at the Jag, in which Martin could be seen to be watching them. 'Do you think he likes me or what?' he asked lightly. For some reason, Phil felt it to be important that he make Jon laugh.

'Do you want to take care of him?' said Jon. 'Or do you want me to do it?'

Phil's hand was at the door handle. 'Are you joking?' He stood on the gravel, leaning against the car as he stretched his cramped legs. He flexed his fists, withdrew a pistol from an inside pocket and walked to the old Jag. He stooped low at the window and, as Martin contrived once more to fix him with a supercilious sneer, he smashed the driver's window with the butt of his pistol. He leaned awkwardly through the hole. Martin threw his hands across his head and his self across the seats in an effort to avoid Phil's clumsy blows. Phil wriggled from the window, snagging his jacket on jagged glass, and opened the car door. He grabbed Martin's ankle and yanked, once, twice, three times. Martin spilled like a new-born calf from car to gravel. Phil let him struggle to his knees before striking him on the jaw with the butt of the gun. As he groaned and curled on the floor, Phil kicked him and kicked him and kicked him. After a minute or so, Phil paused to catch his breath. He lit a cigarette, took a puff or two and finished the job in a more leisurely fashion. Martin began to crawl on his belly. His shirt lifted clear of his trousers, gathering about his chest. Phil walked alongside him, kicking him occasionally and bending to sneer into his ear. Eventually Jon tired and, sighing, walked to Martin, who was prone on the floor, bleeding from both ears. With the blade of the shovel, Jon hit him in the base of the skull. He began to twitch and jerk, spilling gravel this way and that. He made circles and arcs that reminded Jon of a Japanese garden. Phil prodded the corpse with the toe of his shoe.

'Wanker,' he concluded.

Jon handed him the shovel.

'Oh, Christ,' said Phil. He looked at the body and sagged.

Jon clapped him on the shoulder. 'That's not all,' he said. 'Remember the fat man. . .?'

The cottage was a place of fairy-tale innocence. Furniture and carpets had been replaced. The four men unwound with glasses of whisky and whatever passed among them for light conversation. With a degree of difficulty, Jon and Phil dragged the body of the fat man, wrapped in a length of tarpaulin, behind the house and into the darkness where the woods began. The grave took a long time to dig. The earth was soft and moist, but the hole was deep and wide. They rolled the fat man's body into its maw. Jon straightened, bones clicking in his spine. It was four a.m.

'Right,' he said. 'Fill it up and disguise it. The boss wants to be driven home about dawn, so if you're snappy you'll have time to take forty winks.'

Phil spat into the hole. 'What about you?'

Jon retrieved his jacket from the branch upon which he'd hung it.

'Shit,' said Phil. 'Don't leave me alone. I hate the fucking dark. It gives me the fucking creeps.'

Jon smiled.

Phil looked sour. 'Say a prayer to the baby Jesus for me.'

As he trudged back down the field, Jon could hear him muttering as he shovelled earth: 'As I lay me down to sleep, I pray the Lord my soul to keep.'

Jon dragged Martin into a weighted sack, and took a moment or two quickly to sew the lips closed. He dragged the parcel across the gravel and heaved it into the boot of the old Jaguar. When he had closed the lid, he snorted the last of the cocaine. He strode back to the cottage and into the front room.

'You're filthy,' said the Tattooed Man. 'Watch where you step.'

Jon retreated to the threshold. 'Is there anything else?'

96

'No,' said the Tattooed Man. 'Do what has to be done and you can knock off. I'll be in touch.'

The albino offered a cool, pale hand, the texture of pumice. 'It was a pleasure to meet you,' he said.

Jon shook the limb, bid goodbye to the others and left.

As dawn began tentatively to glow on the horizon, as if peeking into the edge of darkness to ensure that nothing resided there, he tipped Martin over a country bridge into a shallow but swift-flowing river. Ten minutes later, as he turned right at a crossroads a Range Rover turned after him and he cursed to himself. He slowed and let it pass. Its lights disappeared over a hill.

At eight-thirty, he pulled into the garage. Rickets, hung-over and surly, waited with a mug of tea, a copy of the *Sun* and a rolled cigarette. He looked Jon up and down, the smart, muddy suit, the wide pupils, the shaved head.

'You're late,' he complained.

'It couldn't be helped.'

He looked at Jon. 'Nice car.' He traced the curve of its bonnet with an index finger.

Jon retrieved a bag from the back seat. 'Just get on with it,' he said.

Rickets looked at him for a second too long, then got on with it. Within minutes there would be new plates, new documents. Later, there would be a new colour, with a new history to match. The vehicle identification number would be altered. It would be meticulously cleaned, then meticulously cleaned again, until there remained no organic trace of human ownership.

Jon walked to the filthy, tiny toilet. A pornographic calendar hung on the wall. He climbed from the muddy, blood-spattered suit. He changed into the clothes he had stuffed into the bag: jeans, a black t-shirt, a blue cotton shirt, his black overcoat. He filled the bag with the suit, splashed cold water on his face and scrubbed his hands with a tiny sliver of white soap. When he emerged, Rickets stared at him enquiringly. Jon looked unchallengingly back.

'Long night?' said Rickets.

'Don't ask,' Jon replied quietly.

The manner in which Rickets regarded him made him recall a conversation with Cathy. He had asked how Andy was enjoying his job.

'Oh,' she said, 'oh, fine. He loves it. He and – what's his name? – Gibbon seem to be thick as thieves already.'

'And Rickets?'

Her eyes crinkled introspectively. 'I'm not so sure about him,' she admitted. She brushed a strand of hair behind her ear and began absently and gently to tug on the softness of its lobe. 'He looks at me funny. You know.'

'I don't like the way he looks at me, sometimes, either,' said Jon, and Cathy had laughed because she could not have known that he'd meant it, nor that the thought of Rickets – of anybody – looking at her or her child or her husband in an inappropriate manner filled him with revulsion.

'I don't see the harm in asking,' said Rickets. 'I don't see anything wrong in making conversation.'

'I don't enjoy conversation,' he replied.

'Tell me about it.'

Jon held an index finger to his lips and bowed his head, one hand cupping an elbow. He closed his eyes and stood like that for a while. Then he laughed and produced the knife and grabbed Rickets by the scruff of the neck. 'I'll fucking tell you about it,' he said through his teeth, pulling Rickets's ear close to his mouth. 'I'll fucking tell you about it if you like.'

After a moment he released his grip. Already he was beginning to regret what he had done. He pocketed the knife and he and Rickets faced one another.

Rickets was breathing quickly but confidently, expelling air through his nostrils. 'Fuck me,' he said, a little raggedly. 'So it *has* got blood in its veins. Who'd've thought?' A vein pulsed rapidly beneath the thin skin of his temple.

'I'm too tired for this,' said Jon. He meant it.

'Yeah,' said Rickets. 'Long night, right?'

He regarded Rickets a moment longer before walking from the garage and on to the street. The confrontation did not concern him as much as his reaction to it. There had been similar problems before – where there were men like Rickets, there would always be similar problems – but they had always been resolved to Jon's advantage. He might, however, be forced to deny to the Tattooed Man that he had done something as unprofessional as pull a knife. It had, undeniably, been a long night. He did not find lying to the Tattooed Man easy or rewarding, especially if the lie concealed weakness or unnecessary indulgence. Duplicity, however insignificant, squatted like an indigestible knot of matter inside him.

He stuffed the bag containing the suit into a wheelie bin. It was a winter morning. The air was icy and cars nudged nose to tail on congested roads. It took two hours to walk home. When he arrived, he had no wish to stay there. He had no wish to think. He stayed long enough to inject amphetamines in his arm and sit out the orgasmically intense rush that followed. He ran cold water over his head, spluttering. Although the events of the previous night seemed distant, dreamlike, the morning felt equally unreal, as if he was watching himself. The morning, his breathing, the sound of the passing traffic, had the quality of documentary footage. Intrusively, nakedly normal.

He went to see Jagger. Although the pubs were yet to open, Jagger was already drunk. Since Jon had seen him last, he had yellowed and shrunk around his bones. Spores of corruption had found root in Jagger's bowels, wrapped tight about the insides of him. He was dying. He was dead already. Jon followed him into his house. The half-light of curtains across windows and endless hours of solitude and bitterness and silent recrimination. Jagger offered a beer. They drank in silence until lunchtime when, upon unspoken agreement, they left the oppressive stink of cancer, and went on to Fat Dave's, substituting the stink of sluttishness and corpulence. The three of them played cards and drank cheap sherry. Gambling was joyless and the drunkenness was of the worst kind: the steady-handed, sour-faced inebriation of people for whom there was joy neither in the world nor in escape from it. At seven in the evening they staggered to the pub to spend their winnings from one another on one another in a bitter communion, a malevolent fraternity. The pub was thick and humid with pressed bodies and the residue of breath. Nausea overcame Jon. He walked unsteadily to the lavatory. A thick, yellow stream of urine oozed the length of the urinal. Excrement had dried to concrete on the walls of the cubicles. Jon poured horribly bitter amphetamine sulphate down his throat, then stepped unsteadily to the tiny sink and washed it down with handfuls of water. He stood with his head over the grimy bowl, watching water spiral down the plug. Eventually the trembling began to subside. Waves of cramp passed over his stomach and he dry-retched, knuckles whitening at the edges of the sink. Eventually there came a point when his inebriation subsided. Physically he was still unsteady but his mind sharpened behind the dull pillow of drunkenness. He thought with distant, crystalline clarity, along arbitrary and tangential lines, but each of these paths converged to a vanishing point. The Tattooed Man, naked, wearing faces, the syringe in his hand. The infinite purity of the Oblivion Suite. The Tattooed Man, holding the sweating creases of his own palm to the flame of one of those massive candles, grinning at him with incomprehensible malevolence. 'Darkness is alien to me, Jon. I'm a creature of infinite illumination. I'm the bringer of light.'

Jon splashed water on to his face, rubbed himself damp with a filthy loop of blue cotton which hung from a battered dispenser. There were two drinks waiting for him: a pint of stout, impenetrably black with a white head, and a whisky chaser like a urine sample in chipped glass. He listened to Fat Dave and Jagger and tried not to think, or remember.

Jagger's wife had left him. This despite the malignancy squeezing the life from him. How she must have hated him. Fat Dave was in trouble with a loan shark. Exponential interest rates whose prodigious fertility he lacked the capacity to understand had grown at the rate of Jagger's tumour. Fat Dave too feared for his life.

As he listened to them, trying to imagine what it was to be like them, to be inside those heads which were closed to him, a hand fell heavily on his shoulder. He turned his head. At the end of the arm which rested on him with aggressive familiarity was Rickets. He wore jeans and expensive, very new trainers. He smiled wide. 'All right, Jon? I didn't know you drank in here.' His smile indicated that this was a deliberate lie.

'Now and again,' said Jon. He glared a warning, but Rickets was drunk and stoned. His eyes were red, bloodshot and unspecific. He was accompanied by a group of perhaps fifteen other young men, kagouls and trainers and baggy denim. Each of them was a stranger to the pub. Jon understood such young men. To enter a strange pub in numbers was, if not a challenge, then at least an indication of aggressive intent. The pub fell silent.

Rickets swayed and grinned. 'Aren't you going to introduce me to your mates?' His teeth seemed very white.

Jon glared into his glass. 'Not today,' he said, 'if you don't mind.'

Rickets leaned over and spread his hands across the table, lowered his head such that he was able to stare directly into Jon's eyes. 'What is it with you?' he said. 'Are you a miserable cunt or is it just me you don't like?'

An intense cone of silence focused on Jon. Fat Dave and Jagger shifted subtly sideways. Rickets's companions looked on, pint glasses pausing at lips. One or two wore knowing smiles. Jon scowled, seemed to think. He knew what was going to happen. He knew that a man like Rickets was incapable of nurturing a dislike – a jealousy – of the magnitude of that which he nursed for Jon without acting on it some day. He exhaled as he resigned himself. 'It's just you,' he said levelly.

Rickets stood straight and laughed, half-turning to his friends. 'Did you *hear* that?' He made an expansive gesture of disbelief. He picked up a half-full pint glass and brought it down across Jon's head.

Like all such events, it was quick and savage and prosaic. Jon fell heavily to the floor and with a flurry of kicks Rickets beat him half-unconscious. Jagger and Fat Dave stood, but were held in check by Rickets's mates, each of whom was evidently eager for escalation, but each of whom, equally, seemed to acknowledge tacitly that at least a nominal excuse was required to embark on such action. Drained of colour, under the weight of too many eyes, Fat Dave and Jagger sank back into their seats and watched.

It was over in half a minute. Jon lay curled on the floor among shards of glass and cigarette butts.

Rickets wiped a hand across his lips and prodded Jon with the toe of a trainer, the pristine white of which was flecked with blood. He swore to himself and spat on the floor. Jon cupped his face and stomach and curled tighter about himself and groaned. Rickets and his entourage left all but immediately. One or two pointedly lagged behind draining their glasses before swaggering towards the door.

The pub had fallen silent and watchful. Fat Dave and Jagger helped Jon to his feet, hands heaving beneath his armpits. His legs hung limp beneath him.

Shirt-sleeves rolled to reveal inappropriate, amateur blue tattoos representing the crucifixion, the landlord waddled to their aid.

Bemused and furious, he addressed Fat Dave. 'What the fuck was all that about?'

Fat Dave looked back at him. 'I dunno, Ted,' he said. 'The black bastard laid into him for nothing.'

The landlord looked at Jon. 'I'd best call you an ambulance, mate.'

Jon shook his head. A shallow, half-inch gash ran across his temple, oozing the blood which had smeared across his face and neck. His eye was beginning to swell and he suspected, in the oddly logical haze of mild shock that he would be pissing blood for days. 'I'm all right,' he said, His voice trembled. 'I just need to clean myself up a bit.' He tried to stand unaided and staggered, falling against Jagger.

'Come through,' said the landlord, 'there's a first-aid kit. Do you want me to phone the police?'

Jon shook his bleary head and allowed the landlord to support him through the pub, behind the bar and into his flat, where he gave Jon a red plastic first-aid box and a half-bottle of whisky. 'On the house. To steady your nerves.'

'Thanks,' said Jon.

The landlord shrugged. 'Any mate of Fat Dave's,' he said. Then, 'It was obvious they were out for trouble tonight. I had my eye on them. I should have been more careful.'

'There was nothing you could do,' said Jon.

'Fucking black bastard,' spat the landlord. The four of them passed the whisky round to steady their nerves.

In the bathroom, Jon washed and disinfected the wound across his head. It was not as dramatic as it looked. Then he stripped to the waist and washed his body, which was grazed and bruised and dotted here and there with black spots of caked blood, marking tiny wounds where he had rolled across broken glass. The blood hardly showed on the dark cotton of his shirt. He drained the remnants of the half-bottle of whisky and returned to the pub. He drank for free for the remainder of the evening. The landlord, by way of Matehood, guilt and gratitude that there was no police involvement, allowed the first few pints on the house. The remainder were supplied by Dave and Jagger.

Jagger: 'I don't know what's wrong. Everything's fucked up. Everything's fucked. Everything's gone wrong.'

Jon could not bring himself to speak.

They left the otherwise empty pub at midnight. The landlord bolted the door behind them, and they staggered unsteadily in the direction of Fat Dave's squalid flat, by way of the Taj Mahal take-away. Still incensed and impotent, Fat Dave called the man who served them a fucking Paki monkey. It occurred to Jon for the first time that Dave was eaten with self-loathing, that he woke every morning or afternoon hungover and filthy with a dull throb of misery in his guts and only himself to blame.

They sat cross-legged upon Dave's bitty and malodorous carpet, faded and worn, and drank tins of super-strength lager and ate vindaloo curry and yellow rice. Jagger talked for the first time of his cancer, Dave of his financial tribulations. There was an exhausted despair in everything that was said. There were things they had wanted to be which they had never been, things they had done they wished they had not.

Jon began to doze, warmed by the unfamiliar intimacy and rhythm of their voices. He had loathed these men. Now he was lulled as, in the face of their extinction, they spoke to one another with something not unakin to tenderness. As Jon slipped from consciousness, he was aware of Jagger tucking a blanket about him and slipping a stained and coverless pillow beneath his head. He was unable to speak. He wanted to say that he understood and forgave them both, but could not.

He woke bathed in dishwater daylight, the glow of impossibly distant, exploding hydrogen filtered through a gap in the rotting curtains. Letting light in.

Fat Dave and Jagger were unconscious and snoring, one on the sofa, the other flat on the carpet, both with forearms crossed against their eyelids. He looked at them with something like pity as he stood, then stumbled unsteadily to the bathroom. He bolted the door and leaned against the peeling wall, shaking and groaning. He kneeled before the filthy toilet and hacked and strained until he vomited a bitter yellow-green liquid that dangled like an umbilicus of egg yolk between his lips and the water. He waited until the shivering had passed. The dressing was crusty brown. His eye was swollen and purple. His mouth felt fetid and his clothes were rumpled. He knew he smelled of cigarettes, of alcohol, of Fat Dave's filth and Jagger's cancer. He loosened his jeans, which fell about his ankles as he squatted on the toilet, his face buried in his hands. After interminable peristaltic waves of agony, he passed a thin, malodorous diarrhoea. Squirt groan. Squirt groan. His piss was thick and yellowy orange, like half-set jelly. It reeked. He retched and puked more thick bile into the avocado bath.

There were perhaps four grammes of speed left in the small plastic bag in his pocket. He wrapped some into a square of toilet tissue which he dry-swallowed like a pill. He could find no toothpaste. He splashed his face with cold water. Another wave of cramps passed across his guts, and again he dropped his trousers and passed burning liquid shit, biting his lip against crying out in pain. When the attack had passed, he tiptoed into the front room, arranging his belt and flies, and retrieved his jacket from the floor. Quietly he left the flat. Outside the speed began to take effect. He shuddered with borrowed energy, beneath which he could feel his body protesting. He needed rest, he needed to eat. He needed to soak in hot, soapy water. He needed to sit across the kitchen table from the Tattooed Man as Phil read a tabloid in the corner and talk to them about cricket, or that day's leader column in the *Daily Telegraph*. He needed to retrieve some normality. He needed the thought of that cottage and that gathering of men, the memory of Rickets kicking him to the floor, the inexplicable tenderness he had felt towards Jagger and Fat Dave, to be assimilated in memory, where everything could be contextualised and understood. While he shivered with a combination of the hangover, the speed he had taken to eradicate it and the exhaustion of the body from which he felt so distant, these things remained part of the present.

The winter sunlight hurt his eyes. He had speed-freak eyes: wide pupils, pools of blackness that allowed in too much light, more light than he needed to see by. Details were crisp and immediate and the world dizzying with signs whose meanings and relationships were supernaturally clear. He knew that if people were staring at him, if heads turned in cars as they passed, if people looked over their shoulders at him, if people spoke about him in hushed whispers, it was because he reeked of alcohol and sweat and puke and shit, because the filthy dressing on his head marked him out as something peculiar and threatening. It was not because everyone sensed what he was, and what he had done. Yet the urgent eruption of a siren nearly caused him to lose control of his bowels. He found himself avoiding people's gaze with a transparent desperation.

He stopped in a café to drink a cup of coffee and smoke a cigarette, but the weight of all the eyes, of all that perceived insight, was too great. He staggered into the street and walked from nowhere to nowhere, ricocheting from lamp-posts, moving aggressively onwards. He looked at himself reflected in a department store window, the hollows of his eyes in juxtaposition with the smiling mannequins within, modelling ski-gear and winter coats. People swerved to avoid him. He looked at their reflection behind his own, two layers of perception reflected in the unreal window of commerce.

He remembered the favour he had asked of his friend. Something within him warmed. It was a long time before a taxi would stop for him.

Cathy's first reaction upon seeing him was a bright smile. Then her face fell. The toddler, Kirsty, stood behind her, in cotton vest and knickers, a doll dangling from her sticky fist. 'My God,' said Cathy, 'what happened to you?'

Jon stumbled over his words, shivered. Found himself unable to speak.

'Come in,' she said. 'Come on in, for Christ's sake.'

He followed her into the living room. She set Kirsty down in her chair, and faced him, hands on hips. She was wearing a long white T-shirt and black leggings, hair pulled into a casual ponytail. She smelled of soap and shampoo and Johnson's baby talc. She lit a cigarette and sat, crossing her legs and arms, holding the cigarette centimetres from her mouth, speaking from behind it. 'Sit down before you fall down.'

He was loath to sit: his filthiness made him an alien thing in this place. As he sank into the chair, his clothes pressed into him and his flesh crawled at their touch. He was shaking.

Her brow was knitted: 'What the bloody hell happened to you?'

He buried his head in his hands. 'I'm sorry I came.'

She spat the words with genuine contempt. 'Don't be an idiot. You look *ill*. You look like *death*.'

He smiled with some bitterness and not a little irony.

'Who did that to you?' She reached out as if to touch his brow. Her hand hung in the air between them, its eventual trajectory undecided. She withdrew it.

He touched his forehead, winced. 'Just some idiot in a pub.'

'You look like you haven't slept for a week.' Decisively, she stood and held out her hand. It was a peculiarly maternal gesture: a command to come along this *instant*. He surrendered his hand. She took it and pulled him to his feet, leading him upstairs. On the landing, she said, 'Men,' with a kind of disgust born of familiarity, 'I swear you don't know how to look after yourselves.' She showed him through to the bathroom and bent over the bath to run the taps. Steam began to rise. 'Take those filthy clothes off,' she said.

She softened at his reaction and said, 'Don't worry, I'll turn my back.' She did just that and, self-consciously he stripped, handing over his jeans and shirt and t-shirt. He stood absurd in his socks and pants. 'Right,' she said, 'have a long soak. It'll take an hour or two to wash and dry these things. There's plenty of hot water. Then we'll make you a decent breakfast. When did you last eat?'

He didn't know.

She tutted and left the bathroom. Jon removed his socks and underpants and held them in one hand, looking around for somewhere to put them. Nowhere seemed particularly appropriate so he dropped them to the floor. The door opened a crack and he immediately kicked them behind him with his heel. Cathy's hand poked through the crack, holding a blue towelling dressing-gown. She dropped it to the floor without saying a word and closed the door again.

He slid into the bath when it was still only half full and running, the water painfully hot, making his flesh pink, heating even the chill of his bones. He exhaled half in pain, half in relief. He lay there and listened to his heart and the sounds of the washing machine as it ran through its cycle. When the bath cooled he let in more hot water. He dipped his head beneath the surface, the heat threatening to suffocate rather than drown him, then thoroughly soaped his body, washing away the recent past. He lay in a half-doze, the delicate fluttering of arteries beneath his skin like fronds shifting in a tiny tide. At last he stood, dripping, and tenderly began to towel himself dry.

As he stood there, Cathy walked in. She carried his jeans and T-shirt folded in her arms. He could smell that they were freshly laundered. She dropped them and put her hand to her mouth and said, 'Oh, God, I'm sorry, I didn't think.' But Jon knew, or felt he knew, that this was not so, that, if she had not actually intended this to happen, then it was the thought of doing it which had distracted her to the extent that it became possible. He knew also that seduction was not her intent but something else, something immediate but inarticulable, as if bursting in on his nudity was a way to establish an intimacy. He knew that she would spin on her heel before the words had died in her mouth and slam the door behind her, and they would giggle about it over breakfast and be friends. In a tenth of a second all this passed his mind. But in the expected act of turning away she paused, as if registering what she had seen, and turned slowly to face him, pushing the door quietly closed. She shook her head and said, 'My God, look at you.' He dropped the towel and hung his head as she stared at him. She reached out a trembling hand and with the tip of a tentative finger traced the length of white scar tissue that ran across his ribs, across his chest. His body was a lace of scars, a brutal tattoo of his violence. She ran her fingers along the white relief of the stab wounds that crossed his stomach, then the indelible record of a gash that ran from hip to knee, a hairless trace across his thigh. She walked behind him and, her breath rapid and warm against his nape, traced the wounds that dotted his shoulders and crissed and crossed his spine. He shook with something like shock when, with excruciating tenderness, she wrapped her arms about him from behind, her breasts pressed flat to him, and kissed him at the base of his neck. She turned him and nursed his head, whispering, 'My God. Look at you. Look at you,' over and over. He heard with a knot in his stomach that she wept for him. He held her at arm's length. She leaned forward and pecked him on the lips, touching his face. He had not been touched for so very long.

She turned and left the bathroom without speaking. When she returned, only seconds later, announcing her arrival this time with a rap on the door, it was like a different world. He had pulled on his jeans by then, and she walked in carrying a pair of socks and a shirt. 'These are Andy's,' she said, 'but I'm sure he won't mind if you don't. I hope the shirt fits: I'll never get the blood out of the other one.'

'Keep it for rags,' he said, and took the things from her.

Downstairs, she redressed the wound on his head with the contents of a small first-aid box she kept beneath the sink. Then she fried him an enormous breakfast: sausages, eggs, bacon, fried bread and tomatoes. He sat at the kitchen table as she did so and amused Kirsty by making her dolls dance to the tinny sounds of the portable radio. Although the drugs suppressed his appetite, his guts craved carbohydrates and he was able to wolf down the breakfast and three mugs of milky tea. After he let Cathy demonstrate how to change a nappy, since she insisted that he'd have to learn some time and it might as well be now. And by the way her friend Liz was really quite taken by him. She hadn't said anything in particular, mind you, but it had been a while since the party and she always seemed to find an excuse to bring it up. He was astonished at the sheer awfulness of toddler shit.

Kirsty perched herself happily on his lap and, to his astonishment, dozed as he and Cathy watched an old black-and-white movie, chatting inanely. When it was time to go, he gently laid the child along the sofa. She made an irritated little scowl, then put her thumb in her mouth and, sucking on it, fell asleep.

'Tell Andy I called,' Jon said.

'He'll be sorry he missed you.'

'I've got to go,' he said. 'I need to get some sleep.'

She crossed her arms. 'At least you look a bit better than you did this morning.'

'Thanks to you.'

It was her turn to shrug. 'Look after yourself,' she said.

'I will,' he said.

As she opened the front door for him, she said, 'You know we're always here to wash the blood from your jeans. If you need us.'

He nodded, and smiled. For a second, he was sad, and wished that things might be different. Then he put his hands in his pockets and turned away, and she closed the door. He could feel her watching his progress through a gap in the downstairs curtain.

Three evenings later he was startled into consciousness by the telephone ringing. He scratched the crown of his head wearily and as he lifted the receiver settled back into a chair, slinging his legs across one of the arms. He patted blindly on the table for a pack of cigarettes.

For a moment he thought he recognised the voice as Cathy's, but it was not Cathy. The woman identified herself as a WPC and for a nauseated moment the world shifted beneath his feet and before his eyes. Gently she had him confirm his identity, before asking whether he knew two people whose names were not familiar. Andrew and Catherine.

The police car arrived within five minutes and as it pulled off with him in the back seat – he always seemed to travel in the back seat – he experienced a sense of childish dislocation. He had never travelled in a police car and had certainly not expected to under such circumstances. He watched as soporific wipers wiped away the rain and the two polite but unmoved officers surveyed the road they travelled. He could not speak.

Andy's parents were there, but it was Jon that Andy had asked to be present. It was Jon that Andy had thought of first. He sat in the hospital waiting room, hands clasped into a double fist between his legs, gazing ahead, dumbfounded, as if incapable of thought.

There were others in the room – police, family, doctors – but Jon hardly registered their presence. They milled unfocused in the periphery of his mind like revenants, ghouls sensing fresh carrion.

It was only when Jon reached out and uselessly placed a hand on his shoulder that Andy moved, violently shuddering, as if somebody had walked across his grave.

He reached out and closed his fingers about Jon's wrist and

began to slowly pull the hand towards his face. He planted a deliberate kiss on the back of it before letting go. Jon was stunned for a moment by the shock of contact and wondered what was expected of him. Then he settled on the carpet before Andy, chin resting on knees, hands cupping his ankles.

That afternoon, at the local shops, Cathy had stopped on a zebra crossing to retrieve a plastic doll that Kirsty, intent on a lollipop, had dropped. A car that was going too fast smashed the life from her in an impact so terrible she was thrown from her shoes.

Kirsty, whom the car had dealt an indirect blow, fought hard for the life that Cathy and Andy had granted her. It was fully three days before she too died, without ever in her life having voiced a proper word.

Six The Guaranteed Eternal Sanctuary Man

There were two greedy black holes and two boxes, one smaller than the other and there was freezing, driving rain and two black heaps of earth and there was a man reading from a black book, the blackest book in the world. And there was Andy, supported by his father-in-law, who could not take his eyes from the silent, yawning, arrested fertility of the soil.

The wake was muted. There were sandwiches with the crusts cut off and wines and spirits to toast the departed. People milled about and wanted to say things but did not. Instead they sipped sherry and warm bitter and were ashamed, although they did not know why. Death was suffocating in its power to suck one beneath its surface. It had hit with the juggernaut force of tidal flood water, chaotic with filth and debris.

Jon said hello to those he recognised from the party. The red-haired woman he'd danced with (and who he had supposed he would remember for the way she looked at her friends before speaking to him, the way she bent a little at the waist as she laughed) he was shocked to recognise as a terribly frail thing, freckled skin drained pale against the black of her dress and the startling auburn of her hair. Her eyes were smudges on the surface of her face and when she kissed his cheek he wanted to take her hand and squeeze it gently but could not.

The girl who had fallen asleep on Andy's lap in the garden – Cathy's niece, Kirsty's cousin – was made a child again by her inability to comprehend that such a thing as this could occur, was *allowed* to occur. Jon watched her, tiny and tearfully bewildered. He even followed her from the room, hoping to stop her in the hallway and say something meaningless and comforting, but without seeing him she strode into the bathroom, slamming the door and locking it behind her. Jon heard her noisily vomiting and quietly retraced his steps.

He kissed Andy's mother on the cheek, shook his father's hand, was introduced to Cathy's parents. Her mother told him that she knew all about him. He was ashamed.

The priest was there. He was a family friend. He had christened Cathy and he had christened her child and he had fed them to the ground. Jon thought he could feel the priest's eyes follow him. When they met in the doorway, the priest stood aside only after a momentary pause that was nevertheless almost marked enough to constitute a challenge. Jon met his gaze for a violently luminous instant. The priest was broad and tall enough to be slightly stooped, still solid of muscle and powerful. His nose was Roman and broken, an authoritative, imperious and possibly stubborn beak. His hair was curly and dirty grey, a little too long, a wino's mop, and he wore a thick, heavily greying beard that rode up his cheeks and crept under his collar. There were clumps of white hair nestling in his ears and tufts of it sprouting from beneath his cuffs. He wore steel-rimmed spectacles and Jon thought he could detect a severity in his demeanour the source of which he was unable to place.

In twos and threes the mourners began to leave. The woman he'd danced with hugged him very tightly and kissed his cheek again. She wore the same perfume she had at the party but a different black dress. He cuddled her head briefly to his shoulder. Soon there remained only the two sets of parents, Jon, Andy and the priest. The women set about tidying up, clearing paper plates from the table, sweeping sausage rolls and Scotch eggs together, to be stored in the fridge so that Andy might wake the next day and think, 'I'll eat the leftovers from my wife's funeral.' The thought was terrifying. That there could be a tomorrow and another tomorrow after that was incomprehensible. Cathy would never again turn her key in the lock and walk in, flustered and irritable, Kirsty nagging stickily at her sleeves.

Jon imagined Andy sobbing on the bed, his face buried in a handful of her clothes, inhaling the ghost of her fragrance, terrified that it would fade.

The women were still tidying. He understood why. The three men, two fathers and a Father, stood in the corner. Andy's dad linked his arm through Jon's and said, 'Father Chapman, this is Jon. He's been a very good friend to our Andy.'

There was another pause, not long enough to become uncomfortable, and again Jon had the impression that the priest was subjecting him to minute scrutiny before offering his hand. He was visited by a momentary, dizzying *déjà vu*. 'I think Keith will do. Call me Keith.'

Jon dropped the priest's hand and noted that Chapman seemed unconsciously to wipe his palm clean on the lapel of his jacket. They exchanged an equally quizzical smile.

'It's good to meet you, Keith,' said Jon.

'And you, Jon. And you.'

Sure now that the priest was as obscurely uncomfortable as he, Jon made a non-committal noise, clapped Andy's father gently but encouragingly on the shoulder and went into the kitchen, where the two mothers were washing up. 'Look,' he said, 'leave that. I'll do it.'

'No, we'd rather. Really.'

He had no function here. He kissed them both goodbye, pulled on his black overcoat, shook hands with the three fathers, and left. It was dark, and the rain was freezing and filthy, and he was filled with the extravagant urge to punish.

His lack of knowledge of life was such that he knew nothing of the proper human reaction to death. Where he saw the pantomine of grief in others he felt in himself only a power that resonated like the strings of an untouched violin. The chords of his musculature sang with it.

For Cathy he felt nothing that might properly be called grief. Instead there was a nagging sadness that seemed to sneak up on him at inappropriate and arbitrary times: walking into the kitchen, brushing his teeth, even lifting a buttock from a chair to facilitate a fart. He would find himself choked by a sob that was too big for his throat and which was yet too big to swallow. He would sit without moving, his eyes threatening to pop in his skull, until the feeling dissolved into his throat. Now and again he was possessed by a strange rage: veins would stand livid on his neck and forehead and his teeth would grind and he longed, briefly, for release. But this, too, would pass.

He saw Andy often, three or four times a week, although he was particularly busy and despite the fact that it was often the sight of Andy that instigated the barely contained attacks of fury. Sometimes he wanted to grab him by the throat and squeeze and squeeze and squeeze. When the attack was past he would want to cradle Andy's head in his arms and whisper wordless and meaningless comfort to him. He did neither.

Andy grew fatter. His stomach spilled from under his t-shirts and above his jeans. His features were becoming lost in his spreading face. He perpetually wore three or four days' worth of filthy ginger stubble. He smelled, and his hands shook as he chainlit cigarettes. Each time Jon visited the house he found it filthy, the kitchen and the living room strewn with the detritus of a diet of take-away food: pizza boxes, foil tubs containing cold noodles curled like worms in greasy sauce, chip and kebab wrappers, beer tins and whisky bottles, empty cigarette cartons, heaped ashtrays. The stink was almost unbearable, the squalor of a descent whose nature he could only guess at. Andy would sit in silence, smoking while Jon pottered about like a maid, gathering wrappers and tins and ashtrays and filling black bin-liners. He opened windows and doors, letting in the freezing but relatively fresh winter air. He washed up endless cups and glasses and cutlery, and cleaned the kitchen with specially purchased bottles of this and that until it once more resembled the new kitchen of which Cathy had been so proud, and heralded a rush of fury that left him shaking over the sink, a sponge crushed in his fist. He Hoovered the carpets and the stairs as if they had in some way offended him. He cleaned the bathroom in which Cathy had wrapped a soft white towel about him.

The first time he performed this function, he left the kitchen with his shirt-sleeves rolled, and went to enter Andy's bedroom, steeling himself for the mess he would find there. Andy stood at the foot of the stairs, a can in his hand.

'That's my fucking *bedroom*,' he said, and shuffled back to the living room.

'Sorry,' Jon called down the stairs, and went to get the vacuum cleaner. He didn't go near the bedrooms again, despite an urge to do so that bordered on the neurotic.

Christmas approached and things got worse. Andy was restless, unable to sit still, equally unable to concentrate for any appreciable period of time. He was absent from work. He smelled so sour that Jon felt uncomfortable standing close. In Jon's presence he would sometimes walk aimlessly up and down the room, muttering to himself. Once Jon saw him punch the door and winced as Andy screamed in response and buried his hand between his thighs.

'Come on,' Jon said, standing. 'Come on, mate.'

The hand swelled and purpled. For a while he ate, drank and smoked with his left hand, which made him clumsy and slow and irritating. Jon wanted to hit him.

The week before Christmas Andy's parents arrived. Jon was in occasional contact with them. They visited on days when they knew that Jon would not, so that Andy's time in the company of others was maximised. Each understood the reason for this, although it went unspoken. Thus he was surprised to answer the door (Andy was unwilling to do this) to see them huddled outside, hand in hand. Their trepidation was transparent.

They stepped inside without invitation and removed their heavy winter coats, which Jon took and hung up. Andy's mother shook out a black and white polka-dot umbrella. 'How are you, Jon?' she said. She was a short, plump woman who Jon remembered sadly as a source of gently ribald wit. She and her husband seemed to feel it necessary to dress up to visit their son. She wore a cream trouser suit and patent leather shoes.

'Fine,' he answered. 'Fine.'

'And how's our Andy?'

He allowed himself to communicate a degree of his frustration with a shrug of his shoulders and a slightly despairing wave of the hand. 'Much the same.'

Andy's father, as was his habit, shook Jon's hand and pronounced his name once, investing it with monosyllabic gravity: 'Jon.'

Jon followed them through, then went into the kitchen, from which he returned with a tray of tea and biscuits.

'Thanks, love,' said Andy's mother. She and her husband perched side by side on the edge of the sofa, facing their son, who sat slumped and sullen in an armchair. Jon could smell him from the corner of the room.

'So how have you been keeping yourself?' she asked, taking a cup and saucer and balancing it in her lap.

'I haven't,' he said. 'You and Jon have been doing all the keeping for me.'

She looked at Jon. He shrugged again, minutely. 'You're looking a little better,' she said.

Andy rolled his eyes.

'Have you thought about getting yourself back to work?' said his father. He did not resemble his son. He was slight, with narrow shoulders and skin stretched tight over his temples. Jon had often wondered if their physical dissimilarity was not in some secret way the root cause of their long-running antipathy. He wondered if this man was actually Andy's father. 'You should make the effort,' he continued. 'It'll do you good, and you don't want to go losing your job on top of everything else, do you?'

Andy's lips silently formed the protest: 'For fuck's sake.' Then he pointed at Jon and said, 'How can I lose the job when he's the boss?'

Jon could almost sense the effort it took for Andy's father to keep his mouth closed. He watched his Adam's apple bob and the muscles in his jaw flex.

'Come on, now, love,' said his mother. 'Your dad's only trying to help.'

Father and son (or otherwise) regarded one another levelly.

Jon intervened. He sat in the second armchair, able to view the other three. 'The job's not a problem,' he said. 'I've sorted it out with the boss.'

'He's been ever so kind,' said Andy's mum. 'You will thank him for me, won't you?' She said exactly this every time she and Jon spoke.

'He says not to worry about it,' said Jon. 'He says Andy's job will be there for as long as he needs it.'

'He must be an angel,' she said.

Andy's father muttered, 'He must be something all right,' a little too loudly. She nudged him in the ribs and through the corner of her eye looked pointedly at him.

'Anyway,' she said, 'the reason we came round tonight is', she took a sip of tea and paused, – 'to ask if you'd like to come round to your mum and dad's for Christmas. We can't have you all alone, can we? We thought it would be best if we spent a quiet couple of days alone. You know, with the way things are. We've already got the turkey.'

Things was apparently the only word it was possible to use with reference to the death of Andy's wife and child. Jon was as guilty of it as anybody else: the way things are, the way things have been, these things happen, nobody understands these things, these things make you wonder don't they? These things.

'And, of course,' she added, 'Jon's invited, too.'

Andy stood and marched unsteadily to the kitchen. He returned with a can of lager, which he opened with his left hand. He snatched a cigarette from the pack and lit it. 'I'm sorry, Mum,' he said through the smoke, 'but that's about the most stupid idea I've ever heard.'

'Fine,' she replied. 'No, of course. Whatever you think is best.' Jon thought she might cry. 'We just thought. We thought it was an idea.'

Andy glugged beer.

'Anyway. You know you'll be welcome.'

'All *right*,' he said. 'Thanks. But no. Can we change the fucking record now?'

Andy's mother blinked rapidly. 'Don't swear so much, love,' she said softly. 'There's no need for you to swear so much.'

His father's jaw flexed in impotent fury.

'And have you been back to the doctor?' she persisted.

'For what?'

'To ask him if he has anything to – you know. Give you.'

'Give me for what?'

'To help you sleep.'

'I don't want to sleep.'

'To help you feel better.'

'I don't want to feel better.'

His father could contain himself no longer. 'You've got to help yourself to help yourself, Andrew,' he said. 'None of this is any good. Nobody's expecting you to carry on as if nothing has happened, but it's not doing *any* of us any good, you wallowing in it like this.'

'What do you mean, "any of us"? Sorry – am I being a *bother*, Dad?'

'All I'm saying is that you've got to face your responsibilities some time. That's all I'm saying.'

Andy reached for the pack of cigarettes. He muttered, 'Piss off, you mad old cunt.'

Andy's father slapped his son across the face. Andy roared and launched himself at his father. There was a sudden squall of chaos. Andy punched his father in the head. Andy's father fell back and tripped over the sofa, sending it and a standard lamp toppling to the floor. Jon grabbed Andy and wrestled him to the floor. They landed heavily. Jon banged the back of his head on the skirting board. Andy's mum was screaming in the corner of the room. Andy wriggled and writhed furiously to free himself from Jon, who struggled with equal vigour to pin Andy's arms to the floor.

His father retreated to the far corner. 'You little bastard,' he yelled, 'you ungrateful little bastard. You filthy mouthed little bastard.'

'You old cunt,' Andy screamed back at him. Veins stood prominently against the purple flesh of his bursting face.

Andy's mother was yelling for them to stop. Jon was yelling for Andy to lie still. Everyone was yelling at everyone else and nobody was listening.

Andy's father strode for the door, sniffing blood. He paused to say, 'Are you coming?' to his wife.

She hesitated. Looked at Jon struggling with her son. Regarded her husband with eyes that had the intimacy of years.

'Fine,' he said and slammed the door behind him.

It was not until they heard the sound of his car pulling away too quickly from the kerb that things began to calm down. Andy began to weaken. Jon rolled from on top of him. They lay alongside one another, staring at the ceiling.

'I forgot how strong you were,' said Jon.

'So did *he*, by the look of things,' said Andy.

Incredibly, they began to laugh. It was not good laughter, but it was better than nothing.

'I hope you're finished,' his mother said. 'I thought we were done with all this nonsense long ago.'

Jon and Andy sat. Looking at them, dishevelled and sweating, her face softened with nostalgia. 'Pick yourselves up,' she said, 'and tuck your shirts in.'

They did as commanded.

'You shouldn't have done that, Andrew.'

Andy shrugged.

She sat on the sofa, wiping at a patch of spilled tea. She patted the seat next to her. 'Come here.' Andy did as he was asked. He sat next to his mother. He looked too big. 'Let me look at that hand.' He offered his bruised hand. She took it in hers, examined it palm up, palm down, tutting and shaking her head. 'Look at the state of you.'

He began to cry. He buried his head in his mother's neck and shook and shuddered. She toyed with the hair on the crown of his head. He wrapped his arms around her.

Jon walked to the kitchen, but could not bear it there. He walked on into the garden and stood beneath the sky, smoking a cigarette.

He hoped the worst of it had passed with that evening, but he was wrong. Although he realised that the invitation to spend Christmas with Andy's parents was made more in gratitude than anything else he was also aware that it was a request to convince Andy to go home for the festive period. He tried his best. Andy was intractable. In the end Jon said that, if that was the case, he would visit Andy for Christmas. He hinted that he would be very bad company if forced to do so. Andy gave in. He promised to go to his parents.

On Christmas Eve, as his parents slept and dreamed dreams of Christmases long gone, Andy sat on the toilet and slashed his wrists and forearms. They found him at seven in the morning. He lay with his forehead on the floor as if kowtowing, wearing an old pair of his father's pyjama trousers. Neither his mother or father had imagined that a human body contained so much liquid. Blood seemed to have exploded from Andy's veins and arteries like water from a balloon dropped from a height. For years his mother would be troubled by a nightmare, in which her dreaming self realised that *of course* no one body could contain so much blood. In the dream her son lay face down in the bathroom sopping and sodden with the blood of his butchered wife and child.

The ambulance man and woman were patient with her and sympathetic. It was the worst time of year for such things, they told her. She wondered how many times today they would have to repeat this unreassuring piece of information. She was filled with a directionless dread. The ambulance, too, would figure in her dreams. So would the horrible, inappropriate spectre of Cathy, disguised as Father Christmas, in beard and wig and red hat, recognisable by the familiar crow's-feet at the corner of her eyes. She carried her giggling child in a sack swung across her shoulders. She was going to surprise her husband, to hang his child in a bag at the foot of his bed.

Jon found her at the side of her son's bed, gazing at a portion of Christmas pudding that sat on a paper plate on her lap. Someone had made an effort to decorate the ward with tinsel and streamers and a synthetic tree. Christmas in hospital was a hollow and desperate thing. Christmas and death went together. Christmas and dying were made for each other.

He pulled up a chair and sat beside her. She held his hand. He was surprised to find that he didn't mind. Her husband had retreated to the pub with his mates. He had wept as his son was hustled into the ambulance. She had never seen him weep before. She told Jon she wished Andy could have seen it.

Andy was bandaged and sedated, unaware of their presence. If he was able to dream, Jon surmised with grim Christmas sentimentality, that at least he was able to spend one last

Christmas with his wife. He left the hospital shortly before midday.

He and the Tattooed Man ritually spent Christmas Day together. Jon's favourite part of the day was the Queen's speech. He enjoyed watching the Tattooed Man relishing every cut-glass syllable of it. Every year, when the Queen had finished, the Tattooed Man would cackle and say, 'Silly old tart, how's your grandma?' Jon never asked why.

Following the speech they enjoyed a meal, the absurd extravagance of which the Tattooed Man seemed to find intellectually rather than physically delicious. This year, as in others, it was a lavish spread of kitsch Victoriana, complete with goose and suckling pig. 'Vietnamese pot-bellied,' explained the Tattooed Man. 'Sautéed in napalm.' They ate in agreeable silence, punctuated by short bursts of conversation.

The Tattooed Man bit down on a turkey thigh, peggy teeth puncturing the crisped and golden skin. He had grease smeared around his mouth and jaw. It shone like varnish. 'I feel for your friend,' he said. 'Christmas is a terrible time to be alone.'

Jon had no desire to be forced into betraying the Tattooed Man by resenting his sense of irony. He shrugged.

'No,' insisted the Tattooed Man. 'Really. I can remember some terrible Christmases. I can remember going hungry on the streets on many a Christmas Day.'

Jon had never heard him talk about himself like this. His pulse quickened 'Really?'

'Really.'

'When was this?'

The Tattooed Man waved the turkey thigh non-committally. 'A long time ago.'

'Tell me about it,' Jon insisted. 'I'd like to know. I don't know anything about you.'

'There's nothing much to tell,' grinned the Tattooed Man. 'It was all such a long time ago.'

After lunch, they settled before the television in deep

armchairs. They drank sherry from small glasses. On one of the satellite channels the Tattooed Man found a film he particularly liked. He settled down with an arch purr of contentment. They watched it in loaded silence. When the credits began to roll, he stretched and reached for Jon's arm.

'I agree, don't you?' he said. 'It's a *wonderful* life.' He lifted the crystal decanter. 'Shall we drink to it? To a wonderful life!'

Jon could not help but grin. He felt bloated and slow. His arm was heavy as he lifted the little glass. He gave the Tattooed Man a look.

'Well,' protested the Tattooed Man. 'You know my philosophy: You've got to accentuate the positive, to eliminate the negative, latch on to the affirmative . . .' He leaned over and squeezed Jon's knee once, fixing him with an impish grin.

Jon looked up from beneath his brow, taking a sip of sherry. 'Don't mess with Mister Inbetween,' he concluded.

The Tattooed Man nodded sagely and raised his glass. 'Exactly,' he said. 'So: a toast?'

They clinked glasses.

'To a wonderful life,' said Jon. 'You old bastard.'

On New Year's Day, Jon found Andy propped up in bed, a pile of pillows supporting the small of his back. The glitter and decoration hung tired and subdued, as if they had surrendered to the insidious depression that soaked into the ward's bilious green walls. Although physically Andy had almost recovered, Jon understood that he was being kept in for psychiatric observation. Apparently, attempting to take one's life was considered a dangerously irrational act. The balance of Andy's mind was disturbed. Jon knew this was nonsense. It was the balance of the world that was disturbed. He mentioned this to nobody but the Tattooed Man, who clucked indulgent agreement.

Andy looked like he needed fresh air. His wrists and forearms were bandaged, and he wore dark rings beneath his eyes, which were piggy black marbles in his pudgy flesh. He had a tabloid spread across his lap.

Pulling up a chair, Jon said, 'I don't know how you can bear to read that rubbish.'

Andy looked up. 'I didn't hear you come in.' He was vague and slightly dreamy.

Jon crossed his legs. He handed Andy a large Toblerone. 'Happy New Year,' he said.

Andy took the chocolate. 'Cheers.'

'So how are things?'

Things.

Andy threw him the newspaper, stabbing at one article with a rigid finger, pinning the paper to the bed.

'Look at this,' he said.

'Look at what?'

'They found Rickets.'

'Oh yeah'?

'In his flat,' said Andy. 'Somebody cut him to bits,' he said. 'He was there for weeks. In bits.'

'Christ,' said Jon.

'Dead right,' replied Andy.

'Couldn't have happened to a nicer bloke.'

Andy concurred with a grunt. 'Still,' he said. 'Nobody deserves that, do they?'

Jon opened the Toblerone and took a chunk. His answer was obscured by the triangle of chocolate passing from cheek to cheek. Andy took a chunk of his own.

'Weeks he was there,' said Andy. 'Imagine that. Weeks. The police think it's drugs related. Imagine *that*. You don't know anything, do you? The things that go on.'

'Look on the bright side,' ventured Jon. 'It means instant promotion for you, when you're well.'

Andy retrieved the newspaper, folding it closed. The front page, in half-inch bold, read: 'Top Cops in New Year Bomb Horror'. The subheading was: 'Festive Outrage Shocks PM'.

There was a photograph of a mangled and twisted car. The previous night two senior policemen, on their way to a New Year's Eve party, had been killed by a car bomb. No organisation had yet claimed responsibility. The men left two wives and five children between them. The Prime Minister, true to the headline, had expressed his 'shock and outrage'. Jon reached out and turned the paper over, pretending to scan the back page for the football results, although unsure if there were any.

Andy leaned back and lifted his head. He sighed. 'You don't have to do this,' he said.

'Do what?'

'Try to cheer me up.'

'I didn't know I was.'

'Come off it,' he said. 'Rickets is dead. He's been cut to *pieces* –' he opened the paper, found the story, and quoted, ' – "in a brutal and frenzied attack".'

Jon shrugged. 'What can you do?' he said. 'Do you want me to cry and say what a great bloke he was?'

'Somebody *killed* him, for God's sake.'

'Things happen.'

Exasperated, Andy closed his eyes. 'For fuck's sake,' he whispered. Jon was visited by a passing sense of empathy. Rickets was dead and Jon seemed to him to regard it as a piece of meaningless gossip, less important than the sharing of a Toblerone and banal, profoundly meaningless trivialities such as 'Happy New Year' and 'How are you?' The way he said *things* instead of *Cathy*.

He reached out and closed his hand about Andy's upper arm. It was doughy to the touch. 'Look, I'm sorry. I knew days ago,' he lied. 'The police came to interview me. I didn't want to worry you. I'm sorry.'

Andy opened his eyes, gazed across the ward. 'I never knew anybody who was murdered before,' he said, blankly. 'I hadn't thought about any of it really. Dying. What have you.'

'Come on,' said Jon. He was beginning to recognise this as his mantra of helpless wordlessness. When there's nothing to say, say, 'Come on.' Say anything but, 'I agree with you. Everything you say has a perfectly understandable basis in reality. Why not die and be done with it?'

'Come on,' he said. 'Come on.'

Andy snapped off a chunk of chocolate and popped it in his mouth. 'I don't half fancy a kebab,' he said.

'As soon as you get out of here,' replied Jon, 'I'll buy you the biggest bastard kebab you've ever seen. As long as you promise to behave yourself.'

Andy laughed.

An hour later his parents arrived. His mother leaned over on tiptoe to kiss his forehead. Jon heard her whisper, 'Happy New Year, love.' Andy's father shook his son's hand stiffly. 'Hello, son.'

'Hello, Dad.'

Andy's mum kissed Jon's cheek. 'And you, love. Happy New Year.'

'Here's to a better one,' Jon said.

'Hear, hear,' she said, and squeezed his hand.

Andy was showing his father the paper. 'This bloke. This is the bloke I worked with. The one who didn't show up for weeks.'

His father took the paper and scrutinised it minutely. 'Bugger me,' he concluded. '"A savage and frenzied attack". Look at this, Joyce. This was our Andy's boss.'

'Put it away,' she said. 'I don't want to know.'

Father and son exchanged an intimately knowing glance.

Jon and Andy's father left to get coffee and tea from the Maxpax machine that stood just outside the ward doors.

'How are things?' Jon said, inserting money into the slot.

'Better,' admitted Andy's father. 'Getting better.'

'Good,' said Jon.

Not much later, he went home.

All the way he was oppressed by a sense of threat, which clung about him like a localised atmosphere. He stepped into the house with exaggerated caution, even withdrawing the stiletto knife from his pocket.

The Tattooed Man sat in the leather armchair, tabloid newspaper open on his lap.

Jon fell against the door. 'Jesus Christ,' he said. 'What are you doing here?'

The Tattooed Man stood, folding the tabloid. 'Reading,' he said. 'I was sat here reading.'

The relief left him. He straightened slowly, concealing the knife in his palm.

A man emerged from Jon's kitchen. It was another of the Tattooed Man's drivers, an enormously tall, gangling sociopath who wore a dark grey suit, crisp white shirt and shined shoes. His name was Olly. He and Jon shared a long history of antipathy. As an unspoken matter of course, the Tattooed Man usually arranged things such that Jon and Olly rarely, if ever, crossed each other's path. Olly regarded Jon over the rims of the mirror-lensed sunglasses he affected to wear, and which Jon found unbearably aggravating. He carried a mug of tea in his hand. Jon's mug. Jon's tea.

'What the fuck is going on?'

The Tattooed Man bunched the tabloid in his fist and threw it at Jon. It unfurled as it flew. '*This* is going on.'

'What?'

'*Rickets*,' bellowed the Tattooed Man. 'Don't pretend to be an *idiot*, Jon. Don't pretend you can *lie* to me.'

Olly hid a cool, satisfied smile behind the back of his hand.

Jon was cold with fury for seeing this man, whom he loathed, invited into his house as a calculated insult. He spoke to the Tattooed Man but regarded Olly. 'Tell that cunt that if he laughs at me again I'll cut his fucking throat.' He revealed the knife.

Olly took a step forward, reaching into his pocket. The

Tattooed Man restrained him with a hand against his solar plexus. '*Rickets*,' he hissed at Jon, arid sibilants forced through spitless teeth.

'He had it coming,' said Jon.

The Tattooed Man whirled on his axis, howling, his arms spread wide. The windows shook. '*He had it coming*?'

Jon said nothing.

The Tattooed Man faced him. 'Do you know what I hate?' he said. 'I'll tell you what I hate. I hate someone who knows the cost of everything but the value of nothing.'

Jon lowered the knife. 'What does that mean?'

The Tattooed Man levelled an accusing finger: 'It means that it's not your place to decide who lives and who dies. Do you *understand that*? That's *my* decision. That's my prerogative. You're not qualified. You don't *know* enough.'

Jon swallowed. 'For Christ's sake,' he spat, as if expelling a sour taste. 'What was Rickets to you? He was more trouble than he was worth. I did you a favour.'

'You don't *know* what Rickets was to me!'

'He was nothing. Admit it. He was nothing. You're angry because I did something off my own back for my own reasons. You can't stand the idea that I made a *decision*!'

'A decision?' The accusing finger was so tense, it might snap. 'Rickets was nothing. Do you know the value of nothing?'

Jon clenched his fist in frustration, too angry to speak.

'People saw him,' muttered the Tattooed Man. 'They saw him give you a kicking in that pub. How long do you think it'll be before they start sniffing around you?'

'So what if they do?' replied Jon a trifle petulantly. 'Do you think they'll be able to *prove* anything? The day Rickets died I was at the funeral of my friend's wife and child. Who goes revenge killing on a day like that?'

'Don't try to psychologise,' warned the Tattooed Man. 'Don't try to second-guess. Rickets leads them to you. You lead them to me. For all I know they're watching me now. For all I know they're *listening*. *Now*, of all times.'

'Oh, don't be such a *martyr*,' spat Jon. 'The Law represents no threat to you. You've got them eating out of your hand.'

'But it's not just the Law, is it?' The Tattooed Man advanced slowly upon him.

Jon stooped and picked up the paper, flattened it. He held it aloft and pointed to the front page. 'No, it's *not*, is it?' He stabbed at the lead story. 'Look at what I do,' he accused sadly. 'Look at what I do for you.'

'And I, of course, have done nothing for you.' His jaw was set.

'You can be such a fucking parasite,' said Jon.

The Tattooed Man bunched his fists at his sides. 'I should have known,' he said. 'I should have known you for Judas.'

Jon took a step forward. 'The suffering servant, you bastard,' he replied, and punched the Tattooed Man in the side of the head.

Olly leaped forward, hand inside his jacket. Jon lashed out with his left hand and slashed Olly's face lip to ear. He kicked him twice in the testicles. When Olly had fallen to the floor he kicked him twice in the back of the neck, once in the knobbly curve of his spine.

Jon turned to the Tattooed Man, opened his mouth to speak, to accuse. The Tattooed Man reached out, grabbed his throat and squeezed. Jon gagged and his eyes bulged. Step by step, the Tattooed Man drove him backwards until he had pushed him flat against the cool wall. His breath was forced from his lungs, between the Tattooed Man's fingers. His vision began to blur. 'Don't think you're that good,' the Tattooed Man warned quietly. 'Don't ever think you could ever hope to be anywhere near that good.'

He released his grip. Jon fell in a heap, his hands at his throat. He fought to stand. The Tattooed Man kicked him half-way across the floor.

He scrambled to his knees, his feet. He wiped his hand across his mouth. 'Go on, then,' he said. 'Go on, if you think you can. Do us all a favour.'

Olly had regained his feet. He looked like he'd gone face-first through a windscreen. He levelled a pistol at Jon. The Tattooed Man slapped the gun from his hand. 'Don't you dare,' he warned. 'Don't you fucking dare.' He turned on Olly and punched him full in the face. Olly's nose splintered with a dry crack. He whirled this way and that, howling, and stumbled over the leather sofa which the Tattooed Man had purchased for Jon.

Meanwhile, Jon had retreated to the bookcase, which he used to support himself. He was unable to catch his breath. 'You ungrateful bastard,' he said. The bookcase could not support his weight. It fell spectacularly to the floor, spilling across the carpet the volumes the Tattooed Man had given him.

The Tattooed Man was breathing heavily through his nostrils. He stood like that for a long time. Then, lifting Olly to his feet by the scruff of his neck he turned his back on Jon and left the house.

He left a vacuum behind him.

Jon sat with his back propped by the fallen bookcase. He fumbled for the cigarettes that lay in his pocket. Each one was crushed and bent and beyond smoking.

At length, he stood. He walked in a daze towards the Oblivion Suite. He walked, fully clothed and bruised, into its familiar frigidity, its comforting endlessness. He curled like a foetus on the floor. Infinitely reflected, infinitely repeated and infinitely meaningless. All the time he saw before him the image of a pair of bright blue shoes with a buckle on the side, and a plastic doll without a head.

Two days later the police came for him. Plain-clothes detectives, one an asthmatic Welshman in a Marks & Spencer's suit, the other a powerful man with fine blond hair and a face marbled and mottled like corned beef. They asked if they could come in. They showed him their badges. He said, 'Come in, please.' He offered them tea. They declined. He asked if it was about Rickets. They said yes it was and added his given name: Clive Thompson. Jon had trouble attributing the name. He found himself imagining Clive Thompson's life. An incapable or unwilling student. Perhaps a violent father, perhaps a string of 'uncles'. He wondered what was happening to him.

As the two detectives sat, he noticed the eyes of the Welshman settling on the bruises he wore like a necklace. A professionally suppressed reaction. A mental note.

They knew about the 'incident' in the pub. They had spoken to Ted the landlord and Fat Dave and Jagger. They had interviewed other patrons. They had spoken to Rickets's mates, each of whom, Jon suspected, had been reticent in the extreme, for fear of sharing something like Rickets's fate. Jagger and Dave, too, had been loyally evasive to effectively, if unintentionally, incriminating effect.

Murder was easy and usually the murderer was a lamentably stupid creature, whose crime, though endlessly fantasised about and mulled over, was committed in haste and frenzy and stupid fury. Frequently, the victim was known to the murderer. Equally frequently, alcohol was involved.

They asked him where he'd been and he said, 'A funeral.'

They asked him when the funeral had ended and he said, 'I left the wake at about six o'clock.'

The Welshman said, 'Mr Thompson was last seen alive at –' he checked his notes, 'about eight fifteen or thereabouts. That would have given you plenty of time to leave the wake. Don't you agree?'

Jon shrugged. 'I suppose so.'

'Can you remember where you were at about eight o'clock that evening?'

'Of course not.'

The blond policeman withdrew a pack of cigarettes and said, 'Do you mind?'

Jon said, 'Of course not,' again. He offered an ashtray.

In return the blond policeman offered him a cigarette which he took with a steady hand, and lit from the Welshman's match, leaning into the flame.

'Would you mind', said the blond policeman, whose name was Marlowe, 'if we took a look around?'

'For what? The murder weapon?' He snorted. 'How stupid do you think I am?'

'It's nothing personal, Jon,' said the Welshman. 'Do you mind if I call you Jon? It's just procedure.'

'Procedure,' he mimicked. 'Leave my house alone.'

Each man regarded him through slow-lidded eyes.

'Why, Jon?' said Marlowe, the blond detective. He leaned forward a tiny increment.

Jon smiled at him. He could see something in the detective's eyes. He wondered how these men saw him, men who were attuned and immune to the inexpert mundanity of everyday violence. He wondered if they suspected, if they *intuited*, as he believed policemen were wont to do, the nature of the man to whom they spoke. He wondered if they had seen Rickets's – Clive Thompson's – body, or worse, if they had seen only photographs. He wondered if they had lain awake in bed next to their wives, or sat alone late at night in their kitchens, smoking themselves to a headache, wondering what kind of creature could *do* that to another human being?

'I've always wondered', Jon said, 'if the way the police are portrayed on television affects the way the real police behave. "It's a fair cop" and all that. "You're nicked". You know.'

'We're only doing our job –' Marlowe said.

'There you go,' said Jon. 'There you are!'

Marlowe shook his head. 'That was supposed to be a joke,' he said, 'or aren't you a man who appreciates a joke?'

Jon shook his head once. 'I enjoy a joke as much as the next man,' he answered, looking pointedly at the sober-faced Welshman.

Marlowe guffawed and slapped his thigh with a stubby-fingered, powerful hand. 'Very good!' he congratulated. 'Very good. Very dry. Did you kill Clive Thompson?'

'Yeah,' said Jon. 'I broke into his flat and I hacked him into tiny pieces. I made him eat bits of himself. I made him eat his toes.'

He almost laughed.

Jon had seen many arrests, mostly on television. He stood, obscurely incredulous, as the Welshman, whose name he had forgotten, closed the handcuffs about his wrists. As they entered the unmarked car, Marlowe was barely able to touch the end of his cigarette to the wildly waving lighter he held to his face.

Jon sat in the back seat and watched them. They didn't exchange a word.

He looked out of the window. Afternoon shoppers milled apparently aimlessly. Shop windows bore seasonal legends, each of which announced a SALE!, as if taken by a national mood of mad, seasonal philanthropy.

'I expect when I tell you about the others,' said Jon, 'you'll beat me up. I expect the tape machine'll break down, and I expect you'll take it in turns to take your righteous anger out on me. I expect you can't wait.'

Detective Constable Marlowe took a corner with studious calm. Jon saw his face reflected in the rear-view. His mouth was set firm, but the muscles of his jaw were working, grinding away.

'I expect', said Jon, 'that you're worried I'm going to tell you about the others I did the same to. I expect you're going through the missing persons list in your heads right now. I expect you're picturing the mess all those missing prostitutes and schoolboys might be in. I expect you're wondering exactly how they suffered, and for how long. I expect you're wondering why I did it.'

The Welshman swivelled in his seat and regarded him. 'Shut up.'

Jon grinned at him and rattled his cuffs. He had seen it in a film.

Although he made a full confession, the interviews were interminable and infuriatingly repetitive. He never once wavered from the detail of his tale, because it was true and he had a memory for such things. He recounted exactly what he had done, and in what order, then recounted it again. He spoke to psychiatrists and criminologists, but mostly there was just Marlowe, the Welshman (whose name resolutely refused to stick in his mind), and one of any number of uniformed officers standing stony faced but clearly disturbed at the door.

He was unsurprised to find that, on the third day of his interrogation (of his *helping the police with their enquiries*), the Welshman with the elusive name indeed took a suspiciously perfect opportunity to knock him from one side of his cell from the other until he fell, threatening to gag on his own vomit, to the floor. He was equally unsurprised to see a forged doctor's report imaginatively recounting how his (rather minor, considering the beating that had been so skilfully administered) injuries had innocently been come across.

The next day, before the tape machine could be turned on, he levelled his gaze at the Welshman and whispered, 'I'll have *you* next.'

By then, Marlowe was red-eyed and sour smelling. The weight of Jon's confession hung heavy about him. He seemed exhausted and penitent.

Jon told him, 'Don't worry. None of this is your fault.'

Marlowe stared at him for a long time before throwing a sheaf of photographs on the desk before him. He asked Jon if he recognised any of the faces. In truth Jon did not, with the possible exception of one or two he remembered from the television news, the school–photo grins of the recently disappeared, the recently deceased. Still, he denied knowledge of them with a smile which he hoped would be carried with them for many a fitful night. He fended off their questions until all were exhausted. As the tape was to be shut off, he said, 'But I'll tell you about the others if you want.'

'What others?'

'Tomorrow.'

'How many others?'

'Tomorrow.'

They pressed him for as long as they were able before concluding the interview. As Marlowe and the Welshman left the interview room, Jon said, 'See you in the morning.'

But he didn't see them, or at least not together. He sat out a morning and afternoon alone in the cell. Finally it was another policeman who opened the cell door and told him he was free to go.

He stood at the desk as they returned to him the belongings taken from him at the time of his arrest, with the exception of a small bag containing three grammes of cocaine, upon the existence of which no comment was passed. He nodded goodbye to the Desk Sergeant.

As he turned for the door, his way was blocked by two men. One was Marlowe. The other took a second or two to register as the Yorkshireman with the oiled black hair who had shaken his hand at the cottage and greeted him and Phil with the word, 'Lads.' They exchanged a look.

'Mr Bennet,' acknowledged the Yorkshireman, who was considerably better turned out than the last time Jon had met him. Despite this, he looked strained and worn out. He looked at Jon with polite contempt.

'Inspector,' said Jon.

Marlowe stuttered as he passed, 'Mr Bennet?'

Jon faced him and the detective recoiled slightly but noticeably. 'Yes, Detective Constable Marlowe?'

'I'd like', said the detective, 'to apologise for any inconvenience we might have caused you.'

Jon allowed himself to look once more into the eyes of the Yorkshireman. 'Think nothing of it,' he said. 'I quite enjoyed myself. Give my regards to your colleague. Inspector –'

'Llewellyn.'

'Llewellyn, yes. Tell him I'll remember him.'

He walked out on to the street and hailed a taxi. Only when he was safely inside, and half-way home, did his composure collapse. He began to shake and laugh uncontrollably into his clenched fist for what he was capable of when betrayed, of what surprising mischief.

Seven   Idiot's Limbo

Stepping from the taxi Jon continued to stifle giggles of such a nature that the driver squinted at him through rheumy blue eyes as he handed over a twenty-pound note. He examined it minutely, holding it millimetres from his face as if to demonstrate his myopia. Jon could hear his laboured breathing, all the pies and chips and curry sauce hanging heavy on his slow-beating heart.

'Keep the change,' Jon suggested.

He smelled of police stations, a vague, institutional odour of polyester armpits, filing cabinets and tepid coffee. He itched. The taxi pulled away, the driver throwing him one last glance as he performed an illegal U-turn.

As he approached his front door, spinning a single key on a ring around his index finger, he heard the sharp beeping of a familiar horn. He turned, pocketing the key. Across the road he saw Phil, impassive at the wheel of the racing green Aston. He wore a pair of gold-rimmed aviator shades and a subdued chauffeur's outfit: dark suit, leather gloves. He slid across the front seat, and pointedly opened the passenger-side door.

Jon dodged traffic. He patted the boot of the car as he walked around it, then slid into the passenger side. He left the door open.

'You look the part,' he said.

Phil brushed a lapel and smiled delicately.

Jon lit a cigarette. 'Watch what you do with the ash,' said Phil.

Jon inhaled. 'I see,' he breathed. 'It's like that, then, is it?'

'And then some,' Phil confirmed. He hesitated, then

accepted a cigarette. The flame of the match as he bent to light it reflected on the lenses of his sunglasses. Jon flicked the spent match into the gutter. Phil sat back and looked ahead. 'You should've been around him the last few days. It's like being a gofer for Jack the fucking Ripper. Do this. Do that.' He blew smoke through the open window. 'I need a holiday,' he said.

'I can well imagine,' said Jon.

'I'm not sure you can.'

He thought Phil might be right. 'Sorry,' he said. 'I suppose that's my fault.'

Phil accepted the apology with equanimity. Then he said, 'He wants to see you.'

Jon felt sick. He put a hand on the dash to steady himself, although the car was stationary. He ran his tongue over his teeth. They were furred with plaque. 'Give me five minutes,' he said. 'I need a wash.'

'I'm not sure that's a good idea.' Phil's eyebrows rose above the thin gold rims of the sunglasses. 'I think you'd better just come as you are.'

Jon shrugged and pulled the door closed. He buckled the seat belt across his chest and waist, passed the cigarette to his left hand and rested his elbow in the open window frame. It made him feel oddly like a teenager.

Phil avoided the necessity of further conversation by cranking up the stereo to a level which made it impossible. He had a weakness for American industrial music, relentless and electronically apocalyptic, which Jon shared only when under the influence of a chemically aided rush and at all other times considered somewhat juvenile.

Without relinquishing control of the car, Phil beat the steering wheel in time to the sampled percussion and mesmerisingly repetitive riffing guitars: 'Resurrection,' he bellowed tunelessly and unselfconsciously, 'Coming in stereo . . . If you think so!' He had to swerve a little to correct the car's course, brake a little to legalise its speed.

Phil had once talked Jon into going with him to a night-club which specialised in such music. Phil had supplied the drugs and had been eager for the night to be a success. Each of them had been dismayed by the age of the clientèle, which, with exceptions, did not appear to rise much above twenty. Further, the unwillingness of either to participate in proceedings by dancing – even though, given the crowded conditions afforded by the squalid hovel they had paid seven pounds to enter, dancing consisted of little more than vigorously and enthusiastically attempting to maintain one's balance on the circular dance-floor – compounded with the volume of both music and cocaine ensured that both were beaten into dumbfounded submission for the hour or two they were able to stand it.

Jon sat back and closed his eyes. He had never been so tired.

'Assassin,' hollered Phil in zealous abandon. He took his hands from the wheel to beat a drum-roll on the dashboard. 'Kill for a thrill!' he bellowed.

Jon knuckled his eyelids. Bursts of grubby colour.

'Supply and sanctify!' shrieked Phil. 'I only kill because I'm alive!'

Jon leaned forward and turned off the CD. 'Are you taking the piss,' he said, 'or what?' His had intended a quiet, threatening tone but ringing tinnitus necessitated an oafishly offended roar.

Phil's hand went to his mouth. The car swerved a little. Behind reflecting lenses, he closed his eyes, taking the car fortuitously through a set of lights which were half-way through a change. He looked imploringly at Jon. 'Oh, shit,' he said. 'I'm sorry. Shit. I wasn't thinking.'

Jon rubbed his brow. 'That's all right,' he said. 'No harm done.'

They drove in silence.

Eventually, Phil looked at him askance. 'Do you mind if I put the music back on?'

Jon waved his hand non-committally.

'So what?' ended the song in a looped sample. 'So what? So what?'

They pulled up outside the Tattooed Man's. Phil killed the engine and Jon's hand went immediately to the door release. Then he paused, hand on handle and stared for a while at the house, the sightless windows, the autistic flowers, the topiary cockerel which rippled slightly in the breeze. He glanced at Phil. 'Aren't you coming in?'

'You're joking.' Phil grimaced and shook his head. 'Not on your nelly, mate. No way. Not on your effing nelly. I'm going home.'

Jon pinched the bridge of his nose then opened the door and stepped on to the pavement. He stared at the house. The cockerel looked especially ragged and in need of a trim. It stood in a small heap of shed leaves, and its twiggy innards were visible here and there, like a nervous system in formaldehyde.

Phil poked his head through the passenger-side window. 'Good luck, mate,' he said.

Jon patted the roof of the car with something like fondness. 'Thanks,' he said.

Then the car pulled away. Phil acknowledged him with a single, backward wave of a gloved hand.

The gravel path had never seemed longer, nor the house more of a physical threat. It seemed to lean toward him with bullish aggression.

He licked his lips and rapped on the door, rubbing sweat from his hands. From inside, he heard the Tattooed Man: 'Come in. The door's on the latch.' For a moment he was staggered, unable to move. It was as if all that had transpired had been an illusion, a super-accelerated dream that had taken place between knuckle meeting door and the knock being answered, such was the naturalness of the Tattooed Man's response. He pictured his expression, imagined the clothes he might be wearing and smiled to himself, as if with nostalgia. Then he remembered.

He stepped inside as if expecting a blow, pushing the door silently closed behind him. The Tattooed Man's house had its own special, subtle smell, something like a cross between soap powder and a bookshop. Standing as it did on the brow of a hill, it caught beautifully what little light there was left outside and filtered it down the hallway. Through the kitchen window, but for the enormous apple tree, it would have been possible to scrutinise much of the city spread below. Once, from the top floor, Jon had leaned against the wide sill and scanned the city until he was able to identify his own house. Since then he had always found it comforting that, whenever he was home, the Tattooed Man could almost see him.

'In the kitchen,' called the Tattooed Man.

Jon stepped from the carpeted, half-lit gloom of the hallway into the light of the kitchen. He shielded his eyes. The sun was low in the sky – the shortest day of the year had passed less than a fortnight ago – and the kitchen glowed with surgical brilliance. Through the huge windows, and through the naked branches of the apple tree, he could see that much of the city already squatted glumly in the blue-grey gloom of a winter evening. It was dark everywhere but here.

It was an extravagantly large kitchen, with all the white-enamelled, wood-panelled perfection of a brochure. In it stood the Tattooed Man, shirt-sleeves rolled to reveal the snakeskin of countenances etched on to his dermis. He was leaning over the sink, fastidiously skinning a breast of chicken. He might have been wearing surgical gloves, so naked did his hands look beneath the tattoos, which terminated in a neat border at his wrists. A half-empty bottle of white wine stood at his side. As Jon entered he turned, sipping from a glass. He followed Jon's eyes, which had fallen on four copper pans that bubbled on the hob. The odour of boiling vegetables was snatched by a humming extractor fan.

'I keep meaning to get a steamer,' explained the Tattooed Man, drying his hands on a dishcloth. 'I prefer my vegetables with a bit of, you know –' he folded the dishcloth and put it behind him on the work surface, ' – *crunch*. You lose so much of the goodness this way.' He reached into an overhead cupboard, removed a wineglass, filled it, and set it on the table. He had not yet properly looked at Jon.

His Alsatian ambled over to Jon, who bent to its level and scratched behind its ears. The dog nuzzled its head in Jon's stomach and Jon scratched it where skull joined backbone. 'Hello, boy,' said Jon. 'Hello.' The dog responded with a lazy, weighty swipe of its tail.

'Clint!' the Tattooed Man instructed it. 'Come on. That's enough. Leave him alone.'

The dog lolloped obligingly off. It curled in its basket, regarding Jon through heavy lids. Jon stood, brushing stray hairs from his trousers.

'He wasn't doing any harm,' Jon said.

'He's shedding all over the place,' said the Tattooed Man. 'Did you see the state of the carpet?'

Jon hadn't.

The Tattooed Man looked at Clint and said, 'You old bastard, why don't you keep your hair to yourself?'

The dog thumped its tail once.

'You old bastard,' repeated the Tattooed Man. He refilled his glass and faced Jon. The sun was behind him, and Jon had to squint to see even the suggestion of his form.

'Well, well, well,' said the Tattooed Man. 'What is there to do with you? What is there to do?'

Jon licked his dry lips. He had not yet been invited to sit, and his legs were like rubber prostheses. He looked into his wine, took a shallow sip. 'I don't know,' he admitted.

The Tattooed Man unrolled his shirt-sleeves and buttoned the cuffs.

'How's Olly?' said Jon.

'Forty stitches in his cheek,' answered the Tattooed Man. 'Another twenty in his gums. A good chance he's going to lose some sensation on the right side of his face.' He tapped his cheek. 'Here,' he said, 'beneath the eye.'

'Sorry,' said Jon.

The Tattooed Man shrugged. 'Nobody asked him to do what he did. I don't know what else he expected.'

Jon couldn't look up.

The Tattooed Man stepped forward from the sunlight. He was pointing to his temple. When Jon's eyes had adjusted, he saw that he indicated a bruise, most of which was hidden by hair. 'Look at that,' the Tattooed Man said. He turned his back again and stood again at the cooker. He took a wooden spoon from a drawer and began to stir the pots in turn. He paused to reduce heat on two of the burners. Then he asked, 'Do you know how long ago it was that anybody lifted their hand to me?'

'No,' Jon admitted.

The Tattooed Man sipped from the wooden spoon, withdrawing sharply, sucking in a quick, cooling breath. 'Do you know how long ago it was that anybody last raised their *voice* to me?'

Jon's hand was locked around the stem of the glass. He murmured a vaguely negative monosyllable.

Once more the Tattooed Man turned to face him. He leaned over the kitchen table, his hands spread upon it. 'Look at me,' he insisted.

Jon looked at him.

With a rigid index finger, the Tattooed Man beat emphatically upon the stripped pine table-top the rhythm of his address. 'Do you think', he said, index finger emphasising each carefully enunciated syllable, 'that I'm such an idiot and so very fond of you that I will allow you to treat me in such a fashion?' He paused, the finger raised an inch above the table-top.

'Well,' he said. '*Do* you?'

He brought the flat of his hand suddenly down on the table-top. Jon winced at the concussion.

The Tattooed Man began to pace the length of the kitchen, up and down, down and up, rubbing his stinging palm. He stopped to Jon's right, haloed by the setting sun. One hand cupped an elbow, an index finger pressed his lips.

Very quietly, so that Jon had to lean towards him, he said again, 'What am I to do with you? What am I to do?'

He regarded Jon from beneath his brows. From the shadow of his face his eyes shone like icy beacons. He put his hands in his pockets and scuffed his feet once, contemplatively.

'What you did to Rickets,' he said, 'that's one thing. I could almost understand it. I know Rickets never treated you with any respect, and I know that what he did was unacceptable. But you should have come to me.' He withdrew a hand from his pocket and pointed to his solar plexus. 'You should have spoken to me. I might have needed Rickets. Or at the very least – ', he scratched the base of his skull, 'at the very least, you could have waited. You know how things are at the moment. You know the last thing I need is my name popping up on some police computer, even if only as a distant connection between you and Rickets. You know what things are like at the moment, Jon. You're out there doing things. Do you think I ask you to do these things for fun? You know what's going on.'

'I know nothing,' said Jon, not without bitterness.

The Tattooed Man took a slow step forward. 'You know,' he muttered. He gripped the edge of the table. Jon saw that his knuckles, the scarred and twisted knobs of an arthritic old pugilist, were white. 'Don't tell me you don't know.'

Jon thought of the cottage. He looked at the floor.

Clint the Alsatian whined and twitched in its sleep.

The Tattooed Man relaxed his grip on the table's edge. Jon saw his knuckles redden as blood rushed to fill starved capillaries.

'Nevertheless,' said the Tattooed Man. He seemed to be holding the table for balance, as if he felt faint. He closed his eyes for a second then stood abruptly upright and turned his back once more on Jon. His voice was louder and he waggled an admonishing finger like a melodramatic defence lawyer in an American courtroom drama. 'Nevertheless,' he repeated, 'I might have understood. You haven't been yourself since this friend of yours turned up. And don't think that it's escaped my attention that you did away with Rickets the day this friend's –'

'Andy,' said Jon.

'This *friend*'s', emphasised the Tattooed Man, 'wife and child were returned to their maker. Don't think I haven't noticed that. So don't think I'm stupid enough to assume that you did *that* to Rickets –' with the word 'that' his lip curled with distaste: the look of a puritan reacting to decadent self-indulgence, ' – because the stupid bastard got drunk and decided to beat you up one night.

'What you did to him was a *weak* thing, Jon. It was childish and petulant. Don't pretend to yourself that I imagine for a moment that it had anything at all to do with Rickets. I know you, remember. I *thought* I knew you.

'It had nothing to do with Rickets. If you wanted to get Rickets, you would have scared the shit out of him. You'd have terrified him. You'd have made him piss himself with terror.

'You wouldn't have done what you did. You did it because this woman was dead and you were furious about it. You stupid bastard.'

Jon pressed his palm to his cold lips and closed his eyes.

'What's wrong?' the Tattooed Man scoffed. 'Did you *love* her, Jon?'

Slowly Jon shook his head. His eyes were tight closed.

'What, then? What was it? Were you *fucking* her? Is that it?'

Jon felt giddy. He reached out for the comforting plane of the table.

The Tattooed Man was shouting now, accusatory and violent. 'You weren't even *fucking* her? *What*, then? What could possibly have caused you to do all this? You *dreamed* about fucking her? Is that it? You wanted to fuck your friend's wife so you got him a job to get him out of the house? Is that it? Or did you just hope that his gratitude would be so overwhelming that he'd *pass her on* to you? How much did you want to humiliate that poor fucker?'

Jon's testicles shrivelled tight to his groin. Behind his palm, he opened his eyes. He saw the light shining red through the web of skin where his fingers met.

It occurred to him to him that the Tattooed Man was reacting as if he had rehearsed every word of what he said, as if to calculate passion rather than surrender to it. The Tattooed Man had taken Olly to Jon's house that evening not as a calculated warning. He had taken Olly simply and singly because Jon disliked him. He wanted Jon to see how he trusted others whom Jon could not bear.

The Tattooed Man was jealous.

Jon had tried to be too clever: he had tried to psychologise, he had tried to second-guess. Even now the Tattooed Man, perhaps despite himself, was hinting to Jon the truth. But Jon had been arrogant. He knew the cost of everything but the value of nothing.

He lost his footing. He was exhausted and disorientated. He stumbled forward, against the table.

'Oh, for Christ's *sake*,' the Tattooed Man spat with exasperated venom, as if the very sight of Jon disgusted him. 'Sit down before you fall down.'

Jon pulled back a chair and fell on to it. He rested his elbows on the table, and buried his face in his hands. 'I'm sorry,' he said.

'Can't you even *look* at me when you speak?'

Jon looked up. His fingers dragged down his lower lids,

revealing much of the lower half of his eyes, which were raw and dry and red. 'I'm sorry,' he repeated.

'You're *sorry*.' The Tattooed Man turned back to the cooker and stirred furiously. He turned off one of the hobs. 'Listen to him,' he said to the ceiling. 'He's *sorry*. I don't care how fucking sorry you are,' he said. '*Sorry* isn't a pacifier. *Sorry* doesn't make anything better. *Sorry* doesn't undo anything.' He threw the wooden spoon into a copper pot. Even from across the room, Jon could see that he fought to control his upper lip. It trembled as he sipped his wine.

The Tattooed Man looked almost small. For the first time in their acquaintance, Jon wanted to protect him. He ran his hand through his greasy, cropped hair. 'Bill,' he said, 'What can I say? I'm sorry. I'm really, really sorry.'

The Tattooed Man turned on him, and immediately Jon regretted using his name. His fists were clenched and Jon remembered, or perhaps imagined the power of those arms. The Tattooed Man, he thought, might smash the heavy wooden table with a single punch, might pick him up by the throat and, with the other hand, pulp his head like a ripe apple.

The dog whimpered in its sleep and its legs twitched with an urgency which seemed to suggest that in its dreams it was pursued rather than pursuer.

The sun had slipped beneath a bank of high cloud that sat on the horizon. From this elevated perspective it looked like a tidal wave on the point of crashing over the city, crushing it with the force of the hand of God. The dim light in the kitchen was faintly pink.

'I might have forgiven this', said the Tattooed Man, 'because I understand something of your motivation. I warned you once that sentimental love was the worst, the most profound weakness, and I knew that you understood not one word. I allowed you your dalliance with your friend and his wife because I knew that sooner or later you'd come to understand what I meant. I thought experience of its', he waved his hand, looking for the word, 'debilitation would eventually strengthen you. Obviously I've been stupid. It made an idiot of you. It made you act like some spoiled brat wailing because a bigger kid stole his favourite toy.' Sadly he shook his head. 'I warned you, Jon. You didn't listen. Even this I might have allowed to pass. But you have been so stupid, have acted in such a fashion . . .' He broke off. 'I warned you once – it was the same day, I think, part of the same conversation – that, for all that I love you, if ever you were anything but loyal and trustworthy, if you were ever anything but *useful*, then I'd have not the slightest hesitation in –' with theatrical finality, he clicked his fingers. He raised an eyebrow.

'Not only', he continued, 'did you *strike* me. Not only did you *raise your voice* to me. You tried to *threaten* me. Did you think your behaviour with the police was *clever*?' He had, by now, regained his composure. The momentary glimpse Jon had been given of his vulnerability might have been calculated to emphasise the frigidity of his current malevolence. Jon was dismayed that he had been sufficiently stupid to think that the Tattooed Man would ever let him see anything but what he wanted him to see. The idea that the Tattooed Man had acted through jealousy seemed now absurd and childish – selfish, even, as if Jon had wilfully dampened his fear by attempting to convince himself that he was somehow more *important* that he was. He felt manipulated and frightened.

'Do you think,' resumed the Tattooed Man, 'do you *imagine*, for a second, that even if you were to confess to everything you've done in my name, that your confession would ever leave the room in which you made it? Do you think you'd be alive to repeat it? Do you imagine', his mouth twisted into a viscously supercilious sneer, 'that even if there was one policeman – just one, unlikely as that might be – who for some reason felt the desire to pursue what he had heard, do you imagine that he or she might be brave enough to do so?

'Or do you imagine, Jon, that they would try and forget

everything in their own best interest? Do you imagine them requesting a transfer? Do you imagine them leaving the police force? Do you imagine them finding an as yet undreamed of imaginative capacity as, every time they close their eyes, they picture the terrible things that could happen to their children; and then the horror as they remember for – what? – the hundredth time that day, that for every terrible thing that they can imagine, for every unspeakable thing they feel ashamed for even being able to conceive, there are things that defy even the worst excesses of their imagination, and that there are people willing – people longing – to do these things to their family, these things the like of which they can't begin to conceive?' He walked towards the table, stopped in a pink patch of sunlight.

'Stand up. Come here.'

Jon stood and faced him. His fingers traced the wooden surface of the kitchen table as if it might be the last surface he would ever touch.

The Tattooed Man closed his hand across the back of Jon's neck. With the remorseless leisure of something industrial he began to tighten his grip until the pressure there became unendurable. Jon bent double. His fists clenched into his stomach. An inarticulate groan forced itself through lips rigid with pain.

Jon imagined with stupefied detachment that, should the pressure increase by even the tiniest increment, he would hear the sticky crunch of his spine being crushed an instant before a fragment of splintered bone severed his spinal column and his vision faded, the bright colours behind his tight-screwed lids fading with the speed and finality of flowers rotting in time-lapse.

The Tattooed Man forced him straight (he thought he might pass out then) and put his lips close to Jon's ear, so close Jon could not tell if they brushed his flesh as he whispered through gritted teeth, 'Did you think you could *hurt* me, Jon?

Did you think you could *damage* me? Did you think,' and here his hand tightened a further increment on the back of Jon's neck, 'did you think you could *frighten* me?'

He began to exert downward pressure, forcing Jon to his knees. He shifted his grip so that his spatulate thumb was pressed tight to the weak spot at the base of Jon's skull. Jon imagined it cracking bone like a crust of ice formed over a pool of dirty water, pressing through his meninges, inexorably tunnelling through to the secret tissue of his cortex.

The pressure was such that he thought his knees might splinter against the hard kitchen floor.

'Do you know what I could *do* to you?' the Tattooed Man said. 'Do you have any conception of what I could put you through?' Maintaining the pressure on Jon's neck, he stooped heel to haunch and whispered. Over the bass roaring in his ears the Tattooed Man's whisper was like an internal voice, like a possessive demon speaking through the very beat of his tissues, inseparable from his own flesh.

'Not even you can imagine, Jon,' he said, 'not even you can imagine what I could put you through.'

Jon pissed himself. Hot urine flooded his crotch and the length of his legs. The Tattooed Man looked at the small yellow puddles the piss made, watched them spread and embrace one another, making a single pool which spread round Jon's shoes and towards his own. He whispered, 'I can see you think you've got some idea,' before releasing his grip and standing straight.

As the restricted blood seemed to erupt in a wave against the back of his eyes, Jon gasped and fell face down on the floor. In a puddle of cooling urine he curled around himself, nursing the back of his neck and moaning. He sobbed. The pain was such that he wanted to thrash this way and that, as if to shake it from his body. It was also such that he was unable to move beyond a gentle, almost neonatal rocking.

Arms crossed, the Tattooed Man waited until this rocking

had stopped. He tapped Jon's shoulder with the toe of his shoe. 'Stand up,' he commanded.

Jon struggled to his knees then slipped to the ground like a boneless thing. One hand closed about the cuff of the Tattooed Man's trouser. The Tattooed Man shook it off. 'Get to your feet,' he repeated.

Somehow Jon regained his footing, although he could do no more than bend double, his hands knitted at the base of his skull.

'Stand straight.'

Jon obeyed. He thought again that he must faint. He felt his eyes roll in their sockets as his vision faded at the corners. He felt himself tip sideways. He corrected himself, reaching out for the edge of the table. Something solid: something outside the metallic bolts of bright light being shot through his spine, flashing shapes across the inside of his skull.

His eyes refused to focus. When finally they did, he saw that the Tattooed Man held a kitchen knife at the soft skin between his clavicles.

'Do you know why I'm not going to do any of those things?' he said.

Jon could not have spoken even if he knew how to answer.

'Do you think it's because I'm scared?'

Jon shook his head as far as he was able; a tiny shift in one direction. He screamed.

'Do you think it's because I love you?'

Once again, the agonising half-shake of his head. He bit his lip this time. He bit through it – teeth met teeth. His mouth flooded with saliva and blood.

'Quite right.'

The Tattooed Man drove the knife forward. It slit the delicate skin beneath Jon's throat and entered him a millimetre or two. The Tattooed Man withdrew the blade. Jon felt the skin of his neck clinging to it as it slipped away.

'Not at all,' confirmed the Tattooed Man. 'It's because

there's *no need* to do those things. I would be doing them not because they served any purpose, but because I *want* to,' on the word *want*, his visage decayed momentarily into such bestial savagery that Jon found himself praying for relief, for the knife to slice his neck open and have done. 'And that would be weak of me – that would be for me to commit the same mistake as you. And I'm nothing', he said, 'if not a man who practises what he preaches.'

Jon fought the flutter of relief in his intestines, fought to remain stock still.

'However,' the Tattooed Man said, 'there's clearly a problem. I'm not about to let you go unpunished. I have held you in such high regard that it seems only reasonable to allow you to display the contrition I'm sure you feel.'

Jon's breath left his nose in short, sharp bursts. His chest barely inflated. He and the dog, twitching in its dream-filled sleep, beat perfect respiratory time.

'I take it', the Tattooed Man said, 'that I'm correct in assuming you want to make amends?'

He took Jon's dry swallow as an affirmative.

'Open your eyes.'

Jon was unaware that he had closed them. When he opened them the point of the knife hung unfocused and double before his right eye.

'Keep them open,' said the Tattooed Man, 'and stop shaking.'

When the knife bit minutely into the nerveless tissue of the white of his eye, Jon fell still. Only his eyelid moved, fluttering against the tip of the intrusive blade like the wings of a moth.

The knife, in the Tattooed Man's grip, remained perfectly unmoving. 'Walk on to it,' he commanded.

Jon's eyelids flickered more erratically.

The Tattooed Man smiled. 'Walk on to it. Take one good step forward. It won't hurt much if you do it that way. If you're weak, if you're indecisive, it'll take one or perhaps even two steps more before the point pierces your frontal lobes. I don't think you could take that, Jon. I think that's too terrible a thing for you to do yourself. Do yourself a favour. Take one good step, and it'll be over. I'll be able to think good thoughts about you.'

Jon found himself fighting to lift his leg.

'You know you're going to die.' the Tattooed Man insisted. 'How much better to do so a free man? How much better to take your destiny in your own hands than surrender it to those of another? One free act, Jon. One final act of redemption. One step, one firm step forward, one act of self-love. It's a fine choice I offer you. It's a freedom most human beings are denied, or choose to deny themselves. It's my parting gift to you. If you refuse it, you know I'm going to kill you anyway. For your own sake, and for the sake of my memory of you, don't let me down again.'

Jon's head was suffused with a bright, directionless light. He clenched his fist, and lifted his foot. Before the thought had formed to do so he thrust himself firmly forward, towards the blade.

There was no pain. The Tattooed Man was pulling the knife away even as he sought, for his sake, to impale himself upon it. The Tattooed Man was smiling a dead smile, the look of a fox caught for a sweeping instant in a car headlight.

What strength remained in Jon chose that moment to leave him. As he fell the Tattooed Man, with a delicate flourish, carved a half-moon into the flesh beneath his eye, scraping across the bone of its socket. Blood burst like flak behind his eyes, blood oozed warm into them, into his nostrils, his mouth.

The Tattooed Man poured another glass of wine and drained it.

'Get out of my sight, Jon,' he said. 'Pull yourself together and get out of my sight.'

Jon did not know how he managed to stand. As he leaned

against a kitchen chair, the Tattooed Man regarded him with a distant, removed disdain.

Jon stumbled the length of the hallway, his hand finding purchase on the beautifully cool brass handle of the front door. The Tattooed Man watched him from the kitchen doorway. 'You're worse than dead, Jon,' he said. 'I cast you out.' He seemed unable to resist a final act of self-indulgence. 'You lack the intelligence even to carry the responsibility and freedom of your own sins,' he said. 'And finally, I must accept the fact that your sins are in fact my sins: since you are a fool, since you are incapable of accepting responsibility for your own actions, I cast you out. There is no hell for fools, Jon, but there's no Heaven either. There's neither punishment nor reward.'

Jon set his jaw and pulled open the door to the dead air outside. Behind him, the Tattooed Man said, 'Look outside, Jon. No freedom. No responsibility. A limbo for fools. It's all yours.'

Jon slammed the door closed behind him, and ran in a half-balanced stumble the length of the gravel driveway, past the lewd topiary cockerel, and into the wide, straight street. He did not look back over his shoulder, nor was he able to fully ascertain in which direction he moved. It was dark now, and the night air was a series of icy lacerations in his parched larynx. He saw no one, nor any hint that there was anyone to see. It was as if even God obeyed the demands of the Tattooed Man, and had removed everyone from the world. Even the windscreens of the parked cars were frosted and opaque.

He feared to look at the sky because he understood the distance of the stars. They were dead things, their light gone cold.

He leaned against then slid down a lamp-post. His feet folded beneath him.

It might have been hours before the yellow Ford Orion, patched with rust and filler, slowed to a halt alongside him. Its nearside tyres interrupted the flow of water into the gutter. By then the sky had clouded and it had begun to rain, great fat icy globs, that had first pittered and occasionally patted against the crown of Jon's head like insistent fingers reminding him to wake, then gushed in an icy torrent upon him. He was drenched.

Phil stepped from the Orion and walked around it. He was wearing jeans, a woollen sweater and an old sheepskin flying jacket that stank when it was wet. He bent in the gutter, resting one forearm across his knee. He squinted in the rain. Water dripped from his brow, in rivulets alongside his nose, channelled by the deep furrows that ran from the corner of his nostrils to dangle from the line of his jaw. Then he whispered 'Jesus Christ' through his teeth. He stood and jogged to the car, fiddled impatiently with the boot, finally removing an oily blanket from beneath a toolbox and various assorted spanners.

This he wrapped about Jon's shoulders, muttering all the time, 'Jesus Christ. What did he do to you?'

Jon could move his jaw only with great difficulty. The top half of his body was rigid. To turn his head he had to swivel at the waist. Even this was painful. 'Did he send you?'

'Did he fuck,' spat Phil.

Jon attempted to extricate himself from the blanket in which Phil had wrapped him. Phil helped him to his feet. 'Don't talk to me, Phil,' said Jon thickly, as through an anaesthetised tongue. 'Don't let anybody see you with me.'

Phil dismissed him. He opened the door of the Orion and bundled Jon inside. The roar of the rain subsided to a pleasant background percussion. The car smelled of stale biscuits and unemptied ashtrays. Phil sat beside him, throwing his sopping hair from his eyes as he turned the ignition. The car started on the third attempt. Phil looked over his shoulder as he reversed from the awkward position in which he had parked. He had searched the streets for some hours and his trepidation had become a terrible tension. When he caught sight of Jon, sitting like a tramp in the rain, he had hit the brake so hard he barked the skin of his ankle.

He leaned to peer through the rain. 'What did he do to you?' he repeated. Before Jon could begin to answer, he spat, 'I don't know who he thinks he fucking is, sometimes. I really fucking don't. Does he think he's *royalty* going about treating people the way he does? The fucker.

'Remember how those blokes spoke about you at that cottage? Remember how effing proud he looked? Then what does he do? You overstep the mark a bit – just *once*, after all you've done for him – look what he does. I can hardly believe it. Look at the state of you. Are you all right?'

'Yeah,' said Jon through stiff jaw. 'Apart from my neck –'

'Your *neck*!' The Orion came to a halt so abruptly that Jon bent double the nail of his index finger as he threw his hand out to steady himself against the dashboard. He did not find this surprising. 'Fuck this,' said Phil. 'I'm taking you to hospital.' He reversed the car with all the lack of care of the professional driver.

'Phil –' insisted Jon. 'You don't want to be seen with me. He won't like it.'

'*Him*?' said Phil. 'Fuck whether he likes it or not. He can fuck right off. I'll tell you this,' he said, 'if I hadn't sold my soul to him years ago, I think I'd be seriously considering alternative employment prospects at the moment.' His eyes narrowed. 'Watch that neck,' he said. 'Try not to move it. Keep still.' He couldn't tell if Jon was laughing or weeping.

Naturally, there were doctors to whom Jon and Phil were familiar clients, but each of them knew that to approach any of this private network of clinicians would serve only to further raise the ire of the Tattooed Man. Jon tried to convince Phil to drop him in the car park of the nearest casualty department and go.

'Look,' said Phil, 'I can do what I want on my nights off. He doesn't *own* me, you know.'

It was the wordless reply in Jon's look that convinced him to leave, though not without five more minutes of 'Are you *sure* you'll be OK?' and, 'Do you need any cash or anything?'

Jon accepted a fifty-pound note, and stood in the rain watching the yellow Orion aggressively negotiate the various obstacles of the car park, before screeching on to the road. Distance and the rain washed it away. He walked towards the casualty department with some difficulty. A great nothingness inflated him from inside and a great nothingness outside pushed down upon him. Between these pressures there was the thin shell of his skin, defining his form like a toy soldier stamped in tin.

It had been many years since last he had experienced the oddly lit, disinfected carnival that was a National Health Service casualty ward after dark.

As he gave the disinterested receptionist details he did not think to fabricate, he realised that it had been with Andy. They had both been fifteen. Or perhaps Andy had been sixteen then. Jon pictured him wearing those blue shoes. A friend of theirs, whose name he had forgotten and whose face he feared he might be inventing, had slipped drunkenly on a broken cider bottle which had been thrown from the upstairs window of a party they were leaving. It was a Saturday night during the Easter holidays, that dreadful run-up to the 'O' level examinations that had seemed so monstrously important. He remembered because it was a shirt-sleeves' night. Andy in a short-sleeved white shirt and jeans and those blue shoes. Jon could not remember what he had been wearing. Their friend, whose name and face were forgotten, hadn't seen the broken bottle. Andy and Jon watched him fall flat on his arse and slide along the points of glass as if it were a patch of ice, opening a shallow but singularly unpleasant-looking gash that ran from above his Achilles tendon to the back of his knee and along to the flesh of his buttock, where the glass shard found final purchase. Even though the blood flow had been copious, even though the injured boy was howling (to his later chagrin) for his mother, Jon remembered that his first thought was: *Oh, no. What are Mum and Dad going to think?*

He smiled at the memory, then found himself wondering if it were true. Perhaps it was a sentimental distortion. Perhaps he had made of his childhood something akin to a false idol, a golden calf in which he banked a little of his belief even though the bulk of that account had gone to the Tattooed Man. Perhaps the Tattooed Man had known this and tired of it. Perhaps the Tattooed Man had encouraged Andy's reliance on Jon in order that the idols of his memory be brought up to date, removed from their museums and temples and dragged into the unforgiving scrutiny of the present. Two biblical passages came to mind; 'I am a jealous God' and 'Thou shalt not bow down before any graven image, nor worship at any false idol.'

But as the woman behind the desk continued to enter his details into the computer he remembered that he and Andy had sat in this very corridor while very similar nurses wearing very similar uniforms pushed about very similar trolleys and wounded drunks made wounded drunken fools of themselves. Jon remembered their immense, unspoken pride in each other that they had taken control of the situation, that Andy had not hesitated to call an ambulance, while Jon had attempted (without great success) to fashion a tourniquet to apply to the grisly leg wound, that they had sat silently and grimly in the back of the ambulance, jostling this way and that, as it made its way to hospital. Not everything was a lie.

Then he remembered the circumstances in which he had encountered Andy once more. He had been merely one of a docile crowd which stood dumbly by and watched an old man die in the street. Perhaps the boy he remembered was an inaccurately sentimental construction after all. This way of meeting again seemed to reflect too perfectly what Jon was sure the Tattooed Man had been trying to tell him but which he had secretly resisted.

He began to fear that everything, his entire existence might be a manipulation by the Tattooed Man. Perhaps Andy was somehow in his employ, used as a means to drive him to these conclusions. Perhaps the Tattooed Man had instructed Phil to drive him to this exact casualty department, so that his fondest memories might be rendered redundant. He saw the Tattooed Man's gaze in every nurse, every patient, heard his laugh in the squeak of every rubber wheel and every rubber-soled shoe.

Perhaps the Tattooed Man was like an *idiot savant* on a cosmic scale. The Newtonian dream of the rational mind: to be able, by observation of the position and properties of all particles in the universe in one freeze-framed micro-micro-second, to predict all future states and by informed intervention model them to one's own design.

Perhaps the Tattooed Man had been responsible for the death of Cathy and the child.

Jon's head snapped up. A bright fork of pain ran the length of his spine.

The floor seemed to recede beneath him, the walls to rush away. The world expanded and grew diffuse.

For the first time since adolescence, he seriously considered whether he might be insane and whether the company of madmen might not make madness the norm.

'It's Jon, isn't it?'

He forced his eyes to focus. First there was a black shape like a gaseous bat hanging in a haze before him. Bit by bit, particle by particle, it solidified into the shape of a priest, like a hole punctured through the white projection of the waiting room, through to the nothingness beneath.

'You look like a rip in the air,' said Jon.

'I beg your pardon?' the priest said. It was then that Jon recognised him. It was Chapman, who had consigned Cathy to the grave.

Jon repeated what he'd said.

The priest stooped before him, actually reached out and took Jon's chin in his hand. 'What on earth happened to you, Jon? Have they seen to you yet? You look like you need looking after.' He took the flutter of Jon's eyelids as a negative. 'That's the way it is, these days,' he said. 'Unless you're practically dead on arrival, you have to wait.'

'I suppose that's why you're here,' Jon heard himself say. 'Waiting for those who are almost dead on arrival. Holding out for the carrion.'

Chapman's face creased into something not dissimilar to curiosity, although it had about it an intensity that lit his ice-blue eyes predatory yellow. Perhaps it was apprehension, although Jon surmised that he might be hallucinating this. Certainly the angle of the walls seemed subtly to have shifted and somebody seemed to have turned up the lights. Chapman's clothing was of a profound, impossible blackness.

'Something along those lines,' Chapman said, as if he were not listening to himself, answering a question he had not quite heard or not quite registered. 'Do you mind if I sit?'

Jon wanted to fall against the priest's chest but was kept rigid by the pole that seemed to have been inserted along his spine. He had to speak through clenched teeth, so what he had to say sounded more like a threat than he had intended. 'Do you mind', he asked, 'if I make a confession?'

Chapman seemed to him as unmoving and observant as something basking on a rock. 'Are you a Catholic?'

'Do I have to be?'

'Not *absolutely*, no. But confession is −' he bit his lower lip, '− well, is not a thing to be entered into lightly. It's not a convenient means to vent one's anguish, however profound it might be.'

'Who says there's any anguish?' His jaw was so stiff that Chapman had to sit uncomfortably close to hear his words. Jon could feel the wiry tickle of the priest's beard touching the skin of his face. 'I was only asking.'

He could feel priest gazing at him steadily and intently, taking advantage of Jon's immobility. Taking advantage, for all Jon knew, of the twisting, half-glimpsed shapes that danced in the periphery of his vision, for which the black of the priest's garb acted as a convenient screen.

A set of double doors burst open and Jon was able briefly to observe the bustle of doctors and nurses clustering noisily but calmly around a trolley which they proceeded to wheel away to God knew where, there to do God knew what to God knew who to God knew what eventual purpose.

The priest had yet to drop his gaze.

'Do you think . . .' muttered Jon. He could not stop the sentence once it had started. It was a sentence whose prepositions were unfamiliar, whose concerns were not his own, whose words were not part of his vocabulary, 'that as intellectual currency the Newtonian idea of a mechanistic universe is entirely devalued, or do you think that there will come a new theory to unite classical and quantum physics? Does God play dice with the universe?'

The priest shifted a little in his seat, as if unaware that he had witnessed an example of glossolalia. 'I'm not sure,' he said. 'I'm not sure it matters. Science speaks a different language from theology.'

'And if He did,' continued the possessive dybbuk that seemed to have annexed control of Jon, 'would He win? Or would He accept some handicap to make things fair? And who would calculate the handicap? I mean, who *could*? Although I am of course willing to accept the *a priori* assumption that God would not cheat. I'm fully happy as far as that's concerned.'

Chapman ran a hand through his hair, which was a little too long to be merely unkempt. It bordered on the intellectually dandyish, an unforgivable affectation. He continued to examine Jon from just beyond the edge of his vision. 'I find a quantum God rather unsatisfying,' he said, after a long pause for consideration. Jon suspected that it was not the discussion at hand upon which he ruminated. 'Even a little threatening if the truth were told. On the other hand I'm afraid that the purely mechanistic universe proposed by Newton tends by implication to rather do away with the necessity of the God I pray to and feel to be immanent in the world. If the universe were like a huge spinning top set in motion at the beginning of time and space, left to unwind itself to some inevitable conclusion, then some sticky theological problems arise. So I don't know. I really wouldn't like to say. I'm something of a cosmological agnostic. Does that answer your question?'

Jon forced a dry laugh. 'And what about the devil?' he said next. 'What about old Nick?'

The priest placed a hand on Jon's knee and squeezed once. Again Jon suspected an ulterior motive. It was as if Chapman were checking that he was of solid flesh.

'That old chestnut,' he said.

'What does that mean?'

Chapman turned and sat back in his chair so that they sat like acquaintances in a cinema, watching the barely maintained order of the casualty ward. Jon could see him only as the vaguest of black hazes in the very corner of his eye, like a blind spot caused by the pressure of a spreading tumour.

'I'll tell you what I believe,' Chapman suggested. His intonation had changed slightly. He emphasised certain consonants as if pressing them bitterly with his tongue through gritted teeth. 'I believe that, through the Grace of God's love and the Holy Sacrament, there is no individual in creation who is beyond salvation. However, I'm equally convinced that evil exists in the universe as a power independent of the individual or individuals in which it is manifested.' From some possibly secret pocket he removed a pack of cigarettes, one of which he lit. 'I believe in the existence of actual, objective, evil,' he continued. 'As to the nature of that evil, I can only say, with all due caution, that I remain to be convinced by Augustine's thesis that it is merely an absence, the lack of goodness, in the same way darkness is merely the absence of light. From what experience I have . . .'

'Oh, yes?' said Jon. 'What experience might that be?'

The priest's voice hardened further, not unkindly. 'Nothing special,' he said then corrected himself. 'Nothing unique. Nothing that every human being has not in some way encountered in their lifetime.'

'I see,' said Jon, apparently satisfied. He asked the priest if he might have a cigarette. Chapman lit one and placed it in the corner of Jon's mouth.

Someone, somewhere, screamed. The priest tensed and Jon was visited by a passing fancy that it had not been a patient at all, but a young doctor burned out by pressure and nicotine and sleeplessness and amphetamine sulphate, peering into one hideous cavity too many, unable to contain his despair for a moment longer. When whoever it was screamed again, Jon was almost sure: he could even picture the doctor. Less than thirty, white cotton shirt with a soft collar and a desperately cheerful tie. Messy curly hair. He had handfuls of the curtain in his hand, the curtain which frighteningly efficient nurses had drawn about the intimate suffering of whoever it was, of whatever sex, of whatever age that lay dehumanised on the trolley.

Jon felt all the madness he imagined himself to have faked rising within him, as if something genuinely insane had lurked within him all this time and had somehow manoeuvred him into releasing it. Now it was free, he imagined that it would exhaust him, that it would twist the world into distortions so subtle he could not see them, but progressively, by degrees and degrees. With the cunning of many years spent planning and waiting it would manipulate what he saw until he had no choice but to surrender to the greater validity of the malevolent spirit he had assumed to be a creature of his imagination. Something seemed to be gripping him, attempting to throw him from the chair and make him take the priest about the neck and squeeze him until he was dead.

He noticed that the priest was learning forward. 'I beg your pardon?' he said.

Jon could barely force out the words, 'I think I might need help,' he said. 'I think I'm losing control.'

Chapman leaned closer still. He revealed himself to be other than the man Jon had thought him to be. His hand closed around Jon's wrist and squeezed with something like concern. Jon was astonished to realise that the priest had not been hiding vengeful thoughts at all. He seemed to be seeing the world all wrong. In stepping from it he seemed to have forgotten how properly to interpret it.

'In what way, Jon?' asked the priest. 'Please. You can speak to me. You can trust me.'

Jon smoked the cigarette to a stub without moving it from the corner of his clenched lips. 'Do you know what I am?' he said. 'Do you have any idea what I am?'

Chapman placed his hand flat across Jon's chest. 'I believe you need help,' he said.

'What sort of help is there for someone like me?'

'Professional help,' the priest said, without removing his hand. 'Psychiatric help.'

'Spiritual help?'

The priest paused and regarded him with a scrutiny that defied pretence. 'Of course,' he said. 'Of course, if need be.'

Whatever it was in him that he fought, it spurted within him to form an expanding, steely ball of hatred for the priest. It narrowed his eyes to pinpricks. The priest instinctively retreated a little. Jon shifted in the seat and faced him. 'Do you know what I am?' he hissed, in an invidious whisper. 'I'm a fucking demon, you charlatan, you cunt.' All this in a rushed whisper so quiet it registered on no other ears, recited like somebody imparting urgent intelligence in a businesslike hurry, as if there was little time and perhaps much danger. 'I'm a fucking demon,' he repeated. 'I kill people I've never met who have done me no harm and receive a satisfaction the like of which you wouldn't begin to understand or believe . . .'

The priest tried to take Jon's wrists in his own: he wore an urgent, determined face. The struggle, which, in the larger chaos of the ward, had gone unnoticed or unremarked, had further dishevelled his hair and knocked his collar askew. 'Jon,' he insisted firmly. 'Jon. *Jon*. Jon. Come on. Come on.'

But Jon continued the confessional monologue with abandoned relish. 'I've been cast out,' he insisted. 'I've been thrown into limbo. I have been absolved of the responsibility of my own sins. Hell's closed to me. So's heaven. Isn't that freedom, Father Chapman? Haven't I been granted a certain freedom? Do you have any idea how much blood is on my hands?'

The priest persisted. '*Jon*. Stop now. Stop. That's enough. No more.' He took Jon by the wrists. 'Listen to me. The doctors are going to come for you shortly. I expect that they'll keep you in tonight. I'll come back tomorrow and we'll talk. We'll talk then. When you've rested. Please. I promise.'

Chapman stood and began slowly to back away. He fixed Jon with the benevolent intensity of his scrutiny before disappearing through a set of double doors that Jon imagined were reserved for the use of staff. He pictured the priest talking quietly and hurriedly to a harried doctor, the way the doctor first frowned then sagged wearily. As he did, a sense of what he had just done was visited upon him. The hallucinatory aspect of the ward seemed to have faded. He wondered if was true that he had spoken to a priest.

A nurse came for him, helping him into a wheelchair, in which she pushed him to a small, faintly odorous cubicle bordered on three sides by a curtain which hung suspended from a rail by stainless-steel rings.

He was attended first by a nurse who loosened the surgical

collar and examined the trauma at back of his neck. She probed him with firm fingers whose businesslike efficiency rather belied her gentleness. When he winced and sucked in a sharp breath, she said softly, 'I know, I know. It must be ever so sore.' She asked if he would mind removing his clothes. He replied that he would rather not.

She told him that he would make her job a lot easier if he would do as she asked. He looked at the bright light which hung from the sickly green ceiling. He seemed to have surrendered any illusion of control over his own life. He motioned for the nurse to help him slip his shirt from beneath the surgical collar they'd given him. Because movement was causing him some pain it was she who undid the buttons and slipped the shirt from his shoulders. He helped as best he could by slowly wriggling free his shoulders. She took a half-step back. She looked at him for a moment. He could not hang his head, although he wished to.

She excused herself and stepped between the curtains. 'I'll only be a moment.'

She was lying or perhaps mistaken. Jon listened to her low murmur, its hurried insistence. After the passage of a very few minutes — remarkably few, he supposed, for a busy casualty ward — two new nurses slipped through the orange curtains to attend him. He didn't see the first nurse again. They were accompanied equally scant minutes later by an undoubtedly personable but somewhat condescending man in rather pretentious half-moon spectacles whose very nature — whose very transparent *approachability* — bespoke stratospheric superiority. He spoke with academically soothing depersonalisation. 'Mr Bennet,' he said. From a breast pocket he removed a disposable pen. He leaned in so that Jon could hear the in- and out-take of his breath. 'Let's have a look at you, shall we?' He spoke with the relaxing, intimate burr of a Scottish Anglican.

Jon's hands went to the surgical collar. The doctor blocked their movement with the end of his pen: 'We'll take a look at your neck in a moment,' he said. 'But first I'd like to examine some of this less serious bruising on your ribs, and these –.' Two nurses helped Jon to an upright, sitting position. The doctor bent close to him, tracing with the chewed end of his disposable pen the lines of wounds recent and less so, so close to the skin Jon could almost feel its touch. The doctor was humming deep in his oesophagus. At length he stood, ' – at these scars,' he concluded. Intent, he asked Jon if he could sit forward just a little and repeated the procedure. When he was done he said, 'OK, you can relax.' He looked as though he wished to hold a clipboard. One of the nurses held it, so he prepared himself instead by carefully slipping the Biro into his breast pocket, next to the clip of his bleeper. Finally, he said, 'Who did this to you, Jon?'

Before Jon could answer the doctor leaned towards him again and asked him to look into a small torch and follow it with his eyes first up then down, then left, then right. Satisfied (or having had something confirmed), he next examined the slash beneath Jon's eye, pulling to one side the temporary gauze dressing and coming in very close. He left that, too, and began to poke and prod with degrees of gentleness at the bruising on Jon's neck, which was flowering into a discoloration of thunderous drama. He apparently had yet to notice the shallow wound between Jon's clavicles.

He stepped back and suggested, 'It looks like somebody's put your head in a *vice*.'

Jon refused the clear offer to unburden himself.

'But it doesn't look as though there's going to be any permanent damage, although naturally we'll take an X-ray to make absolutely sure.' He put the pen in the corner of his mouth. The three others, two women and a man, looked first to him then to one another in turn. Eventually, he said, 'And as for the rest of you . . .' He sat on the edge of Jon's bed, hitching his white coat clear of the seat of his trousers. 'I'll be perfectly honest with you, Jon. Some of this scarring I find rather worrying. I wouldn't normally expect anybody who wasn't a lion tamer to have any more than say, just the one of these.' He indicated a scar which twisted just beneath Jon's armpit. 'This is somewhat in excess of what I would normally expect to come across in the course of my everyday duties.' As if to take in the full panorama of barbarity he saw before him, he took a step back. Finally he pointed the end of the pen at the wound beneath Jon's eye, scabbed and puffed and bruised. He made as if to speak, paused, half-turned away. Once more he put the pen back in its pocket. He put his hands behind his back, wrung them for a moment, chewed his bottom lip. Although he did not look directly at Jon, wishing to pose no challenge, he spoke with the same, vaguely hypnotic burr.

'You know that nobody can hurt you while you're here, don't you? Aside from my colleagues and I, nobody can hear what you say. And you know what trustworthy souls we National Health staff are.' He sat again on the edge of the bed, turned slightly away. 'Who did this to you?'

Jon could think of no satisfactory answer. He began to doubt the wisdom of coming here.

The doctor changed tack. The burr became infinitesimally more inquisitorial, more authoritative: 'Are you an intravenous drug user, Jon?'

'Occasionally,' Jon admitted.

'What drugs?'

He listed them.

'And how often?'

He answered.

'Would you describe yourself as an addict?'

He didn't know. He didn't think so.

'And how do you pay for all these drugs? I don't have to tell you how expensive drugs are.'

He didn't answer.

'Are you a practising homosexual, Jon?'

He replied not.

'Have you been tested for the presence of the HIV virus?'

No, he hadn't.

'Have you ever suffered from a psychiatric illness?'

This time he hesitated. The doctor looked directly at him.

'Have you had any mental problems?' he elaborated. 'Have you received treatment for a disease such as schizophrenia?'

Such as, thought Jon. What else was there? He knew that the doctor had access to his medical records. He had not thought to lie to the receptionist and was anyway unclear as to whether this would have achieved anything. Indeed he could imagine it being counter-productive. He was too exhausted and in a deal too much physical discomfort to extricate himself from what, were he to present anything like a belligerent attitude, might prove to be an insurmountable problem.

He told the doctor all about it, or at least as much about it as he had told any other doctor.

'I see,' said the doctor. He chewed the end of his pen. 'Jon,' he said at length, 'I'd like you to agree to remain here for a few days, under observation.'

Jon grimaced. 'What I'd really like to do is go home to bed. Can't you just prescribe me some painkillers and let me go?'

The doctor prodded again at the bruising on his neck with the end of the pen. 'That might be possible,' he said, 'but you've taken quite a battering. It couldn't hurt to keep an eye on you for a couple of days, could it?'

Jon looked away. 'And what if I were to discharge myself?'

'I think you probably know', replied the doctor, 'that I have the power, should I believe that you represent a danger either to yourself or the public . . .' He let the sentence drop. 'And let me be candid, Jon. As yet, I am not entirely convinced that you do *not* represent a danger to yourself . . .'

'Or the public?'

'Not so much that, Jon. Not so much that.'

Jon lay back and looked at the ceiling. It occurred to him that he had spent no more than a few hours of this young year outside the company of strangers. He had learned of his fundamental lack of freedom, the fallacy of his sense of autonomy.

He was wheeled to an observation ward. It was the culmination of all he had come to suspect. Its darkness, its twin rows of anonymous, sick bodies, suspended somewhere between death and the recovery of identity. Equally likely to move in either direction. A kind of limbo.

How wrong he had been. What an idiot he was. Confined to limbo. Denied freedom and identity.

It smelled, as he always knew it would, neither of life nor sterility, but something that itself hung between the two. A cretinous dybbuk hung over them all.

He fell asleep, and did not dream of Cathy.

Eight In Limbo, Attended by Angels

Keith Chapman would not have been surprised by the accuracy of Jon's assessment of him. Rather than preternatural insight, however, he would have ascribed responsibility for its precision to the miraculous capacities of the human memory.

He wondered if Jon remembered him.

Less than half-consciously (perhaps even with a malodorous undercurrent of carnivorous aggression) he and Jon had sized each other up. They had circled one another, seizing upon the remnant of an old scent, a fractured recollection of a gesture, the expansion or contraction of a pupil too fleeting to clutch at and hold.

Chapman had withdrawn from Jon at the point when his curiosity had compelled him to know more, to *find out*. He had moved away from Jon in order to protect him.

He leaned back in the swivel chair. The monitor at which he stared remained impassive and flicker-free. Curtains stirred gently behind it. His morning responsibilities were complete. This was his favourite part of the day. He enjoyed the season of solitude in which he was relieved of the imperative that God be the sole object of reflection.

The study was modest enough but he suspected nevertheless that it represented not only something of an indulgence but even an affectation. It was one for which he hoped he might be forgiven. The walls, of course, were lined with books, mostly (he would smile, with self-deprecation, which was indicative at the same time of humourless intellectual and spiritual depths which his drollery could not penetrate) *business* related.

A Protestant friend of his (he suspected that sometimes he dropped this classification into the conversation in much the same way that he had heard self-conscious liberals drop their association with individuals who represented groups with which they neurotically strove to prove they had *no problem*: a Gay Friend of mine; a Black Friend of mine; an American friend of mine) had suggested that too much theology obfuscated the unremitting vitality and immediacy of religious conviction. All that was required, she maintained — he imagined that she was quoting or paraphrasing — was a newspaper in one hand and a Bible in the other. Chapman respected but was unable to fully accept this. He read Catholic liberation theologies, much of which concerned the fact that the concerns of the Catholic Church in the Third World were often identical with the political and economic concerns of the West — and arguably exerted a genuinely evil influence. He thought it fitting, since it was the Catholic Church at its conservative, intransigent worst which perpetuated the problems of the Third World, that it be the Catholic Church at its most politically radical which addressed, in a revolutionary fashion if necessary, problems for which the Church itself was responsible. He saw reflected in the radical politicisation of a spiritual paradigm grown corpulent and mundane an echo of Christ's own mission.

This surrender to a conservative *status quo*, he had once or twice drunkenly opined to his intimates (who were few), was the cause of the Church's waning influence in the West. He feared it to be only a matter of time before it became fully eclipsed by the ascendant pestilential star of evangelicalism. Evangelicalism offered a vulgar, user-friendly method of worship which was devoid of anything recognisable as theology: an image of Christ not as the profound, singular manifestation of God's Love for His Creation, but as *someone to talk to*, someone who would listen, someone who would *always be there*. Evangelicalism's odious politicism came a poor second to this, like a baby brother brought along on a date at the last minute and accepted with resignation as part of the package. Accept Jesus as Friend and Jesus as Friend in unthinking bigotry came as a second, added bonus.

Chapman loathed this tendency. He loathed the vulgarity with which it sought to portray the depthless profundity of the Primal Universal Power wilfully become suffering man. It lacked the ferocity of love he understood to be necessary in order to surrender oneself to God's will. It lacked rage.

Chapman cultivated his rage. It was indivisible from the ferocity of his love of God. This was the heaviest of his burdens. To continue, in the name of others, to love God while he himself sometimes feared he *hated* Him.

His favourite Jesus was the Jesus of the Gospel according to Mark. This was the figure most recognisable as man: Mark's Christ was prone to anger and even impatience, such that the treatment of his disciples smacked sometimes of unfairness, of being fundamentally *uncalled for*. It was this man who had died, rejected and despised not only by those who had claimed to follow him, not only by the Romans who nailed him to a cross for unspecified crimes against the state, but by the very God whose will he had striven only to serve. 'My God, My God,' he had cried. 'Why have you forsaken me?'

For Chapman, this had lost nothing of its terrible power. It maintained an ability to make him weep. The Jesus of Luke moved him in what he recognised as a slightly sentimental way. The Jesus of John excited his intellect. But his was the Jesus of Mark. Meditating as he prayed on that despairing outburst of an unbearably suffering, unbearably alone man, filled him with a love and desire to serve, the intensity of which on occasion had led him to question his sanity. The suffering servant, the rejected servant. The notion of some infinitely gentle, infinitely suffering thing.

He realised that Jon had perceived this conflict within him between fury and forgiveness, and that this had not been a consequence of the frightening mental aptitude which sometimes accompanied mental disturbance. (He was aware that schizophrenics were remarkably attuned to minute unconscious signs of aggression. He considered it to be a hollow irony that their fears of persecution were not altogether irrational: they saw the violence and fear manifested in others, even in those who were unaware that they ever experienced such turbulent emotion.)

Jon *had* remembered him, if not consciously, as he had remembered Jon.

It had taken him a while, weeks, during which time his mind returned again and again to the man he had first noticed at Cathy's funeral and to whom he had been introduced at the wake. Jon had possessed a quality that disturbed him. Partly it lay in his manner, in the rigidity and tension the priest intuited beneath his demeanour of quiet fortitude and support for his bereaved friend. In a way, Chapman suspected that he had recognised *himself* there: beneath his attitude of support, beneath even the primacy of the love which Chapman did not for a moment doubt Jon genuinely felt for Andy, he was filled with fury. This fury, Chapman knew – and again, he was reminded of himself – was not the passing, occasional rage to which every individual is prone, particularly at such times. Rather, it was like (and at first he had been almost embarrassed to voice the word to himself) *wrath*. He had taken the opportunity to annex Jon's gaze and had been chilled by what he saw there. Jon's response to his conversational gambit, though guarded, had served only to confirm his suspicions. It was as if Jon had been seasoned by the bitter vinegar of the world, as if he had imbibed it with his mother's milk, as if it had hardened him to all sense of mercy.

It was this image, which was uncharacteristically hyperbolic and which seemed to enter his mind unbidden, that finally alerted him to the nature of his concern for this young man.

He had lain awake, staring at the ceiling, waiting for the dawn, and remembered.

He had been introduced to Jon's mother by a social worker. She had expressed a desire to speak to a priest, and Chapman was well known to the social services. She arrived in a taxi, from which she emerged clutching a handbag to her chest. It had been raining. He led her through to his office, which at the time he had (rather arrogantly, he supposed, but with the best of intentions) decorated in such a manner that it resembled that of a doctor or a psychologist: brown-panelled walls, a desk (upon which he had arranged photographs of his family and their children because, naturally, he was unmarried and without children of his own) and two rather opulent sofas arranged to face one other. She wore a raincoat, and perched on the sofa with the handbag balanced on her knees. He offered to take her coat and she leaped abruptly and startlingly to her feet. She looked about herself as she slipped her arms through the sleeves and shrugged the coat from her, as if ashamed that she wore it.

He offered her a cigarette, which she took and lit from a lighter he kept on the coffee table between the two sofas. He provided tea and biscuits.

He had worn a neater beard, then. It was shot through with white, but not yet the rather prophetic tangle he now wore. (At least he always thought of it as prophetic and rather fierce. There were those who had said he reminded them of Father Christmas, and he was fond of it for this reason, too.) He had crossed his legs and leaned earnestly forward.

'It wasn't my fault,' she said. He watched her collapse slowly into tears. Her head sank to her chest and she began gently to shake. Her hand went to her mouth before she broke into shuddering sobs of guilt and contrition. She had needed a priest to witness this. It was as if she believed that God required word of her sorrow.

He waited. She wasn't a particularly young mother, he

177

remembered, perhaps five years older than he had been then. He had been thirty-five.

When the tears had abated he offered her a box of man-sized tissues, with which she dabbed at her calamitously run mascara.

She requested confession. Chapman replied that of course he would be willing to administer it for her, but that she might find it beneficial to first have a *chat* (that had been the word he had used, and it was one which he continued to use; he had yet to come across a satisfactory alternative). So she had chatted, and Chapman had listened and consoled and felt a terrible, helpless pity for her and her child.

It had been three days later that he met Jon. The boy had been in custody then for nearly nine months. He was a slight child, though this came as no surprise since the priest understood that he seemed unable or unwilling to stomach more than a little food. He was reserved and anti-social, unwilling rather than unable to bond with any of the other children with whom he shared this place. This place. Chapman could not help but think of it as a *pen*, a place for children who had done terrible things, things of which children should not have been capable, and in the name of which there were equal and contradictory demands for punishment and rehabilitation. It was a limbo for lost children while unseen forces decided upon their nature: sinner, to be punished, or sinned against, to be cured.

He had his own little room, a cell really, with a low bed upon which was spread a blue candlewick bedspread. There was a little wardrobe and a child-sized desk. In nine months the child had made no attempt to stamp his personality on the room. It was so tidy, so transparently institutional, he might have moved in yesterday.

Chapman remembered the childcare assistant as an immensely tall young man with a fright-wig of curly hair, a pair of canary yellow loon pants and a very tight t-shirt that rode above his hairy belly button. He had gently rapped on the (open) door to Jon's room. 'Jon?' he said. 'This is the man I told you about. The man who'd like to speak to you. His name is Father Chapman.'

Chapman stepped into the room. 'Oh,' he said, 'I think it would be all right to call me Keith. What are you reading?' He glanced briefly over his shoulder. In response the gangling assistant nodded 'OK,' and left, pulling the door closed behind him.

'*Spiderman*,' said Jon, lowering the comic. He lay on the bed. Chapman's first impression was of the quiet beauty whose root is a spiritual peace, rather than an accident of genetic make-up, and which only children truly seemed to possess. This quality was called innocence by some, but in the world Chapman perceived, innocence of this kind did not exist. All were born into sin. Innocence was merely lack of information and experience with little to commend it. He hitched his trousers and sat in the child-sized chair, which he had lifted easily in one hand and placed alongside the bed. He hoped he looked faintly comical there.

'*Spiderman*!' he enthused. Back then, he had spent as much time in the company of children as he was able. For children he suffered a sense of envy and joy, alongside a terrible, crippling need to protect them. 'Is Spiderman your favourite?'

Jon closed the comic and shrugged.

'I know who my favourite is,' Chapman persisted. 'My favourite is the Human Torch. I like it particularly when he says, "Flame ON!"'

Jon seemed to ponder upon this. 'I like it when he fights with Spiderman,' he concluded.

'The Human Torch fights with Spiderman?' Chapman sounded astonished, perhaps even put out. 'I thought they'd be *friends*.'

Jon tutted. 'They *are*,' he said, in the exaggerated tone of a child stating the patently obvious. He sighed and rolled his eyes, then rolled over so that he hung over the edge of the bed. From a neat pile of comics he withdrew a slightly larger edition. He sat up again and showed it to Chapman. 'It's an Anniversary *Special*. That's why they fight.'

Spiderman hung precariously by one hand from the spike of what Chapman suspected to be the Empire State Building. One arm was withdrawn, about to deliver a terrible blow to the Human Torch, whose long trail of fire told that he had circled from behind Spiderman. The Human Torch's manner was such that he seemed about to deliver a piledriver blow, fists clenched at shoulder height. He looked absolutely furious about something or another.

'Mayhem Over Manhattan!' the blurb read. 'Spidey and the Torch do Battle Above the Streets of New York! You'd be a Fool to Miss it!'

Chapman asked if he might take the comic and made a great show of admiration. Although it was practically mint, he noted that the child indicated no concern that he might damage it. He found this lack of concern troubling.

'Do you like the Thing?' asked Jon.

Chapman felt something like relief, something like trepidation. Perhaps the child was beginning to trust him, and he was proud of that. The child might open up to him the contents of his mind, and although this was what Chapman sought, he feared it too.

'Do *you*?' he asked, cautiously.

Jon shrugged. 'Sometimes. He fights the Hulk soon.'

'The Thing and the *Hulk*? Goodness, what a mess that'll make.' He returned the comic to Jon. 'Who bought you these?'

'Bendy.' Bendy was the gangling man in the yellow flares. He evidently took great pleasure in this: Bendy! someone would shout as he walked past, and he would fold at the knees and proceed to perform a comical walk that lampooned his own peculiar, heron-like qualities.

'I see. That's very kind of him.'

Jon shrugged.

'Who used to buy your comics? I bet you spent all your pocket money on them.'

Jon shrugged. 'I s'pose so.'

Chapman persisted, 'How much pocket money did you get?'

'It depends.'

'On how good you were?'

He felt Jon retreat from him somewhat.

'Did your mum ever buy you comics?'

The child looked at him, and it occurred to Chapman then that the peace which gave him an element of beauty was incongruous with what he had done: the thing he had done. The thing for which he had been consigned to limbo. The child's gaze became more specific, and he turned it on the priest, who had to fight to suppress a shudder. It was not childish contempt he saw there. It was the contempt of something far older than this child, far older than Chapman himself. He fought an automatic genuflection, masking it by making a fist into which he coughed.

'Why won't you speak to your mum, Jon?' he asked softly. 'Do you know how sad it makes her that you won't speak to her?'

'My mum's dead,' said Jon with chilly finality.

The priest reached out and stroked the boy's head. Jon made no attempt at withdrawal. 'No,' Chapman explained. 'No, she's not dead. She had to go away for a while, but she's not dead. She misses you ever so much. She misses you as much as I bet you miss her. I bet you miss her, don't you?'

Jon looked at the priest with eloquent, specific malice. He said nothing.

Chapman knew that it was not unusual for a child to become confused between absence and death, particularly if parents felt it necessary to pollute enquiring minds with euphemism. But he had been granted limited access to Jon's records and knew well that the boy was not unacquainted with the reality of death.

The child smiled. Chapman found himself picturing this smile on Jon's face as he stood at the foot of his father's bed and watched him drown in his own blood. Goose bumps tightened his flesh.

'She's dead,' Jon repeated.

'Why do you think so, Jon? Why, when all these people are telling you that she's not? Would they lie to you? Why would they lie to you?'

'He killed her.'

'Who, Jon?' His voice shook a little. 'Who do you think would hurt your mum, Jon?'

Agonisingly and horribly, the child laughed. 'Stupid,' he accused. 'You stupid *thing*. It was *Dad* that killed her.'

He pierced Chapman for another moment with eyes that burned and froze him. Then he looked back to his comic.

Chapman looked at the carpet until the flood of dizziness passed. 'God bless you, Jon,' he whispered.

God help you, he meant. God help you.

Jon slept easily in the hospital bed. He woke only once or twice, and then only because his sleep was interrupted by a snore or a snuffle or a reverberative fart from one of the surrounding beds. Half-asleep, the ward seemed even less real.

Upon waking, his first thought was of the Tattooed Man.

There was a hollow in his stomach, as if he had been kicked there. Even this was somehow distant, closer to wistfulness than raw regret. It felt like driving past the house in which one had grown up.

Peculiarly, rather than Tattooed Man as he knew him, he was able to summon only the mental picture of a tattered old shoebox stuffed to overflowing with photographs. The Tattooed Man laughing in the summer as he stood at the barbecue in a plastic apron upon which was printed in bright pink a pair of cartoon breasts. There was the faded garishness of the 1970s, complete with sideburns and questionable lapels. There was the Tattooed Man in black-and-white: a baggy-trousered suit, the brim of a fedora throwing his eyes into shadow. One leg, foot laced into shining brogue, rested on the running-board of an old car. There was the Tattooed Man in sepia, faded to nicotine yellow and scalloped at the edges, wearing the uniform of a British soldier and the expression of a different century. The same face stared from them all, unaged and unchanging, more grave than in life.

Jon did not know why he thought these things. He had never seen such photographs.

He was submitted to exhaustive examination. Although his neck was unbroken it had undergone a trauma such that he would require some physiotherapy and perhaps suffer recurring twinges of 'spinal discomfort' for months, perhaps years, to come. His ribs were badly bruised. One of his lungs bore traces of scarring clearly inflicted years ago (probably by a badly broken rib), and which failed to appear on any of his records. This was a cause of some consternation and concern. There was some calcification of his left patella caused by the over-enthusiastic knitting of an old fracture. The gash beneath his eye required ten stitches in an admirably neat half-moon; there might be some subsequent loss of sensation in his cheek. The shallow wound between his clavicles did not require stitching. His many minor abrasions were re-dressed. His equally numerous minor bruises were prodded and tutted over. They examined every curve of every plane of skin, even the inside of his mouth, upon the roof of which they were apparently dismayed to find some scarring. They checked his blood pressure, which was too low, and they checked the volume of his lungs, about which they said nothing. They took blood samples and shit samples and urine samples. They checked his eyes, and asked him if he was aware that there seemed to be some loss of peripheral vision in his right eye, possibly caused by a blow to the head.

They informed him that, if what he had told them about the duration and extent of his drug use was true, there was the possibility, even the likelihood, of liver damage. Which, they warned, was irreversible.

By the time Chapman arrived for the promised visit Jon was tired but calm. The routine of the ward – the snatches of conversation he heard the nurses share as they went about doing this, or setting up that – filled him with a sense of banality, the effect of which was profoundly to deepen his sense of unreality.

As Chapman sat on the edge of the bed, Jon experienced an unsettling moment of *déjà vu*.

Chapman nodded his head in the direction of a departing nurse. 'You can see why they call them angels, can't you?'

Jon agreed.

'I've brought you some fruit and chocolate.' The priest set some small paper bags (two of which bore the legend *Shop Local!*) on Jon's bedside cabinet. 'I would have brought you a book or two, or some magazines, only I didn't know what you like to read. So if there's anything you'd like me to bring along, just say the word. I like whodunits myself,' he confided cheerfully, 'but that's probably because I'm not much of a reader of fiction.'

'Thank you,' said Jon. Once again it occurred to him that Chapman had a peculiar presence, like a black puncture in the white continuum of this odd limbo.

'How are you this morning?' said Chapman.

'Much better,' Jon told him. 'Much better, thanks.'

'I'm glad to hear it.'

Jon opened one of the bags (leaning over awkwardly, the plastic neck brace restricting his movement) and took out an apple, from which he took a healthy crunch before saying with his mouth full, 'Oh, I'm sorry. Would you like one?'

'No,' said the priest. 'No, I'm fine, thanks. I bought them for you. Actually,' he leaned forward and put his hand on the bedclothes above Jon's knee, 'I'm not a man who's over-fond of apples. It's a Catholic thing, I think.'

'Look,' Jon said, 'about last night – '

Chapman dismissed him with a wave. 'Let's hear no more about it.'

'No,' insisted Jon. 'No, really. I don't know what was going on. I don't know why I said those things.'

The priest smiled. It raised into shadowed relief the worry lines of sixty years of loving his neighbour as himself. 'You were in a deal of pain,' he said. 'People react in funny ways to pain. Especially – ' and Jon thought he looked sad, as if it was a struggle for him to maintain even that melancholy grin, 'especially where there seems to have been so very much pain. And for so long.'

Jon wanted to reach out and squeeze the priest's leathery hand. He thought it would be very dry and warm. He thanked him and believed he meant it.

'Is there anything you want?' Chapman asked. 'Anything I can get you? From home, perhaps? Can I contact Andy for you, or any other friends or family?'

'No please don't do that.' He made a reassuring face. 'I'm fine. Thank you.'

'Well,' said the priest, standing, 'this must be a flying visit, I'm afraid. No rest for the wicked. I just wanted to make sure you were OK. I'll be back, though. To see how you're coming along.'

'There's no need,' said Jon.

'Nonsense,' said Chapman. 'It'll help keep me out of mischief. Are you sure there's nobody I can call?'

'Really,' said Jon. 'I'm fine here. In limbo', he said, 'attended by angels.'

'Indeed,' Chapman confirmed. He paused at the door of the

ward and sagged, as if he suddenly felt himself to be an old, old man, and unbearably tired.

Jon knew that it would require effort to extricate himself from this place. In order to avoid being sectioned under the Mental Health Act of whatever year it was he would be required to provide proof of his effective sanity, concerning which, given the extremity of his physical state, there was some question.

He knew well, however, how to lead others away from the apprehension of his nature. He had done such a thing before, although he had been younger then.

The duty psychiatrist was a blank canvas with bobbed hair that was badly in need of a trim and clothes that were too old for her, worn rather self-consciously, as if to cultivate gravitas. She wore rather severe oval spectacles with tortoiseshell rims and smoked Marlboro lights at such a rate Jon was driven to concern for her mental well-being.

She began with his childhood. Jon took pains to indicate a careful balance between assimilation, acceptance of, yet healthy distancing from the events to which she referred. Behind the drifting clouds of cigarette smoke she wore a neutral expression, although she betrayed what Jon interpreted as occasional irritation or boredom by tucking a lock of hair behind her left ear. She also tapped her cigarette rather too frequently on an overflowing ashtray on her desk.

She then briefly tried a more elliptical approach. In response Jon was carefully ambiguous. The second time he saw her she had clearly decided upon a different tactic. She announced the decision unconsciously with a particularly aggressive tuck of the hair. She looked at him from behind reflecting lenses and asked him how he had come to be so scarred.

'I'm a prostitute,' he replied.

She undertook to conceal any response by lighting a fresh cigarette. 'A prostitute for men?'

'Usually,' he confirmed. 'But not always. You'd be surprised.'

Still she was careful not to react. She twisted at the waist and referred to Jon's records, which lay on the desk beside her. She read, closed the notes. 'Your records show no sign of anal trauma. No *recent*', she corrected, and made another note as she concluded with diminishing volume, 'anal trauma.'

Jon indicated that this meant nothing beyond the obvious. He added that it took all sorts.

'Yes, I suppose it does,' she agreed. 'I suppose it takes all sorts, right enough.'

Despite this capitulation, she pursued the subject. Why? Who? How? Did he enjoy it? Did it involve promiscuity?

'No,' Jon answered. 'I'm a sort of personal assistant,' he said. 'Although I have, in that capacity, on occasion been required to cater for parties.'

She removed her spectacles and breathed on each oval lens in turn. As he continued, she polished each one carefully with a soft, yellow cloth. 'And this fellow,' she said, holding one lens close to his eye, then polishing it more, 'are you and he *together*?'

Did she mean, were they a couple?

'If you like, yes.' Breathe on lens. Polish.

Not in the traditional sense.

'But it *is* a long-term . . . association. Or has there been another relationship of a similar nature? Or relationships plural.'

No. It was the only such relationship, and it was ongoing and mutually satisfactory.

She coughed dryly. 'In what sense satisfactory? In the emotional or the financial?'

Both.

'So this fellow,' she said. 'This chap. Would you say that you loved him?'

Jon paused, seemed to think. 'I suppose so,' he said, at length. 'As far as you can say that such a thing as love exists.'

She replaced her spectacles with a certain finality, an action which rewarded Jon with the knowledge that he had chosen wisely the nature of his lies.

There were degrees of insanity, she told him: an ongoing continuum of oddity (whose flow she demonstrated with a wave of her hand), much of which she had encountered in this office or one similar. In her opinion, she disclosed, masochism was an *unfortunate* pattern of behaviour, since its genesis lay somewhere in deep psychological pain. She conceded that in a sense it perhaps even constituted an illness, since she believed that it could be treated and possibly cured, if cured was the right word. But it didn't constitute insanity; instead, she confided, she was often more concerned by people who seemed to think it did.

She saw Jon three times more, each time with clearly decreasing levels of interest. They spent the final session engaging in what she announced to be an Informal Discussion. This sounded sufficiently like a psychological tactic for Jon's suspicions to be alerted. In the end, the Informal Discussion proved to be an interminable discourse on safe sexual practice, in which the word 'consent' was endlessly emphasised. When she was (finally) satisfied, she wished Jon all the best of luck for the future. She reminded him that should he ever require somebody to talk to then, well, that was her job. She shook Jon's hand across the desk for all the world as if ending a job interview. She advised him to look out for himself, and be sure to have frequent medical check-ups. There was nothing wrong with being careful.

Jon thanked her.

When the day came for Jon to leave, he returned from the toilet to find Chapman waiting at the side of his empty bed.

The priest noticed that Jon was dressed. 'Aha,' he said. 'All better, I see.'

Stiffly, Jon demonstrated that he could turn his head, although he had been advised to avoid doing so for a while. He thanked Chapman for taking the time to visit him during his stay. He offered the priest his hand.

Chapman responded that it had been a pleasure.

'By the way,' he added, regarding Jon through slightly narrowed eyes, as if gazing into a distant light, 'I forgot to mention that Andy is well on the mend. He went back to work a week or two ago. I'd almost forgotten that you two knew one another, or I would have mentioned it earlier. He's coming on in leaps and bounds. He's even been promoted. Isn't *that* good news? Apparently he's the new assistant manager of the garage. Or something along those lines. I forget exactly what.'

Jon had neglected the existence of the world beyond the confines of the hospital. He had pictured himself among endless ranks of prone bodies, lost within an infinite, endlessly echoing domain of tiled corridors and rubber-wheeled trolleys. A place without end, without entrance or exit. Numberless, milling hordes of men and women in white coats. Inconceivable numbers of attending angels. Corridors that stretched to the far horizon and beyond, which branched off to form unknown routes to unknown corners, which themselves branched and branched and branched again. All those souls in Limbo, all those helpless souls.

He had quite forgotten what it was that he was to be released into. He considered external time to have stopped, its actors preserved like the postponed characters of a half-read book.

Chapman saw some of this fall like a shadow across Jon's face. He watched his eyes disfocus, then solidify.

'Is everything all right?'

Jon nodded distantly. 'Yeah,' he said. 'Yeah, that's good news.' He looked at his watch. 'Look,' he said. 'I've got to go.'

'Of course,' said Chapman. Then, 'Are you sure you're OK?'

'Of course,' said Jon, 'or they wouldn't be letting me go, would they?'

He patted Chapman's upper arm and walked silently away, along the length of the ward and through its swinging doors. Not one of the nurses paused to bid him goodbye and good luck. They didn't seem to register that he was leaving. He drifted behind them like a cool breeze and was gone. He seemed to leave in his wake no sense of his absence, no trace that he had ever been here.

For a reason he well knew, this troubled Chapman. For the same reason it frightened him.

Nine A Face from the Ancient Gallery

Jon took two days to abrade the stink of institution from his flesh before visiting the garage. He still wore a short, scruffy beard and his hair was shaggy and unkempt. The half-circular scar beneath one eye was livid purple against the winter pallor of his flesh.

Gibbon was hanging about the forecourt, a mug of tea clasped in his paw. His blue overalls were unbuttoned to the waist, revealing an oily t-shirt with a picture of Garfield and the legend. 'Diets start tomorrow!' swelling beneath his impressive musculature and pot belly.

He lacked the facility to mask his surprise.

'How's it going, Derek?' said Jon.

'Fine,' said Gibbon. 'How are you? It's been a while.'

Clearly, Derek Gibbon was privy to rumours Jon hoped Andy was not. 'It has been a while, Derek,' Jon confirmed. 'Things are good. Thanks for asking.'

'Good,' said Gibbon. 'No problem. Nice one.'

'Andy's in the office, is he?'

'Yeah,' said Gibbon. 'In the office. Doing the paperwork.'

Jon walked past him and into the office, which was considerably cleaner than the last time he had seen it. A cigarette in his hand, Andy sat at the desk, Bic Biro paused above a sheaf of papers. He was wearing pressed blue overalls, and had lost a little weight.

'Hello, fucker,' said Jon as he entered.

Andy looked up, startled. He dropped the cigarette on his lap and flustered and cursed as he retrieved it. He called Jon's name like an exclamation of sharp pain and stood. 'Where the fuck have *you* been?' He stepped forward and took Jon in a bear hug. As ever, Jon was surprised at his strength.

'All right,' he said, wriggling from the embrace, 'steady as you go. Watch the neck. Watch the neck.'

Andy stepped back. 'What happened to your eye?'

'I cut it.'

'I'd say! How many *stitches*? Jesus bloody Christ. What happened, like?'

Jon lifted a gentle finger to the wound. 'It's not as bad as it looks.'

'I should hope not. Where have you *been*? What happened?' Andy's *bonhomie* struck him as grotesque and inappropriate.

'Never mind that,' he said. 'I've been away. It couldn't be helped. More to the point, how are you? You look well.'

'You know how it is,' said Andy, 'you can't wallow in these things. You've got to pick yourself up.'

'Good,' said Jon. 'I'm glad for you.' The words were dry in his mouth.

'Cathy wouldn't have wanted me to be sad for the rest of my life.'

It's months, thought Jon. It's only months.

'She would've wanted me to carry on. You know how it is.'

It occurred to Jon that his friend no longer had need of him.

'That's good,' he said. 'Really, that's good. That's all for the best.'

Andy looked away, ostensibly to grind out his cigarette.

You bastard, thought Jon.

'So,' said Andy. With one hand he opened the packet of cigarettes that lay on the desk, removed one and lit it.

'You've lost weight,' said Jon.

'Have I already?' Andy patted his diminishing gut. 'I've started going to the gym with Derek. I need to get myself in shape.'

'I see,' said Jon. He took one of his own cigarettes and lit it with his own lighter, squinting as the smoke curled into one eye. 'Good. Good. And your mum and dad?'

'Oh, they're fine,' said Andy, adjusting the position of the ashtray. 'They're on holiday at the moment. In Wales. The break'll do them good, you know. It was hard on them.'

Thank me, thought Jon. Thank me. Have you any idea what I've given up for you?

He hated himself.

'So,' said Andy. 'What are you up to now? I take it you've got another job.'

He squinted through a plume of exhaled smoke. 'Why should I want another job?'

Andy shrugged. 'He said you'd told him it was time for you to move on.'

'*Who* said?'

'The boss,' said Andy. 'He came to have a chat. Have you seen his *tattoos*?'

Jon had seen his tattoos all right.

'When did he come and see you?'

'A few weeks ago. A month and a half?'

While I was in custody, thought Jon. Before he did this to me.

'He's an excellent bloke,' said Andy. This was his highest form of praise. 'Excellent bloke. He had me in stitches. You didn't tell me he was so *funny*.'

Jon held the back of his neck, massaging it gently. 'Oh, he's funny,' he said.

'He was dead nice. He said that in your absence he felt responsible for my well-being and that he'd put little bits of extra work my way now and again. Just odds and sods when they come up. What an excellent bloke.'

Jon shook his head. *Seduced*. That was the exact word that came to him. 'Good,' he said. 'Good.'

'Right,' said Andy. 'No rest for the wicked – '

Once more, Jon was dizzied by *déjà vu*.

'Best be getting on with it. You know how it is.'

'Yeah,' said Jon.

'Look after yourself,' said Andy.

'I will,' said Jon.

'Give me a call,' said Andy. 'Keep in touch. We should go for a pint.'

'We should,' said Jon and left the office.

'See you,' said Gibbon. 'Look after yourself.'

Jon was unable to answer. He did not want his voice to shake when he did so.

Inside, he perched on the edge of the sofa, elbows on knees, chin cupped in hands. He was unable to move. For the first time since he had first realised that (from one upper-storey window at least) the Tattooed Man could see his house, he kept the curtains closed.

He wondered how it was that he had come to be here, losing control of his own past.

The night passed. When the house was suffused with a dilated pink light, like a palm held up to a glowing bulb, he stood and walked upstairs to the Oblivion Suite. Closing the door behind him he squatted, fully clothed, hugging his knees to his chest. He saw nothing more than a room full of mirrors, a private, ironic funhouse which endlessly reflected the identical, embarrassingly dumbfounded and grieved expression. Dizzy with vertigo, he stood and paced the reflective floor. Splinters of him fell in all directions. Advancing from the rear, retreating to the fore. Above and below they kept perfect pace, head to head and foot to foot.

He had long been discreetly proud of the way he had gone about doing the things he had done. As an institutionalised child he had always been fully aware that his mother was alive. Although it seemed necessary that those who sought to understand what he did thought otherwise, she had not even gone so far as to cause in him some formative psychological trauma.

With hindsight it had long ago occurred to him that despite their academic disavowal of innocence as anything other than a sentimental Victorian fantasy, they had acted with transparent desperation to apportion blame to something other than Jon, to something *outside* him. It was immediately upon the spurious establishment of his fundamental innocence that they began to concentrate on making him better. On letting him go.

Jon never saw his mother again. He often pitied her the necessity that she spend the remainder of her life racked by the mistaken assumption of neglected responsibility and worse, of being the object of hatred. He had in fact borne her neither ill will nor malice.

Sometimes he wondered where she was and hoped she was well, although he expected she was not.

He wondered now if the things he had chosen freely to do were an attempt at definition, to make of himself a single, fixed point about which raged an incandescent maelstrom of universal fury.

He closed the door on the Oblivion Suite, padded downstairs and turned on the television. He had an appetite for a curry.

On the third day he gasped and lifted his head, as if from a doze. He saw that the room was a mess. He had no recollection of how this had come to be. Ashtrays were overflowing. Unwashed plates made a semicircle before the sofa. The television flickered moronically and silently in the corner, a crushed cola tin adorning its crown. Time had leaked into this time-free place. The mess terrified him. The thought of time terrified him. The thought that he had lost control of it.

He felt beached, dumped into a mundane continuum.

He ran yellowed fingers through a short but unruly thatch

of hair, gingerly stood on bare feet and picked up plates that lay cultured with dried sauce and tinned spaghetti, the end of a sausage lying like the tip of a mummified penis between a knife and fork crusted with egg yolk. With the plates balanced like a poor piece of conceptual art, pinned in place with the tip of his chin, he stumbled to the kitchen, upon the work surfaces of which were distributed opened and fragrant cartons of milk, undiscarded tins, the peelings of potatoes, Cellophane wrappers and Styrofoam containers in which lay pooled the drying, watery, bloody residue of the flesh of a pig. From the bin issued a thick, sweet smell, like banana liqueur. Jon felt little fronds of panic in his intestines, like the lazy shifting of a parasite that might reside there.

From a high cupboard he withdrew a roll of black bin-liners, and with hands that shook with distaste withdrew two bags from the roll, opened their flimsy lips by rubbing them between his palms, and in three or four grand sweeps, scooped into their innards all the junk, all the detritus of the time that he had not observed passing. He sealed both of these, as well as the bag that lay corpulent and bursting in the red plastic frame of the swingbin. Frantically, he rinsed his hands under cold running water. They were still dripping when he opened the front door to deposit the bags in the concreted front garden. He noticed cracks in the cement where sickly weeds were beginning to nestle.

He regimented lines of cleaning solutions: disinfectants, bleaches, sprays, foams and mousses, and lines of cleaning utensils: a mop, sponges, scouring pads, dusters, a vacuum cleaner which had a tube-laden chrome exoskeleton like the sculpture of some beast's digestive system. It had been a gift of the Tattooed Man. He had thought Jon would enjoy cleaning it.

He began to clean. First the kitchen. Floor, windows, corners, skirting boards, doorframes, his countenance grim and his pace merciless in its efficiency. He emptied cupboards and cleaned their interiors, then examined their contents to ascertain if they, too, needed to be disinfected. He cleaned the rims of ketchup bottles. He washed the inside and outside of the plastic bin. When the cupboards were dry he replaced their contents, spending half an hour of determined satisfaction arranging them in the way that the space surrounding them seemed to demand; catalogued by type and labels facing straight forward. He washed work surfaces and pulled freezer, washing machine, drier and – with a degree of effort – cooker from their respective niches in order to clean each surface. Then he washed up the remaining utensils; pans, knives, forks, spoons. He dried them and replaced them in their proper place, taking great care not to mark cutlery with thumb- or fingerprints. Then he washed and disinfected the sink and taps.

He knelt at the ostentatious vacuum cleaner and polished the complex, curved planes of its chrome surface before taking it into his front room (the living room, people called it – he snorted and smiled). He kneeled in order to push the three-pin plug into its socket.

Since it was time that he sought to eradicate, it was meaningless to attempt to measure the interval between embarking upon and completing this project. Like a shy guest, time slipped away while he was otherwise engaged. He was unaware that it had left until he began to look for signs of it.

Eventually the house resumed its habitual state, that of a perpetually preserved moment, like a snapshot upon which he was projected as if by a special effect. When it was thus, he felt something in his stomach uncurl like a fern, and begin to dissipate through the pores of his skin. When the sensation had passed he felt light again, like a ghost in this timeless place, a quiet spirit.

He was sweaty and not clean. Dust and fluff had caked on his hands and face, attached themselves to the burr of his beard. His jeans were rumpled and his armpits dark with sweat.

Loose-limbed and with the beginnings of a familiar

contentment, he walked to the bathroom. He looked for a long time at the reflection of his face; uncouth, bearded and damaged, like a man escaped from some hellish nineteenth-century penitentiary. Tiny black knots of dissolving stitches traced the semicircular purple scar that echoed the orbit of his right eye, the centrepiece of a fragile yellow bloom that had been a fierce, black bruise. He prodded the scar just beneath his Adam's apple. He pictured himself in the Tattooed Man's kitchen, pink-edged by the sunset, hands clasped about his throat as his traitorous heart pounded harder with his terror, pumping the thickness of his essence from him in a gushing black plume.

His legs went weak and he sat on the edge of the bath. He opened the hot and cold taps. Steam rose, for a moment suggested form then thinned and split, condensing and rolling on the ceiling.

He undressed, hastily pulling the dirty shirt above his head, the sweaty socks from his pale feet which were purple in places, indented by the seams of his boots. Finally, jeans and underwear: he slipped them over his hips and stepped from them, kicking them from his feet and prudishly stepping from the malodorous pile they made.

He pushed damp hair back from his brow and looked with unspecific melancholy at the diary of violence that had ripped and gashed and broken and spilt and crushed what he supposed might have once been the purity of his body. There was a sense of loss in the thought. Gently, almost with reverence, he ran the tip of two fingers along a ragged white scar that ran across the flat of his stomach, left by the slash of a carpet knife. He remembered looking down at it, vividly recalled the electric moment of certainty that the wall of muscle was split through, that when he moved his guts would spill through the hole and fall like Victorian skirts in a mess about his knees.

The scars left by the jaws of dogs, by broken glass and baseball bats, by the carefully applied ends of burning cigarettes. Even damaged nipples where, on one occasion he had failed to forget, electrodes had been attached. The sewn, puckered mouths of two gunshot wounds that had just failed to kill him. The grim zigzag and hairless patch of knee that testified to shattered patella.

Without disturbing the rising steam, a chill passed through the room. Goose bumps raced up his legs and he felt the flesh on his back tighten as they advanced on his spine and came to a tickling halt at the down at the base of his neck. He shivered.

Then warmth settled on him from above, as if by the gentle draping about his shoulders of a soft, warm towel. He thought for a moment to detect the faint trace of the scent of fabric conditioner. His nostrils dilated but the elusive aroma was gone. He found himself moved by a sudden hollow pity of which his patchwork body was the vehicle but somehow not the object. He wanted to hug himself, to step outside of this frail, damaged frame and envelop it, to forgive and protect it.

Blinking, he imagined that he saw diaphanous tendrils of steam beginning to converge about a point just before his eyes, to grow milky and opaque. He tried to focus on the movement as with agonising grace it slowly appeared to spiral, falling towards a discrete, localised gravity, as if he were observing the unthinkable rotation of a distant galaxy, a spasm of cosmic savagery and explosive grandeur whose impossible heat, in crossing unmappable voids, had exhausted itself, become meagre illumination by the time it reached his eyes. Then, with a heavy, wet thud of his heart, Jon thought that he saw the suggestion of a human face, trailing off to a neck and shoulders that faded transparently into curtains of water vapour. He feared to blink and dispel the image. Indistinct, perhaps a construction of reflecting light and the play of shadow cast by his own form across the steam, he began to recognise the face. It was a face of which he had been dreaming. It was like the projection of an over-exposed film in an over-illuminated room against a white wall. There was a suggestion of movement where he thought her mouth might be struggling to find density, as if she were beginning to smile, and he thought that soon the vaporous sketch in which he saw the formation of her lids might finally pool, then open to reveal indulgent eyes that gazed fondly upon him. He reached out his hand.

There was a click, and the bathroom door sprung open on its latch.

The steam rippled and billowed and split and whipped lazily this way and that. It began to pour from the room, withdrawing to another space.

His heart thudding quick and steady, Jon sat once more on the edge of the bath. He thought of Cathy and something within him broke in two, something improperly mended. With an aching, urgent intensity, he needed to masturbate. It did not take long. He sank to his knees and thought of the smudge of lipstick on her front tooth, of the shy and forgiving way she broke his gaze, flicking a strand of hair from her face and looking at the ceiling when, dancing with her friends, she had glanced over her shoulder and seen that he had been watching her. The vividness with which he recalled the softness of the flesh of her wrist, gently compressed by the strap of the watch Andy had given her as a fifth anniversary present. The way he had wondered with schoolboy shame if she knew or suspected the existence of the urge he had pretended to himself had been a struggle to control, to reach and trace the curve of her breast with a gentle index finger, then cup its full weight in the palm of his hand, and take a step towards her, to nuzzle into the space behind her ear and in one long inhalation which made his lungs ache, to take into himself that scent and hold it inside, where it might flow through his veins like fresh air through the window of a long unoccupied house. How he had even imagined that she might allow him – how she might *want* him – to gather the hair at the base of her neck gently, like twine in his fist, and ease back her head so that her throat was taut and kiss her neck and shoulders and eyes and mouth, luxuriating in each contact, gulping her in like he was parched. The knowledge that, had he attempted to do so, she would in fact have taken a step back, embarrassed, surprised, possibly even pleased, but insistent. The suspicion that, even so, she would have been breathing more rapidly, shallow and quick, and that she would cover the shaky way she caught her breath by coughing into her fist. The knowledge that she had wrapped him naked in her arms and wanted what had happened to him never to have happened.

All of this in a second or two, like a pile of photographs thrown into the air and caught in slow motion, blank side turning to reveal image, image to reveal blankness, upon none of which his mind was allowed to settle: from one incomplete image his mind flitted to the next, the next, the next, desperate both to fix the instant in eternity and to reach the next plateau, for it to be finished.

He spasmed when he came, like a cripple trying to find his feet. The lumps of his spine crashed against the side of the bath, down which he slowly slid, with a moan, until his forehead rested against his knees. Pearly beads of jism rested on the thick, wiry mattress of his pubic hair, between his fingers, had made a pool in his navel. He wiped his palm on one knee and watched intently as the small, glutinous drop of seminal fluid began to form into the temporary jelly state of whose purpose he had little idea. He rubbed the jelly between the tips of his thumb and forefinger, his head full of the concussion of fully open taps emptying water into a bath that was full to capacity. He wondered for the first time in his existence if he was sterile. The thought that it might be possible for him to play any part in the perpetuation – the creation – of life was abhorrently comical.

He thought of Cathy, and the first sob gathered in him, rushing down his spine like flood water and gathering under increasing pressure in his stomach until, before he became aware of what was happening, it exploded from within, forcing open his clenched jaws, gushing through his open mouth. It was an expression of an agony that he had been unaware lurked within him and, as if he had accidentally belched aloud in class, his hand went to his mouth and his eyes opened wide in surprise and humiliated shame. He groaned again, and began to shudder and sob, rocking on the pivot at the base of his spine, all the while holding his face to his knees to muffle the sounds that issued from him, although it took a long while to subside and although there was no one to hear.

When he had done, he stood and, reaching into the bath, let sufficient water flow away for him to immerse and clean himself. He stepped out for a moment, one foot on the carpet, the other in the water, to retrieve from a low shelf a shaving mirror, razor and foam. He dipped the mirror in the water to wash the obfuscating steam from its reflective surface, then soaped and very carefully shaved his face. After drying himself, he ran the electric hair-clippers over his head, brushing the clippings into the sink. He felt he was beginning to recognise himself again, although he didn't look quite as he had always imagined. It was as if he had been looking, all these years, not into a mirror but at a slightly callous caricature, the authorship of which was obscure. He ran his hands across the smooth suede of his scalp.

He stood at the bathroom window and with one finger lifted the blind a notch. He looked at a slate-grey drizzle being kicked irritably this way and that by a petulant wind.

He began to plan his redemption.

When he was ready he knew time to have passed in the world external. It was dark outside. He sat in the blackest of shadows near the phone and lifted the receiver, blowing non-existent dust from the mouthpiece.

Chapman answered on the third ring. His voice was

muffled, and Jon could picture him cradling the phone in his neck, a cigarette clamped in the corner of his mouth as he looked about for an ashtray.

'It's Jon,' he said. 'Jon Bennet.'

His name was an exclamation of something like joy in the priest's mouth. 'I've been hoping you'd call,' he said, 'I've tried to call you many times but there's never any answer. I even called round once or twice but you were out. It's really good to hear from you. How've you been keeping?'

'Fine.' He wet his lips with the tip of his tongue. 'Listen, I'm sorry to bother you at this time of night – '

'Not at all.' The last word was distant but clearer; the head turning from the receiver, the cigarette being removed and its tube of ash deposited into an ashtray, a sigh as the priest eased himself into an armchair and crossed his legs, upon which uneven surface he balanced the phone. 'What can I do you for?'

'It's Andy,' said Jon. 'I wanted to speak to you about Andy. Have you seen much of him lately?'

A moment of silence, a whisper of interference. Chapman sighed clicked his tongue. 'I've popped by once or twice,' he confirmed. There was something guarded in his response. 'Have you not seen him since – '

'Since I got better. No. He doesn't call.'

'Perhaps he's been round. You're very difficult to get hold of.'

'No,' said Jon. 'I'd have known. I haven't been out that much.' Sensing Chapman's eyes narrowing with concern, he added, 'I still looked like Frankenstein's monster until recently. I didn't want to scare any children.'

Chapman laughed, or tried to. He said, 'I hope you're fully recovered by now.'

'I'm on my way,' said Jon.

'That's good,' the priest told him. 'Good for you. Keep it up.'

Jon scratched the base of his skull. 'Anyway, like I said, it's really Andy that I want to speak about.'

'So you did, so you did. How can I help?'

He gritted his teeth. 'How did he seem the last time you saw him?'

'Oh, you know Andy,' said Chapman. 'He's fine, all things considered.'

A passing car threw a dirty, sweeping arc of yellow light through a crack in the curtains and across the room, bathing him for a moment in its glow.

With gentle but sufficient emphasis, Jon said, 'This is important.'

'I know how important he is to you . . .'

'That's not the issue. Just a second.' Half-blind in the darkness, he reached out a hand, snagged a cigarette packet, removed and lit one. The end glowed fiercely and the half-glimpsed smoke taunted him as he expelled it with the faces it refused to draw. 'I want your honest opinion,' he declared, 'unmediated by the need to spare my feelings.'

'I'm not sure it's for me to say,' answered Chapman directly. 'You know Andy far better than I. Would it not be easier for you to pop round and see him at work in the morning – '

'That's not possible.'

'Or to phone him in the evening, then? I'm sure he'd jump at the chance at going for a drink. Especially as it's been so long since you saw each other.'

'I've tried to phone him. He never seems to be in.'

More silence.

'No,' agreed Chapman. 'No, he doesn't.'

'Have you any idea – ', Jon began.

The priest pre-empted him. 'Jon, I'm sorry. I know your concern's genuine but I don't feel comfortable talking like this over the phone. I know it's nothing of the sort, but I can't help but feel like I'm *gossiping*. Why don't you come round for a cup of tea in the morning? We'll have a chat.'

Jon straightened in the chair, almost dropped the phone. Something about the peculiar intonation of that innocuous final word had jarred him. He frowned, and with the hand that held the cigarette pinched the bridge of his nose.

' – Jon?'

'Sorry,' he said distantly, then, 'Yeah. Thanks. That's a good idea. When would it be OK? Don't you have confessions and masses and whatnots to get out of the way?'

'Don't you worry about that. Come round when it's convenient. If I'm busy then someone'll let you in, I'm sure. You can make yourself at home. How's that?'

'Thank you,' said Jon. 'I appreciate it. I really do.'

'It's nothing. It'll be a pleasure to see you.'

No it's not, thought Jon, as he hung up. And no it won't be.

He finished the cigarette and ground it cold in the ashtray, which he carried, still in darkness, and ran beneath a kitchen tap. How he wished to lift the blinds and stand there, bathed in electric lamplight and weak starlight, exposed to the enquiring gaze of the Tattooed Man.

You finally taught me what I am, he thought.

He would not lift the blind because of a childish fear that the Tattooed Man would be standing there, just the other side of the glass, closer than his own reflection, sodium haze casting him in half-formed silhouette. What expression would Jon read there, what form could he not help but impose on that void?

His scrotum crawled with fear and anticipation. For the first time in many weeks he felt charged with energy, unable to keep still. He paced the floor for a while, then began to gather about him all the things he thought he might need. Over a black t-shirt, black shirt and faded blue jeans, he pulled on his overcoat, shrugging himself into it as if to re-establish an old fit. His keys hung from the keyhole in the door. He locked the house behind him.

It was long past one a.m., on what day he did not know, nor even in which month, although he knew the winter had passed its nadir. He took in a lungful of air which tasted faintly of the city. He knew that he had been gone a long time when he could taste the air so specifically – the exhaust fumes, the take-aways, the carrier bags, the sweat and deodorant, the cheap shoe shops, the sterile supermarkets, baby talc and vomit, cigarettes and alcohol, all passed briefly across his nose and palate, lining up to re-introduce themselves. The street was dark and lined with cars. Some bedroom lights still shone, but each house might as well have been a mausoleum like his own for all the vitality it projected. He lit a cigarette, pleased with the sound and scent of the petroleum flame whipping in the wind. He was followed by the reverberations of his footsteps.

It took over an hour to walk to Andy's. There were silent streets then the brief, flickering bacchanalia of backstreet night-clubs and snooker halls ejecting customers to the harsh mercy outside. He saw the Greek, Chinese and Asian owners of late-night take-aways steeling themselves for the racial and physical humiliations that accompanied their nightly commerce. He was affected by their ability to do so. He stepped over pools of vomit, dogshit, discarded chips and through at least one violent altercation between three men around which hovered four women of varying age screaming encouragement. He passed between two of the combatants even as one brought down a broken bottle towards the face of the other, slipping between them as effortlessly as smoke through a crack in a door. He did not seem to have disturbed the tableau in any way. He was filled with a sense of incalculable well-being.

His cigarettes had become stale, like relics preserved by desert tombs with crumble when exposed to the air. After passing through the night-club district, he paused to queue at a twenty-four-hour petrol station. A group of young drunks in off-the-peg suits or jeans and expensively distressed leather jackets loudly jostled one another. The last three or four of them turned to taunt a gangling young man in army-surplus parka and long dreadlocks and his similarly attired girlfriend, who wore orange tights and purple boots. She managed, somehow, to look both overweight and undernourished. She and her boyfriend fought to ignore the drunks in front. He busied himself constructing a miserly, thin roll-up. She gazed glassily ahead. A car drew up, uncomfortably loud, repetitious music pulsating from its windows, a sampled drum break and a one-line chorus. From the car emerged a man in a suit he should have been unable to afford. He scanned the queue, the proud angle at which he held his head defying comment, and pushed in front of the young black man who stood directly before Jon. The young black turned and expressed his exasperation not at Jon, but at whoever was behind him. One of the drunken young men in front unzipped his fly, appeared for a moment to be unable to find his penis, then pissed in a high arc which terminated on the wall of the garage shop outside which they queued. His friends laughed and scattered and one expressed his approval by delivering a rich fart. The dreadlocked couple exchanged a brief but eloquent glance.

Presently Jon bought his cigarettes and moved on. The streets became darker, the lamp-posts smaller and more infrequent. The pavement was bucked and cracked by erstwhile frosts, and in the front gardens of identical houses lay the rusting hulks of cars and the skeletal remains of motor-cycles. Now and again a security light blinked on as he walked by, startled awake by his passing. He passed patches of scrubby grassland where had been erected climbing frames and roundabouts, decayed and vandalised now into obsolescence, although one such fractured construction doubled as a convenient bench for a gang of luminously moon-faced children of indeterminate sex who silently shared between them a bag of glue and a couple of inexpertly rolled joints.

A man hunched deep into his jacket collided with Jon's shoulder as he passed. Jon could not be sure if the action was deliberate. Other than this he saw no one, although he sometimes heard voices emanating from the houses he passed, and twice a distant scream that might have been rollicking teenagers, and equally likely something worse. Once he was disturbed from his reverie by an aeroplane passing so low overhead he feared it might crash; he twisted beneath it as it passed, and wondered at the everyday acceptance of so unlikely a thing.

It was two thirty a.m. when he stopped outside Andy's house. No lights were on. He watched the house's blank windows for long minutes before admitting that Andy was not yet home. Andy kept new hours now.

Jon looked briefly left and right, then bent at the knees and folded himself into his coat, a localised pool of shadow in the deeper shadow thrown by a domestic hedge.

He might have drifted off to sleep. His calves screamed with cramp when the car disturbed him. He bit his tongue against crying out, held back his breath. The car was a fifteen-year-old Jaguar, whose bodywork was in need of some attention although its engine was mellow and smooth.

Three men emerged from it, two with a small degree of difficulty and one with a great deal of protestation from the tiny space at the rear. All wore suits. One of the men was Andy, although clean-shaven and considerably thinner. He wore a suit well, although even from across the street Jon could detect the faint trace of an overdose of aftershave. The man emerging from the back seat was Derek Gibbon, his suit so well fitted to his odd frame that clearly he employed a skilful tailor. The third man, who seemed to take an age to wholly unfurl himself from the car, like a bat stretching its leathery wings, was Olly, the driver whose face Jon had slashed.

They conversed in throaty whispers, softly laughing. Andy produced and jingled a set of house keys. Olly patted his breast pocket. Gibbon murmured something to him and they laughed as they entered the house.

Jon watched the downstairs lights come on, then heard the faint sound of a stereo or television.

He sat, took in the longed-for breath and stretched out his legs across the pavement. His ankles hung over the gutter. He massaged blood into his thighs while smoking a cigarette. Then he stood and approached the house. He stopped outside the living-room window. There was no gap in the curtains through which to peer. He put his ear to the cold glass, keeping a routinely watchful eye on the street. He heard voices and occasional laughter above the music. (It was American rap, for which Andy had previously no taste and which Jon could not help considering juvenile. Olly liked it. It was a big thing with Olly.) He could not hear what was being said, or guess what was being laughed at, although the laughter had a particular tone that he recognised. It was the secret, pornographic laughter of men alone late at night. Women were inevitably its core subject. Jon found himself wondering what Cathy would have thought if she could overhear this, overhear her husband laughing in precisely that tone. He wondered at the humiliation and shock she would have suffered, at the embarrassment and shame for not being able to stop listening. He winced for her. He hurt in his stomach.

He felt the subtle vibrations that testified to somebody approaching the window. He slipped back into the shadows and skirted the borders of the house with neither ostentatious caution nor casual confidence. He assumed that he would not be heard in much the same way that a fakir, wandering across a bed of hot coals, assumes that he will not burn.

He looked in through the kitchen window. Through the window into the kitchen he had bought as a desperate gift.

It was the same kitchen, spotless and ordered and new, but on the door of the fridge, the very fridge above which he had stashed his coat as Cathy and her friends sat at that very table discussing the bottle of Southern Comfort he had bought, was pinned a pornographic calendar. It hung from a small magnet in the shape of an upper case A.

He strode with a firmer stride to the front of the house. Pausing only to light another cigarette, he pounded three times on the door.

He felt it go quiet inside. He felt the three men exchange glances. If Andy knew these men well enough to socialise with them, then he knew by now that an unannounced visitor at such an hour was not an event in which to rejoice. He hoped Andy was scared. He hoped Andy's eyes followed Olly's hand as it slid inside his jacket and for luck briefly touched the butt of the small pistol he kept there, pearl-handled and ostentatious. He hoped Andy had never been more scared than he was just at that moment, that frozen and indivisible instant.

One of them turned the music down. He heard voices: one exclamatory, another monosyllabic, voicing consent with a muffled grunt. Olly explaining to Andy what to do. Andy agreeing, pale-faced and desperate to piss. He heard the creak of floorboards, two men walking in careful time attempting to sound like one. Stopping.

'Who is it?' Andy's voice. Half an octave deeper than usual.

In the distance a siren.

Jon savoured the idea of Olly and Andy exchanging a glance of terrible apprehension.

Then he said, 'Open the door. It's Jon.'

Even as he heard Andy exhale with relief, he could sense Olly tensing, Andy's hand moving automatically to the latch, Olly's cool hand closing about his wrist. Andy's eyes widening suddenly, remembering what he had been told about Jon.

What had he been told about Jon?

Jon scuffed his feet. 'Are you going to let me in or what?'

Andy opened the door. Olly stepped from behind it, retreating a step in order for it to open wide enough to admit him. The light reflected on his spectacles so that Jon could not see his eyes. Although Olly's eyes were not Jon's concern, this did not make him comfortable.

Andy had not only lost fat but added muscle. His neck was beginning to disappear into his shoulders. His jawline had become square and firm. Jon hated to look at him. He stepped aside, allowing Jon to squeeze past his bulk and the cloying Paco Rabanne and into the house. As he entered he pretended to gaze through the glare on the lenses of Olly's spectacles, right through to the delicate orbs beneath. Jon smiled and Olly took an automatic, precautionary step back. His fingers went briefly to the scar that traced one side of his face. Jon stopped for a moment. He gazed at Olly from under his brow and felt his mouth split wide in a feral and predatory grin.

'How's your face?' he said. 'The smile suits you.'

The reflection on Olly's spectacles shifted as he tilted his head in sardonic acknowledging silence.

Jon laid an ushering hand on Andy's shoulder. He felt him tense, as if his flesh crawled.

'I think Olly had best wait out here,' Jon said.

Olly opened his mouth. He was silenced by Jon's intervention. 'He probably needs the toilet anyway. Don't you need the toilet, Olly?'

Olly went half-way to raising an index finger. Before he could reply Jon had guided Andy through to the living room and closed the door. Against the far wall stood Gibbon. If it would have been possible to get further away from Jon whilst being, as obviously commanded, in the same room, he clearly would have done so. Although he attempted a casual demeanour, a can of Stella Artois clasped in one ginger paw, it looked as if he was trying to push himself through the wall and into the garden. Jon rather liked Gibbon.

He nodded. 'Hello again, Derek.'

Gibbon lifted his can in salute. Jon could see that his hand was trembling. 'How you doing, Jon?'

'Not bad,' he said. 'Yourself?'

'Soldiering on,' said Gibbon. 'You know. Like you do.'

Jon agreed with a sympathetic nod. 'I'll tell you what, Derek,' he said. 'How about popping into the kitchen and making us all a mug of tea? There's a TV in there, I think.' For the first time he addressed Andy. 'There is a TV in there, isn't there?'

Andy said, 'You know there is.'

Jon knew there was.

'So you might find some late-night sport if you're lucky.'

'Right,' said Gibbon, raising the can. 'Yeah. Right. Nice one.' He began to shuffle away.

'You can leave the beers,' said Jon, 'if you like.'

'Yeah, right,' repeated Gibbon. He was muttering 'nice one' even as he closed the kitchen door behind him.

Jon waited until he heard the television being turned on, the distant, primary coloured blare of chatline adverts. Then he turned to Andy. 'Sit down.'

Andy looked back at him. Jon realised that his pupils were too wide for the one hundred and fifty watt glow in which they stood. He walked to the coffee table, picked up a can of beer, sparked it, and took a couple of sips. 'Sit down,' he repeated.

Andy sat down. He put his hands in his lap in a curiously infantile gesture.

Jon opened the living-room door. 'You can come in, now, Olly,' he said, 'but only if you promise to be good.'

Olly stalked in on daddy-long-leg limbs. In the middle of the room he stopped. His hand went for his jacket. Jon looked briefly to Andy, who clearly was quite aware of what Olly kept tucked away in there.

'Never mind that,' said Jon with indulgence. 'You keep hold of your spud gun. I know how much it means to you.'

As the gun hand froze, then began slowly to withdraw, Jon watched not Olly but Andy.

'Gibbon's making a cup of tea,' said Jon and inclined his head.

Olly shook his narrow head and stalked through to the kitchen.

Jon drained the last of the beer and opened another. Andy sat in an armchair gazing dead ahead, unblinking. With exaggerated *laissez-faire*, Jon dropped his weight on to the sofa opposite him, withdrawing the cigarettes from his breast pocket. He offered one to Andy, shrugged at the refusal, and lit one for himself. He drew deep on it. He put his feet on the coffee table.

'I expect you think Olly's pretty fucking hard,' he suggested, exhaling. 'I bet the first time he showed you his gun you thought he was Charles fucking Bronson.' He leaned forward confidentially. 'I'll tell you something. Remember that weird kid with the bowl haircut who always stank of stale piss? Remember we caught him pulling the legs off spiders with one hand and tossing off with the other? That's Olly. That's what Olly is. He's one of those kids grown up.' He raised his eyebrows. 'Do you know what I mean?'

Andy shifted and grunted. He gazed dead ahead as if scanning the horizon for distant land.

'Olly's all right,' he said. 'He's a good bloke.'

Jon tapped ash on the edge of the table. Andy noted the disrespect.

'He'd cut you open for fifty pence, Andy,' he insisted. 'The man's a prick. The man doesn't deserve the breath he draws. He doesn't deserve to be allowed through your door.'

Andy muttered, 'It's *my* fucking house.'

Jon laughed and sat back. He spilled ash down his lap and lazily brushed it away.

'Don't be a prick,' Andy said.

'Oh, come on,' Jon taunted, awaiting a response, 'cocaine makes me feel sharp as a pin. Is this the best you can do?'

Andy looked at him. 'They told me about you.'

'Did they now? And what was it they told you?'

'About Rickets. About what you did to Rickets.'

Jon barked a harsh laugh. He capitalised on the moment and leaned forward, marking a tiny increment between thumb and forefinger. 'Tip of the fucking iceberg, mate. That was something I did on my day off because I felt like it. Have you seen Olly's face? Same thing. I cut him open with this – hang on.' He reached into a pocket and withdrew the stiletto knife. He opened it centimetres from Andy's face. Andy did not flinch. 'They didn't tell you all about me because if they tried they'd still be telling. There's things they know about, things they've heard about, things they've heard rumoured, and there's things they couldn't begin to imagine. And that wouldn't be the half of it. I could tell them a tenth of what I've done and it would be enough to make them slit their own throats if I asked them, rather than risk pissing me off. Why do you think hard man Olly stood meek as a lamb in the hallway when I asked him to, when he's got his little popgun strung beneath his sweaty armpit?' He drew again on the cigarette. 'And if we stood and walked to the kitchen now, Andy, what do you think they'd be doing? Do you think they've run away into the night? Do you think they're huddled over the table talking about how to deal with me?' He poured lukewarm beer down his gullet, belched. 'No,' he said. 'I'll lay you a wager any size you want that they're sat next to one another drinking mugs of tea and watching Canadian ice hockey, even if they feel like doing neither.' He stood. 'Well? Do you want to go and check?'

Andy held out his hand. 'Give me that beer.'

Jon crossed his fingers and stepped forward. He handed Andy the can, from which he proceeded to glug. When he had done he said, 'What do you want? Do you want me to be scared of you as well?'

'No,' said Jon.

'Good,' said Andy. 'Because remember that I was there

when you tried to ask Theresa Burton to the fourth-year disco. Remember that?'

Jon remembered that. 'I don't want you to be scared of me,' he said. All the same, he hoped that Olly and Gibbon weren't listening.

'Just as well,' said Andy. 'Because I'm fucking not.'

'But I do want you to trust me,' Jon continued. 'Not them in the kitchen. Not the Tattooed Man.'

Andy rolled his eyes. 'You can use his name, Jon. It's not like I don't know his name. He's been round more than once to watch the boxing.'

'I don't care about his name,' spat Jon, with urgent vehemence. 'He's got so many fucking names I doubt if he can remember which was first, or which is his favourite. And I don't care about how many times he's been round for fucking tea and biscuits.'

He was lying. That, in a way, was precisely what he cared about.

'All right,' said Andy. 'Keep your shirt on. Give me a cigarette.' Jon obliged, kneeling at Andy's armchair. As Andy's head bowed to meet the flame, Jon repeated, 'All I want is for you to trust me.'

'He says not to trust anyone and I think I agree with him.'

'Who says? Who says that?'

'He does,' said Andy. 'Bill.' He put on a nasal, mocking voice, one he had used since he was a pre-pubescent first exposed to *Monty Python's Flying Circus*. 'The Tattooed Man.'

'I don't care,' said Jon. 'I don't care what he says.'

Andy stood and walked to the window. He parted the curtain and peered outside, wearing an expression of incalculable disgust. 'Why should I listen to you', he said, 'and not to him?'

'Because everything you think he's giving you now is to get back at me for what he thinks I did to him.'

Andy whirled on his heel and faced him. His nostrils flared bullishly.

'And everything I thought you did for me came from him!' He levelled an accusing finger. 'Everything you gave to me and Cath wasn't yours to give. It was his.'

'Bullshit,' Jon spat. He was full of something, a complex cocktail of bitterness, murderous rage, jealousy, mourning and betrayal. 'That's lies. It's all fucking lies, Andy. He wants to damage me and the best way to do that's by damaging you.'

'This is *hurting* me, is it?' He motioned to the suit he wore and the new electrical equipment in his living room. 'You think this is doing me *damage*?'

'Don't be so fucking stupid,' Jon whispered. Bowing his head wearily, he pinched the fleshless bridge of his nose. 'Don't be such a fucking idiot.'

'You arrogant *cunt*,' Andy spat. 'You think if you say, "Jump!" I say, "How high?" Bollocks. I'm not scared of you. I know stuff about you none of them will ever know. I know stuff about you I bet you've forgotten.'

'I know!' Jon raised his head and his voice. 'That's the point. That's the whole fucking point. That's why I want to help you.'

'Help me with what?' He drew a great, sorrowful breath. 'Cathy is dead,' he said, 'and so is my daughter. What is there to do? What do you think you can do?'

'It's for Cathy that I'm here.'

Andy turned away. 'Don't wind me up,' he said.

'She wouldn't want this,' said Jon. 'She'd hate to see you hurting yourself like this.'

'Hurting myself? Christ! You don't know the half of it if you think this is *hurting* myself. This is getting better, Jon. This is getting *over* it.'

Then don't get over it, he wanted to scream. *Wake up thinking about it and go to sleep thinking about it and dream about it.*

216

'It's not getting better,' he insisted quietly. 'It's giving yourself up to someone else.'

'I'm good at that,' Andy retorted. 'That's a talent of mine.'

At length, Andy said, 'Is that it?'

Jon lit a cigarette. 'There's nothing I can say, is there?'

'Nothing that'll make me listen.'

'And nothing that'll make you trust me?'

Andy shook his head once and shrugged, palms up, as if the matter was fully out of his hands.

'Do you know how stupid you're being? Do you know what kind of life you're getting involved with?'

'It's *my* life.'

'No, it's not.'

Andy would not drop his gaze. They stared at each other for too long. Finally, Jon stalked to the kitchen door and kicked it open. Huddled over cups of tea, Gibbon and Olly froze momentarily beneath the frigidity of his glare. He pointed to each of them in turn. His fingers trembled. 'When the time comes', he said through blanched lips, 'it'll be neither of you. Because if it is, you know I'd come for you. You know what I'd do.'

Gibbon met Jon's gaze before looking silently into his mug. Olly, mug cupped between both hands, regarded him over spectacle rims and shrugged non-committally.

'Christ,' said Jon. 'You have no say at all , do you? You've no say at all in your own lives.'

Olly offered a placatory smile. 'Come off it, Jon,' he said. 'Do *you*?'

The thrill and terror of his freedom raced like current through his veins. He shuddered with it. 'I do,' he said. 'I've made myself free.'

For the first time since making his acquaintance, Olly looked at him with genuine fear.

Jon closed the kitchen door softly behind him. He took in several lungfuls of icy, sharp night air, then lit one last cigarette. As he stood in the garden smoking it to the filter, he could sense Gibbon and Olly trying to make out his shape past the reflection they saw of the kitchen, the electric light bouncing back upon them, showing their own shadow-hollowed faces, their empty eye-sockets.

He looked at the sky. There were no stars. The city lay beneath a grimy yellow bubble of electric light pollution.

He waited until the anger was gone: the anger and the frustration and the selfish disappointment. He waited until all that remained was love.

Then he went back inside.

Ten   White Noise

Chapman awoke confused and terrified. He scrabbled in darkness for the spectacles which lay on a pine bedside cabinet. Closing his hand around the cool twist of metal and glass, he lay back flat against the bed, staring towards the blank darkness of the ceiling. He pulled the duvet up just beneath his eyes.

Sounds in the street outside were filtered by the hissing concussion of blood in his ears. He longed to reach over and turn on the bedside lamp, but the thought of such capitulation to irrational terror served somehow only to increase it.

He had dreamed of Father Christmas and could not understand why it had been so terrible.

He lay immobile for what seemed many minutes before admitting to himself that he was too scared to move. Cursing his stupidity even as he surrendered to it, he leaned over and turned on the light.

Jon was standing at the end of his bed.

Every muscle in Chapman's body spasmed. He let go an animal yodel of primal ferocity and leaped naked from the bed, absurdly pulling the duvet with him and holding it before genitals that had shrivelled tight to his body. He heard himself shouting, 'Jesus Christ, Jesus fucking Christ, Jesus holy fucking Christ, oh Jesus . . . ' as he retreated to the corner of the room.

Jon regarded him mildly and did not speak.

'How the fuck –' Chapman began. 'What do you think – ' he bellowed. 'Jesus *Christ*, Jon,' he yelled. 'Je*sus Christ*.'

Jon reached into his breast pocket and withdrew a pack of cigarettes. He bent his head and lit one, blowing smoke at the ceiling. Still he betrayed nothing resembling an emotion: no curiosity, no wariness, shame, pleasure, anger. A curious blankness Chapman knew he had seen before: the eyes of a child in a man's face, eyes that had passed through time. Chapman needed to piss. He was trembling. He dropped the duvet.

'I know who you are,' said Jon. 'And I know who I am.'

At the age of seven, in the dawn of a summer morning, Jon had sneaked on slippered feet into his parents' bedroom and sliced his father's neck with an old cut-throat razor kept in the medicine cabinet.

His father had snuffled and done the things that people do when close to waking. Jon stood still, held his breath, the razor in one hand, the other caressing his velvety foreskin through the cotton of his pyjamas. His father's eyes began eerily to move back and forth behind the bluish membrane of their lids. On tiptoes, feet snug in towelling slippers, Jon leaned over the sleeping figure and, with tongue protruding from the corner of his mouth drew the razor in a single, elegant stroke across his father's throat. His father's eyes opened and his hand jerked in the direction of his neck, from which spouted and pumped an impressive plume of black, arterial blood. Jon had pissed himself.

Chapman wondered now what he would do not to die at the hands of that lost boy become a man, what capitulations he would make, what humiliations he would endure. He thought of Christ in Gethsemane, the Christ of Mark, the Christ in the name of whose suffering he had felt the solidarity of fury and unendurable love.

Jon's eyes moved, met Chapman's. Chapman thought he seemed slight and almost inconsequential.

'What on earth do you think you're doing, Jon?'

The bedroom seemed alien, to have taken on subtly different dimensions and qualities of light and shade, like a bad dream of hospital. He stood naked, his duvet bunched at his feet, looking at a man who had murdered as a child and whom he had striven since to love and even to protect.

Finally Jon moved. He went to the window and opened the curtain a crack. 'It'll be daylight soon,' he said.

Chapman became aware of his nakedness. He struggled into an old pair of jeans which lay folded on a chest of drawers. He slipped his sockless feet into his tennis shoes, which lay unlaced beneath the bed. He was shivering and clumsy as he tied them into double bows. Over his head he pulled a navy blue Marks & Spencer sweater which was beginning to fray at one of the cuffs. These were the clothes he liked to wear when he read. Someone had once called them 'people clothes' and he had been very pleased with the idea.

Jon walked to the wall and flicked on the light switch. The glow was savage in its instant purity. It drained the room of subtlety and gradation. The shadows it cast were solid black and for a moment Chapman had to avert his gaze.

'What do you want, Jon?' he said.

He remembered Jon slipping unnoticed from the hospital ward like an unglimpsed apparition. The watery feeling in his legs increased. He prayed for strength. He petitioned God for physical might.

Jon massaged his brow. He looked confused for a moment.

Chapman hoped that he was drunk, that he had broken in here on some inebriated whim, to no purpose other than to shock, to announce that he remembered the ward, the visits paid to a murderous child. Even as he hoped he knew it was not so. He wondered how Jon could have gained entry so silently, how he could walked up the rickety stairs without them creaking, opened the stiff bedroom door without the customary protestation of its hinges. Even ghosts betrayed themselves thus. A rash of goose-flesh burst into bloom upon his arms and back, beneath his people clothes.

'A bad action can have good consequences,' said Jon. 'Is that correct?'

The priest caught his breath. Here it comes, he thought. Here comes the justification for the things he's about to do to me. He glanced at the telephone which sat next to the bedside lamp.

'I came to ask that question,' said Jon, 'and your forgiveness.' He ground out the cigarette on the windowsill and said, 'When did you recognise me?'

Chapman considered the wisdom of lying. He could see Jon watching him consider. He wondered at the adulterated, childish acuity in that passive and terrifying gaze. 'I don't know,' he replied, truthfully. 'Perhaps at the funeral. Certainly in the hospital when I ran into you, although it took me a while to admit it myself. Does it matter?'

Jon shook his head, perhaps to clear it. Chapman wondered if he heard voices in there. If so, what they were urging him to do? Whose imagination was capable of envisaging worse depravities? His or Jon's?

'Why did you visit me in hospital?'

Which time in hospital? he wanted to reply. It occurred to him that perhaps to Jon there was no difference, perhaps there was only one time, blurred and incomprehensible. Chapman's visits had stapled the ripped fragments of his past together with his dissipated present.

'Because it was my duty and my pleasure to do so,' he answered.

Jon licked his lips and looked at the floor.

'Do you love me?'

The question, delivered with a syntactical precision which betrayed depths of bitterness the priest did not want to understand, hit him like a slap in the face. He considered his reply very carefully and stammered when he spoke. 'I strive as far as I am able to love all people.'

'That doesn't answer the question.'

Chapman had one hand pressed flat to the wall as if to draw strength from the building's solidity. He was aware of beads of sweat shining in his moustache. 'You are a child of God,' he replied. 'And as such I'm bound to love you.'

'Despite the sins I might have committed or because of them?'

'Despite *and* because.'

Jon tilted his head a little to one side. 'Does that make you a weak man or a strong one?'

This time Chapman did not hesitate. 'A strong one. Love of one's fellows is the most empowering force there is.'

'And sacrifice in the name of one's fellows?'

He wiped the sweat away with the back of a hand. 'Is something beautiful and difficult which is demanded to some degree of all of us.'

'To sacrifice one's own salvation for love of another?'

'To sacrifice oneself is often to *be* saved, Jon. This is what the cross taught us. It's the sacrifice that perfects us. It's in overcoming, not denying, our fear and our terror and the selfishness of our humanity that brings us closer to God, to the nature of His sacrifice. God Himself cried out in agony on the cross. God Himself was terrified by the thought of His death. But His love was greater than His fear and it is from this that springs His triumph and our salvation.'

'To commit evil, then, in the name of love?'

Chapman needed to sit. He kept that hand pressed solid to the wall, solid to the cool plane of its firm reality. 'I don't think I understand.'

Jon continued patiently, 'To do something that you know will damn you not because it satisfies a desire but because it will save another, whom you love. Is that a good act or an evil one?'

Chapman pinched the flesh between his brows. 'That's entering some complex moral territory, Jon. We need to define our terms, otherwise how do we know we're talking about the same thing? What do you mean by evil? The same as me? Perhaps not. Some people see evil in', he floundered, as he sought rhetorical comfort in cliché, 'in the fact that we live lives of relative comfort while God knows how many millions of people across the world live lives of deprivation the like of which we couldn't begin to imagine. There are many, and sometimes I am one of them, who believe that life as it is lived in the West is intrinsically evil. And there are others to whom evil is not a state of existence, but an act of violation, to whom the economic sufferings of the world are an incontrovertible, inevitable fact of life while congress with a prostitute or the abortion of an unwanted child represents an act of unadulterated evil. How can we know that we're talking about the same thing? How can we possibly know?'

Jon appeared to consider this. Then he said, 'I think we know.'

Chapman did not want to know. He wanted it to be morning. Even a situation such as this would be made more comprehensible by the shedding of natural light, by the passage of cars outside full of people on their way to work. Of milk-floats and lollipop men. 'I don't think I *do* know Jon,' he lied, because it was not morning but the end of the night, because his guts were flittering and fluttering and he was having trouble controlling his bowels. 'You're moving much too fast for me. Don't you think we'd be better off discussing this downstairs over a cup of tea and a cigarette?'

Chapman had removed his hand from the comforting support of the wall and made ready to take a confident stride to the door.

Jon took a step sideways and blocked the exit. 'You know what I mean,' he said.

The priest wiped his brow. 'You have to *tell* me, Jon. If I'm to help you, you must tell me exactly what it is that's troubling you.'

Jon looked at the ceiling. Chapman thought he heard a tiny, trapped whimper. He wanted to play a child's game. He wanted to stick his fingers in his ears and chant, 'I can't hear you! I can't hear you!' at the top of his voice until the night was fully over and the children were gone to school and the 'Today' programme was over on Radio 4 and Jon had been swallowed back into whatever darkness had spawned him.

Jon lowered his head to face the priest and opened his eyes. 'I killed him.'

Chapman leaned back with both hands against the wall. 'Killed who?'

'Andy,' said Jon. 'I cut his throat and threw his body into the kitchen. I ripped up a pornographic calendar and stuffed some pages of it into his mouth and the hole in his neck.'

Chapman could not stand. He sank to the floor, the wall to his back.

'Oh, Christ,' he said. He buried his head in his hands, and rubbed at his eyes. 'Oh God.'

'Is it a terrible thing I've done?' said Jon. 'Was it really so bad?'

'God forgive you,' said the priest, almost silently.

Jon seemed calm and darkly satisfied. 'I knew you'd think it a terrible thing. But it wasn't. It was a sacrifice in the name of love and that is what you worship and call good.'

He walked forward and stood an inch from Chapman. The priest could smell him, smell the sweat of his exertion. 'I saved him,' said Jon. He squatted to Chapman's eye level. 'I did it for him.'

Chapman stuck his finger in his ears and closed his eyes. 'I can't hear you!' he screamed. 'I didn't hear you!' He curled into a ball on the carpet and began loudly to hum, loudly enough that he heard no more of what was said to him, nor even that there was more.

He did not fall silent or open his eyes or take his fingers from his ears until it was morning and Jon was gone and the children were gone to school and there was milk on the doorstep and the phone was ringing and he did not want it ever to be dark again.

There was something televisual in hurriedly tugging one's clothes from cupboards and wardrobes and throwing them in a jumble-sale pile first on to the bed then, after a cursory sort through to isolate the favourite and practical, into a zippered holdall.

Only when he had pushed the last inches of bunched shirt-sleeve through the last straining gap in the zip and tested the bag for weight did Jon take a moment to think about what he usually carried in it – what horrors it had transported, with what grim contempt he had wielded its contents. Grubby and drawn, he sat heavily on the bed and greedily swigged from a plastic two-litre container of tepid Coca-Cola. He belched and ran the back of a hand across dry lips. Balancing the bottle precariously on his sternum, he lay back and found himself immediately slipping into sleep. Fear of dreaming made him wake and drove him to the bathroom, where he splashed cold water on his face and neck.

From a cupboard beneath the stairs he removed a claw hammer and, armed with it, stalked with purpose into the Oblivion Suite. He did not know what to expect – catharsis, perhaps, by means of an obliquely satisfying act of nihilistic, existential triumphalism, but smashing the mirrors proved unsatisfying, labour-intensive and rather more dangerous than he had stopped to consider. He quit very shortly after a small shard of glass sliced through the flesh of his index finger. He dropped the hammer to the floor and left the Oblivion Suite sucking at his bleeding finger.

There remained a nagging desire for some expression of liberation. He considered burning the house to the ground, but the thought of the inevitable violence of the conflagration bored him. He thought about simply destroying the house's contents, but they meant so little to him that taking the time to smash them seemed somehow more petulant than exultant. He thought about squatting and planting a shit in the middle of the carpet and found that, for a moment, the thought appealed. But once the moment had passed so had the thought.

Instead he moved steadily from room to room giving each one a last tidy-round, putting his things in order. He disconnected the water at the stop-cock and pulled all the plugs from the sockets. He ensured all the windows were locked. He gave the vacuum cleaner one last, quick polish.

He had no clear idea of where he intended to go. He felt neither guilt nor anything which might accurately be described as regret. Instead there was unspecific irritation and a restless boredom. And there was tiredness: tiredness which came not from lack of sleep but fear of it.

Finally, resigned to the fact that he was unable to generate a sense of occasion, he paused once more before leaving to retrieve his knife from the sock drawer, his lighter from the kitchen and his overcoat from the hallway, for although it was spring he could not yet shake the winter chill from his bones.

He closed the door on the house, slung the bag over his shoulder and began the walk to where he did not know.

He had not gone far when the familiar Aston drew alongside him. Smoothly and near silent, it pulled up to the kerb outside a local newsagent within sight of a primary school, from the playground of which it was possible to hear the voices of children playing being carried on the grimy breeze.

There was no surprise, no nauseating lurch deep inside him, no urge to drop his belongings and break into a mad, headlong dash for life and freedom. There was just a sense of inevitability which felt more like returning than leaving.

He lowered the overnight bag to the gritty pavement, turned and squatted at the rear window of the car.

Behind the inevitable oval Raybans, Phil wore no expression. The collar of his white shirt was starched and smart, his tie understated and formal. He moved his head not one increment in acknowledgement. Jon was very proud of him.

In the rear sat the Tattooed Man, in a black overcoat and dark grey suit with a subtle, indistinct check. He wore a red floral tie loosened at his neck. He looked relaxed and comfortable and his smile of greeting was as feral and luminous as ever. His face crinkled with the same indulgence, the same unabashed fondness.

'Well,' he said. 'Good *morning* to you Jon. How've you been keeping?'

Jon smiled in return. He could feel the distortion of the skin at the corner of his eyes.

'Oh,' he said. 'You know. So-so.'

The Tattooed Man laughed heartily. He patted the seat next to him.

'You coming then, or what?'

Before he could answer, Phil had emerged from the driver's seat, taken his bag and thrown it into the boot alongside two calfskin suitcases. Jon stood and faced him. Phil broke into a wide grin. Jon could not help but reciprocate. Wordlessly, they shook hands. It was a good moment.

When he was in the car the Tattooed Man offered Jon a Murray Mint. Jon accepted and they sat for a while in companionable silence, the Tattooed Man crunching down on sweet after sweet, Jon making his last until it was a thin sliver on his tongue. The only other movement of which Jon was aware was the occasional flicker of Phil's eyes in the rear-view mirror as he negotiated the city traffic, imposing a stately gravitas on its verminous anarchy.

At length the city began to dissipate, its last tendrils losing hold on the sleek, speeding body of the immaculate old car. The inner city gave way to trading estates, trading estates to the satirical blandness of suburbia, suburbia to uncongested motorway. Eventually they left the motorway for straight, ill-maintained A-roads, then A-roads for quiet country roads upon which there was little to impede their progress and upon which Phil, with stolid solemnity, drove at maniacal speed.

There were cattle in the fields, moronically ruminating and even some early lambs, unsteady on spindly legs and foolishly bewildered. They stopped for a while to watch a ewe giving birth, easing from inside herself a steaming grey lump of tissue which began to form itself into the semblance of a lamb. The farmer or vet who attended wore a red baseball cap emblazoned with the Budweiser logo.

The Tattooed Man watched, enraptured. Jon watched him for a while, then lit a cigarette and offered round the pack. The Tattooed Man took one without shifting his gaze from the neonate in the damp and muddy field.

'Astonishing,' he said.

Jon agreed. Phil remained diplomatically silent, casually tipping ash out of the window.

Soon they were on the move again.

'Where are we headed?' Jon asked.

Redundantly, the Tattooed Man nodded ahead and said, 'Cornwall. Now that everything's quietened down I thought I'd treat myself to a few days off by the sea. It's been a long time since I spoiled myself.'

He unwound his window, placed his elbow in the open frame and placed his jaw on the back of his fist. Jon copied him and despite a cool spring breeze made arctic by the extreme velocity at which Phil insisted upon driving, they sat mirroring each other like this, watching white clouds scud and skim across the horizon like it was the surface of a pond until the wind drew tears from their eyes and it became difficult to see.

They stopped at a craggily picturesque Cornish seaside town that had yet fully to emerge from its annual hibernation. The Tattooed Man bought Jon and Phil a cream tea in a hideously quaint restaurant full of bigoted and evil old women. The Tattooed Man called them the Tory Dead and Phil laughed so much he sprayed the table with moist crumbs of scone.

In an arcade Jon and Phil took turns on a frenetic and

Technicolor arcade game. Despite his apparent inability to resist napalming civilians (for which points were deducted) Phil consistently won. Each time he did so he clapped Jon companionably on the shoulder and called him a fucking loser. Equally companionably, Jon told him to go and fuck himself.

They took a walk on the breezy front, parallel to a beach deserted but for the insane, the foolhardy, dog owners and the newly in love. They stopped at a beach-front shop and Phil bought a football. The Tattooed Man huddled in his overcoat on a striped deckchair and watched the oddly coloured sea while Jon and Phil kicked the ball from one to the other, shouting insults as they did so.

When they were tired, the three of them walked back towards the town. They sat dangling their legs over the harbour wall, eating fish and chips from paper with their fingers. They watched decayed fishing vessels bob lightly on the incoming tide. They talked about the nostalgic aromas in the air, sea water and fresh fish and salt and vinegar. Then they fell quiet and just watched the boats.

Back in the warmth of the car, Jon found himself fighting to stay awake against the hypnotic hum of the engine.

'It's the sea air,' said the Tattooed Man. 'It's tires you out.'

The sun was low in the sky and the breeze was picking up when the Tattooed Man leaned forward and tapped Phil on the shoulder.

Obediently, Phil turned the car on to what was little more than a half-erased impression of a track leading off from the road. The car bounced and jostled up a gentle but persistent gradient for perhaps ten minutes. They passed neither house nor car nor person nor animal.

When they finally reached a plateau Phil killed the engine and the Tattooed Man said; 'Here we are, then.'

Shivery with sleepiness, Jon stepped from the car, huddling

into his overcoat against what had become a robust, chilly wind.

They had parked close to the edge of a cliff. The ragged stone edge of England stretched deserted to their left and right. The descent of the sun into the sea far to the west cast shadows of industrial black on to the fierce solidity of the cliff-face. At the cliff's edge, sparse grass shivered. At its base, water boiled and crashed and hissed against outcrops like broken, fossilised teeth. Gulls wheeled in loose circles against the reddening strata of the sky, which were cross-hatched by luminous vapour trails. Testament to escape and arrival.

'Look at that.' The Tattooed Man had to raise his voice against the wind. 'That's my favourite view in the world.'

'It's a long way down,' shouted Phil. He stood precariously at the edge, the wind buffeting bubbles into his white shirt and tossing his tie over his shoulder.

'There are those with further to fall,' shouted back the Tattooed Man, and laughed at his own ponderousness. 'Phil's right,' he yelled. 'Go to the edge, Jon. Take a look.'

Jon walked forward and looked down at hissing white foam and black rock which shone wet like vinyl. From the corner of his eye he watched Phil perform a little cliff-top jig to generate warmth.

The Tattooed Man put his hands deep into the pockets of his overcoat and stood at Jon's side. They stood wincing against the wind while it whipped at their coat-tails.

'It's all done and dealt,' said the Tattooed Man. 'Done and dealt, chapter and verse. It's time now to move on.'

He took a step back. Without turning, Jon could picture the overcoat being brushed to one side as the Tattooed Man retrieved a pistol from deep inside its folds. He inhaled sharply when the gun was pressed hard to the base of his skull.

The boiling sea far below, stained by the sunset, made white noise in his head.

'There is a single choice which determines the course of

your life entire,' recited the Tattooed Man. 'You elect to jump
or allow yourself to be pushed. Those who elect to jump are of
course free to choose in which direction.'

Courteously, he withdrew the gun and put his hands back in
his pockets.

Jon wanted to turn to him and see his face, to memorise
exactly the expression he saw, ambiguous though he knew it
would be. But the moment was not right and anyway the
sunset was dramatising, casting into the solidity of shadow and
relief what was in truth equivocal, protean. He had no wish to
make a lie of what was to be his final indivisible, incandescent
moment.

He looked into the sun, bright enough still to blind him,
and prepared to jump.